DICKINSON

An
Ivy Malone
Mystery

BOOK 1

Invisible

Lorena McCourtney

Revell
Grand Rapids, Michigan

© 2004 by Lorena McCourtney

Published by Fleming H. Revell
a division of Baker Publishing Group
P.O. Box 6287, Grand Rapids, MI 49516-6287

Printed in the United States of America

ISBN 0-7394-4528-6

Never will I leave you;
never will I forsake you.

Hebrews 13:5

1

The sign arched over the gravel driveway proclaimed Country Peace in rusty wrought iron. Beyond the sign, the havoc in the cemetery challenged that claim of serenity.

The weathered gravestone of one Emil Riptone lay at the edge of the road, a lump of concrete clinging to its base. Beyond it, another fallen headstone had split in two, creating an irreparable rift between William and Bertha Bartholomew. Across the weedy hillside, I could see at least three other uprooted grave markers.

I braked the old Thunderbird at Mr. Riptone's fallen monument. In the seat beside me, my best friend, Thea, touched her throat with a trembling hand.

"I'm afraid to see what they've done to Uncle Romer and Aunt Maude," she said.

Outrage overrode my lingering heartburn, memento of a rash encounter with a Taco Grande Special at lunch. It was bad enough that an unfortunate error had sent Mr. Riptone to his final resting place with a headstone that forever declared him to be a fithful husband and father. He surely didn't deserve this additional indignity.

"We're going to the police," I said.

"I called them the last time I was here, when Kendra brought me. There was just one overturned tombstone then. And now look."

"This time we'll go to the police station in person."

I edged the long nose of the 'bird around the fallen headstone and drove up the winding lane of the sparsely populated cemetery. I doubted vandals could have made any impact on Uncle Romer and Aunt Maude's double headstone. Thea's aunt had apparently selected it on the basis of size and bulk, not elegance, and the tombstone bore an alarming resemblance to a Volkswagen Bug.

I was wrong, I realized regretfully as we got out of the car and trudged across the weedy hillside. The enormous tombstone lay face down across the graves. Nearby torn-up ground indicated vandals had used a four-wheel-drive vehicle and rope or cable to accomplish the deed.

A tear dribbled down Thea's cheek. "Why would anyone do such a thing?" she asked between puffs of labored breathing.

"At least only the headstone has been disturbed. The graves themselves haven't been entered."

It was some solace. The perpetrators had merely been vandals having "fun," not weird cultists after bones or skulls.

The vandals surely were long gone, but I peered around cautiously to make sure. I also fingered the whistle that has hung at my neck ever since a woman had been mugged in the parking lot where I usually bought groceries. Thea had given it to me. Not that the occupants of Country Peace were likely to respond to even the most piercing screech of whistle.

"Aunt Maude would not be pleased about this," Thea said darkly. "Not pleased at all. She had a fit the time Uncle

Romer accidentally backed over her pink flamingo yard ornament."

My private opinion was that a pink flamingo yard ornament deserved demolishing by any available means. A comment left unsaid, of course. Thea's face had paled to the color of pie dough, and wisps like ghostly fingers fluttered out of her white hair. Her hand slid down to her heart, which was undoubtedly also fluttering. In the past couple of years Thea had blacked out several times. A heart problem, her doctor said. Insufficient blood pumping to the brain. Her blood pressure also made grasshopper leaps in all directions. She daily took an assortment of pills so expensive that she declared the drug company should be a dependent on her tax return, and I was afraid she skipped an occasional pill to make them last longer.

I put a hand on Thea's arm. Her skin felt dead-fish clammy. "I think you should sit down and rest for a few minutes."

Thea peered around. "I can't sit on a tombstone!"

"I don't think Aunt Maude would object, considering these extenuating circumstances." I couldn't be certain of that, but Aunt Maude was in no position to contradict me.

Thea looked doubtful, but she sat. "I'm just glad I didn't have Walter buried out here," she declared.

Thea's husband, dead some fourteen years now, was buried back in the city in Parkdale Heights, where locked iron gates securely barred the entryway every night. My sweet Harley was also a long-time resident at Parkdale. At times I wished I'd looked into burying him here at Country Peace, where individuality in memorials to the deceased ran rampant. Atop one nearby gravestone, as yet undamaged, was the life-size figure of a crowing rooster. Another had the nickname "Rowdy" spelled out in old bullet casings.

Harley would have appreciated something other than the flat, featureless markers at Parkdale. Something whimsical, like those castle birdhouses he used to build. But right then I was glad his body was resting at Parkdale, his generic gravestone undisturbed.

Not that, in the eternal scheme of things, this detail was particularly important. Actually, I never really think of Harley as being at Parkdale. More often I envision him happily building birdhouses in heaven, the Lord looking on approvingly. Or fishing, perhaps. No one knew this, but I'd secretly stuck one of the fishing flies I used to tie for him in the pocket of the suit in which he was buried.

"What am I going to do about this?" Thea fluttered her handkerchief like a small white flag of surrender. "I don't even know who's in charge, or what to do about getting things put back in order."

Is anyone in charge? I wondered as I plucked an accumulation of weedy burrs out of my socks. The cemetery wasn't old enough to have pioneer status, but the most recent tombstone I'd seen there was over twenty years old. There'd never been any evidence of maintenance, although occasionally a modest clump of flowers appeared on some grave.

"We'll worry about fixing things later. Right now, I think we should get you home."

Before you collapse, I thought, although I didn't say that aloud. When Thea blacks out, it is not a gentle swoon. She hits the ground like a sack of onions tossed off a truck, and once, when I caught her as she fell, we went down together. Today, the hot summer afternoon was oppressively muggy, an occasional eddy of sullen breeze rearranging the sticky air without making noticeable improvement. Thunderclouds loomed off to the west. Another reason to get Thea home. In a lightning storm, Thea is as skittery as a high-strung cat climbing any available leg in panic.

I have no objection to storms, but a hillside cemetery of oversized tombstones does not strike me as a prudent place to loiter during a lightning storm. I helped Thea back to the car and buckled the safety belt around her. In her agitation, she had forgotten the flowers she'd brought for Uncle Romer and Aunt Maude. I climbed the hill once more to carry the orange marigolds in a mayonnaise jar that Thea had dressed up with blue tissue paper and pink ribbon.

I paused to catch my breath after setting the jar beside the fallen tombstone. A magnificent view from here, city buildings in the distance, new, mirrored bank building rising like some icon transported from the future. The city was inexorably spreading in this direction. So far Country Peace was still surrounded by picturesque farms tucked among the wooded hills, but I could see raw earth where a new subdivision was breaking ground a few miles away.

The thunderclouds hadn't yet moved closer, and I took a moment to admire a boy sitting on a bridge over a slow-moving creek below the cemetery. He wore an old straw hat, and a fishing line dangled between his bare legs to the water below. *Harley would have looked like that as a boy,* I thought. Although the old refrigerator dumped at the edge of the creek added a jarring note to the pastoral scene.

I turned to look behind me, at the top of the hill beyond Maude's grave. I'd always been curious about what was on the other side of the hill. "All that curiosity is going to get you in trouble," Harley had muttered to me more than once. He'd also, I had to admit, been right more than once. Like the time I was curious about something shiny in the bushes and, a minute later, after crawling under the bushes to grab it, found myself holding a gun that turned out to be the weapon used in a nearby gas station holdup. And the time I just had to investigate a tiny opening behind the bed in our rental apartment and wound up with my rear end ignominiously stuck in an undersized vent to the attic.

But there wasn't time to investigate the other side of the hill today, I decided regretfully. Time to get Thea home.

Yet she appeared to have revived somewhat by the time I got back to the car. "I still have Walter's old double-barreled shotgun," she said, a spirited snap now back in her voice. "We could bring it out here and hide, and when these vandals show up, we'll just let 'em have it. Really blast 'em."

I could just see that. Two little old ladies setting up ambush with an ancient shotgun behind a tombstone shaped like a Volkswagen. I couldn't help laughing, and Thea, apparently getting a glimpse of a similar vision, giggled with me.

Thea's color improved as she laughed, and by the time we were back in the city, she said she wanted to go directly to the police. I'd planned to wait until later, but, hoping it would set her mind at ease, I agreed.

We stopped to look up the address of the county sheriff's office and then drove several miles across town to the two-story concrete building with a flag hanging limp in the humid summer air.

Inside the nicely air-conditioned building, we approached a barred, horseshoe-shaped opening in a square of heavy glass. A high wooden partition blocked view of whatever police activity was going on behind the barrier. The counter in front of the opening was also high. Apparently crime in our county mostly involves people taller than I am. It was several minutes before a young woman in uniform came to the opening.

"Sorry," she apologized. "I didn't see you ladies standing here. May I help you?"

I described the problem. The woman asked us to wait until a deputy became available. Thea and I sat on an old, brown-vinyl couch with squishy cushions that threatened to swallow us.

We waited. And waited. Thea leaned her head back and

closed her eyes. A sullen-looking man in handcuffs accompanied by an officer exited the elevator. An officer with a police dog walked by. Both ignored us.

Various people approached the horseshoe-shaped opening. A young man collected forms to fill out. A girl in burlap skirt and gold nose ring was whisked off down a hall. A young couple with a baby were sent elsewhere. Others came and went.

I sorted through the magazines on an end table. *Sports Illustrated. Body Building. Racing Pigeon Digest. Plumbing News.* People connected with crime apparently had eclectic reading tastes. I read about how some young woman acquired a belly that looked flat enough to iron on.

Then I spent a few minutes inspecting the blood blister under my left thumbnail. It had appeared several weeks ago after an encounter with a misaimed hammer while I was nailing a loose board on the back porch. The purple-red stain was slowly growing out with the nail and now bore the shape of a palm tree sprouting from a deserted island. Or perhaps it was a prehistoric creature with an elongated neck.

A different thought alarmed me. Is seeing designs in a blood blister a sign of eccentricity? Or oncoming senility? I hastily abandoned the inspection and dropped my hand in my lap.

Thea woke with a jump and a startled "where-am-I?" expression.

Okay, enough already. We'd been there almost an hour. I picked up my purse and marched to the window. I counted "one thousand and one, one thousand and two" until I'd reached a full two minutes. No one came to the window. The woman who'd spoken with us earlier had disappeared. A man glanced our way from beyond the glass square, but our presence didn't seem to register with him, and he turned back to his computer.

I tried a polite wave. No response. I tried a genteel "yoo-hoo" through the horseshoe-shaped opening. No reaction.

Apparently this situation required stronger action. I suspected the only idea that occurred to me would instantly catapult me into Weird Little Old Lady territory.

So be it.

I put the whistle to my mouth and blew.

2

Two officers rushed to the inside of the window, and another appeared out of nowhere right at my elbow. All eyed me warily, as if uncertain whether to suspect incoherent babble or a bomb in my purse.

If I'd been a ponytailed young man with an earring, the whistle probably would have landed me in handcuffs. As it was, however, what it did was win us an immediate spot at a desk with a solicitous deputy.

Interesting. Perhaps eccentricity is an area I haven't explored sufficiently.

Now there was much shoulder-patting and tsk-tsking. *Are we feeling faint? There, there. Just take a deep breath. Water? Here's two big glasses of it.* After giving our names—"I'm Ivy Malone, and this is my friend Thea Pinkerton"—forms and pens were flourished, and information was taken. After which we were assured that the department would look into this and do everything possible to apprehend the villains.

Yes, they probably would do their best to capture the vandals, I conceded as Thea and I returned to the Thunderbird. But, as the officer had pointed out, their best in this situation was limited by a stingy budget. They didn't have the manpower to do a nightly stakeout, and the patrolling officer was seldom out that way more than once a week.

Thea had again paled by the time we started back across town, and I was concerned she might be headed for another of those blackout spells. The old Thunderbird had come with air conditioning, but it hadn't worked for several years now. Thea's knuckles stood out like parchment-covered marbles as she clutched her purse. I watched her out of the corner of my eye. Thea was so strongly tied to the past. She kept in touch with schoolmates back to the Truman era. She regularly visited two other cemeteries in addition to Parkdale and Country Peace. The vandalism of Aunt Maude's tombstone had hit her like a stomp on her arthritic hands. And probably wasn't doing her heart any good, either.

On Madison Street, I turned the 'bird into Thea's driveway, second door down from my own. The old house on the lot between our two places welcomed us with the thud of another falling shingle. The place had been vacant since Effie McKenzie went to live with her daughter in Texas. A For Sale sign had stood in the yard for months, but they hadn't yet been able to sell the place. Down the street, someone from the Rite-Cut Yard Service was mowing the grass and watering the magnolia trees while the Margollins were off in their motor home, digging into genealogical roots. Boys eager to do yard work no longer lived in our neighborhood.

Thea brightened. "Oh, look, there's Kendra."

Kendra Alexander had occupied Thea's basement apartment for some three months now. Her little red Corolla stood in the detached carport that Thea no longer used. Thea had given up driving after the blackout spells started.

Kendra, carrying a pink plastic sack from Victoria's Secret, came around to Thea's side of the car. Her raspberry-red miniskirt revealed an extravagant length of leg, and her wildly tousled dark hair fit the "mane" description of the heroine of a romance novel, but her smile bloomed as sweet and friendly as a spring daisy.

She leaned down to peer in the window. "So, ladies, what have you two been up to? Dragging Main Street, scouting for eligible bachelors?"

Thea giggled. "We wouldn't know what to do with an eligible bachelor if he threw himself across the radiator. Actually, we were taking flowers out to Aunt Maude and Uncle Romer at Country Peace." She sobered and went on to relate what we'd found at the old cemetery.

"I'm so sorry to hear that. Why would anyone be so destructive?" Kendra's lovely dark brows drew together in troubled indignation. "When we were out there before, I thought that other headstone might have toppled over on its own. They're so old, you know. But to have someone do such a thing deliberately . . . Is there any way I can help?"

"We've just come from the county sheriff's department. We're hoping they'll find out something," I said.

"Aren't you home early?" Thea asked Kendra.

"My boss gave me a few hours off. I'll go back later. We're having our Hot Summer Saturday Night Sell-A-Thon this evening. Free hot dogs and chili." Kendra wrinkled her nose. "If you have a steel-lined stomach, come on over and chow down."

Kendra worked in the office at Bottom-Buck Barney's car lot on Sylvester Street, just a couple of blocks over from Madison. They were strong on "hot." They ran "hot" coupons in their newspaper ads, and their noisy TV commercials promised "hot" deals and "hot" credit for everyone. It is the type of business that is all too common in our area since the relocation of the freeway.

"Would you like to come to church with us tomorrow morning?" I asked Kendra. Thea and I invited her regularly, but she'd accepted only twice.

Now Kendra looked at her watch, as if today's time had something to do with tomorrow's services. "I'm sorry. I'm meeting a friend in the morning." She didn't elaborate on what the plans with that friend were. "But I'll try to go with you again one of these days."

"Any time," Thea said.

"Right now I'm going to go take a shower." Kendra lifted her arms in a chicken flap. "The air-conditioning in the office is on the blink, and I feel as if I've been running a marathon through that hot chili." Her expression suddenly went serious, and she tapped the window frame lightly with a fingernail that sent off iridescent shimmers. "But you two pray for me, okay? It's . . . especially important right now."

Kendra momentarily looked so grim, perhaps even a little frightened, and I wished she'd say more. But she just gave us a fingertip wave and flashed one of her million-dollar smiles.

We both watched her traipse to the concrete steps that led to the basement apartment, her spiked heels shortening her stride.

I like Kendra, and I pray for her. She might dress a bit skimpily, and definitely too flashy for my taste, but she is personable and sweet, considerate and helpful. A wonderful tenant, Thea said. Kendra paid her rent on time, didn't play screaming music, didn't overload the trash can. Yet there was something about her . . .

"Does Kendra ever strike you as . . ." I paused, trying to corral the appropriate word. "A bit mysterious?"

"Mysterious?" Thea raised her eyebrows. "In what way?"

"Don't you wonder why a nice young woman would want to work at a sleazy place like Bottom-Buck Barney's?"

"Jobs can be hard to find."

True.

I fingered the steering wheel, considering. The usual roar of traffic, now punctuated by a wailing siren, billowed up from the nearby freeway exit. At one time, Madison Street had been quietly residential, curving gently to a rural road below, but the city had reached out like a hungry blob of protoplasm and engulfed us. A white church with a tall steeple and a bell that could be heard for miles had stood at the intersection then. Now the street ended a few doors down from my house, at a concrete barrier decorated with red reflectors, with a breakneck drop-off to the busy exit below. Hundreds of cars now drove every day over the spot where the church had once stood.

"This isn't an area most single, well-bred young ladies would choose to live in," I suggested.

"We're well-bred old ladies, and we live here. Besides, I don't charge much rent. And it's convenient to Kendra's job."

"She doesn't seem to have any family or friends."

"Her family is all out in California, remember?" Thea said. "And she hasn't lived here long enough to make many friends."

"But why did she leave California to begin with? I thought half the young women in the country wanted to *go* to California."

"She must be part of the other half." Thea leaned her head back against the seat. Her blue eyes went dreamy. "Maybe she left because of a broken heart. Maybe she was madly in love, and he was killed in some terrible accident. An earthquake, maybe. Or suffered some tragic fatal illness. And she just couldn't stay there anymore after he was gone."

"She doesn't look as if she's pining away. Did she ever mention anyone who got killed or died?"

Thea frowned at my practical line of thought. "No. But

she probably wouldn't. She's a . . . what do they call it? A very private person. And often she seems so . . . lost in thought."

True. In spite of Kendra's usually breezy attitude—and Thea's tendency to romanticize situations—an air of preoccupation did linger around Kendra. I sometimes saw her in one of Thea's old lounge chairs under the weeping willow out back, sitting with a book in her lap but not reading. Just staring into space as if she were concentrating every cell in her brain on something.

Yet I also saw a lot of determination in Kendra. She'd already moved up from just filling out forms at Bottom-Buck Barney's to a position as assistant to the manager. Perhaps Barney's was just a stepping-stone to some higher goal Kendra had planned.

"Did she have references when she rented the apartment?"

"Oh yes," Thea said. "Including a letter from a pastor."

Which seemed odd, considering her lack of church contact here. "Local references?"

"No. California."

"Did you check them out?"

"No," Thea admitted. "I didn't want to spend the money on long-distance calls. But I could have. They all had addresses and phone numbers. She wouldn't have given them to me if the people were going to report that she stole the furniture or left cigarette burns in the carpet."

True.

"Did she put up a security deposit on the apartment?"

"Oh yes. And she didn't try to get me down on the amount. Although she didn't have much in the way of belongings when she moved in." Thea frowned as if she hated to admit any flaw in her perfect tenant. "Just one suitcase and a couple of boxes of household things. Most people have more."

"She probably didn't want to move a lot of stuff all the way from California." My reasons for thinking Kendra mysterious were fizzling under scrutiny. Yet . . . "She's apparently had time to make *one* friend here."

Guilt jabbed me even as I said that. It sounded snide. Sly and gossipy. And probably quite unjustified. Just because Kendra's young man rarely came to the apartment to pick her up, and never came in daylight, didn't necessarily mean anything. Nor did the fact that she'd never introduced him to Thea. Those small niceties were probably as outdated as girdles and beehive hairdos.

Yet there was that evening when Thea and I were coming down the back steps after dark as he was heading for the basement entrance. He didn't see us until he was almost on top of us, and he'd turned away so hastily that he left a big footprint in the marigold border. All we'd gotten was a glimpse of a tall, lanky man with long arms and an angular jawline. Well-dressed but older, and not the kind of hunk I'd have expected Kendra to go for. And rude. Not a word of apology for almost bowling us over.

I expected Thea to come up with an instant counterargument to my weighted comment about Kendra's "friend." Instead she fingered the clasp of her purse and scowled at the moss-covered concrete wall beside the basement steps.

"Sometimes," Thea said, "I've wondered if maybe he's married."

Oh, I hope not. But also an all-too-viable possibility.

"And sometimes she *does* seem a little mysterious," Thea conceded.

Now it was my turn to ask. "In what way?"

"Well, she colors her hair. I've seen the L'Oréal cartons in the trash."

"That isn't mysterious," I scoffed. "Half the women in the country color their hair. We tried it, remember?"

19

"But how many natural blondes go dark?" Thea countered.

"What makes you think she's a natural blonde?"

"She just has a . . . blond air about her. I do remember something about being a blonde, you know," Thea added, her tone a bit huffy. "In fact, maybe I'll go back to being one."

I remember being a brunette before my hair started to go gray. I also remember when Thea and I had plunged into what a magazine ad called "the stunning new universe of color." Thea's gray-into-beige results were passable, but my transformation from mousy to fiery orange-auburn had been so "stunning" that I'd washed my hair twice a day for three weeks. Now Thea had gone elegantly white. And I was still possum gray.

"I'm almost certain she dyes her eyebrows too," Thea said.

Dyed eyebrows? Now that struck me as more unusual. Not something I'd ever thought about trying. Could it be taken as more than a simple cosmetic enhancement, perhaps even a disguise?

"She doesn't *avoid* answering questions about herself," Thea went on. "But when I ask her something, she always seems to take a minute to think it over before she answers."

Yes, that was true, I realized now that Thea mentioned it. Once I'd asked Kendra what her father did out in California, and she had said he was a teacher. Surely nothing out of the ordinary there. Yet there had been that small hesitation before Kendra made the statement, as if she were running an internal check to be sure it didn't contradict something she'd told one of us earlier.

"Or sometimes," Thea added now, "I ask her something, and next thing I know we're talking about me again, not her. So instead of her telling me about earthquakes in California, I'm telling her about making hollyhock dolls when I was a girl, or how I used to turn the handle on Mama's old washing machine."

I now remembered how Kendra had smoothly segued our conversation away from her father and into asking about my years as librarian at the Madison Street branch of the city library.

Thea and I sat in the car a few minutes more, as if watching the basement steps might reveal some significant new information about Kendra. When it didn't, I reached over and patted Thea's hand. "Why don't you go take a nap, and I'll bring some salad and cobbler over later. If Kendra hasn't gone back to work yet, we'll invite her up."

"Oh, that sounds good, but . . ." Thea flexed her shoulders, as if the weight of Aunt Maude's tombstone lay across them. "Actually, I think I'll just fix a Cup O' Noodles and go right to bed."

I looked at my watch. "At 6:00?"

"I know it's early, but I'm so tired. I didn't sleep well last night. But come over for breakfast before church. I'll get some of those nice Sara Lee cinnamon rolls out of the freezer."

Thea had once cooked everything from old-fashioned molasses cookies to *crepe aux pommes* from a French cookbook, but she didn't do much cooking from scratch these days.

"Be sure to take your pills," I said.

21

3

I sat at the kitchen table turning well-worn pages of C. S. Lewis's *Screwtape Letters* and absentmindedly finishing up a bowl of leftover chicken pot pie, which is the way I usually eat these days. I didn't make a cobbler after all, since doing it just for myself didn't seem worth the effort. After washing up the dishes and with a long evening ahead of me, I wondered again about taking up some arts-and-craftsy type hobby. I always feel as if I should be doing something constructive instead of just sitting there in front of the blaring TV.

Then the inevitable question, like some annoying little voice inside me. *And this something constructive would be . . . ?*

I used to crochet pink and blue Christmas angels that were best-sellers at the annual Rummage and Crafts fund-raiser for the church at the bottom of Madison Street. But the big new church that had absorbed the small community church after the freeway relocation is not inclined toward rummage sales, and I already have a rather formidable population of angels gathering dust in an upstairs bedroom.

Tying fishing flies for Harley also used to keep my hands busy. One fly I invented, the Ugly Bug, so named by our son, Colin, was what Harley always called his "secret weapon." He claimed he could catch trout with an Ugly Bug when no one else was catching anything.

But Harley no longer needs Ugly Bugs.

Perhaps a part-time job? I'd done that a few times. Once I helped a wealthy widow organize her husband's library of books for an auction. Another time I worked in a secondhand bookstore, until it closed down. I'd enjoyed the work. The money too. But there isn't a thriving job market for retired librarians anymore.

The thunderclouds that had been rolling around since midafternoon let loose with a *crack!* that jolted me out of my pity party. I dashed around unplugging things and closing windows and relishing the sudden aura of excitement. Gusts of wind whipped around the house, stirring scents of dust and coming rain. Blue bolts lit up the windows like TV screens gone berserk. One seemed to explode right there in the living room with me. The lights flickered off and on. Hail hammered the roof. The phone made ominous tings, like ghost calls from some other realm.

Harley always said to stay away from the phone in a storm, but I tried to call Thea anyway. No answer. I debated running through the hail to check on her. As a small girl, Thea had crouched all alone in a Kansas storm cellar while a tornado ripped the house overhead to shreds, and she was still terrified of storms. I, on the other hand, was blessed with a mother who looped her arms around my sister and me during a storm and told us stories about the Lonely Little Lightning Bolt.

Now I decided that if Thea wasn't answering the phone, she must be sleeping through this, and that was good. No need to disturb her. She'd had enough stress for one day.

23

So I just sat there and rather guiltily enjoyed the tumult of the storm. One close-by hit made the hair on my arms stand upright. Wind lashed the windows like the tail of an angry cat and rattled the old fireplace chimney, long since closed off and bricked up. I ran upstairs to better hear the hail on the roof and remembered Colin's scared little-boy voice once asking in a storm, "Is God mad about something?" Which was my clue to start passing the Lonely Little Lightning Bolt story on to him.

I was sorry when the storm rumbled off and the hail softened to rain. The lights stopped flickering, and I plugged in the TV again. Newspeople were already out picking up reports about downed trees and power outages and nonworking traffic lights. By the time I had brushed my teeth and got into bed at 10:30, the rain was only a gentle patter.

I wasn't sleepy. The storm had left me feeling, as I'd once heard Kendra say of her own inability to sleep, "jazzed." I read three chapters of a Mary Higgins Clark mystery—I always have several books going at once—and then some uplifting verses from the Psalms. I debated writing a letter to the editor about those overturned gravestones out at Country Peace, worried about how much the taxes on the house would go up this year, and wondered how much longer my old refrigerator was going to hold out.

Then I finished the day the same way I have for as long as I can remember, with a final prayer entrusting everything to the Lord.

Next morning, I made my way past Effie's house, where the wind had ripped off more shingles and scattered them like fallen leaves. I knocked at Thea's back door about 8:30. A branch torn from the big maple tree lay in her front yard, but the Sunday air smelled as if it had been routed through heaven for cleansing. The cantaloupe I held to accompany Thea's cinnamon rolls also gave off a heavenly fragrance. I had on old jeans and a yard-sale T-shirt that said "God loves you. I'm still working on it." I'd go home and dress for church after we ate.

No answer to the knock. Surely Thea hadn't slept late after going to bed so early and sleeping right through the storm. I circled to the front door, though it was seldom used, and rang the bell. No response. The Sunday newspaper still lay like a paper log by the front door, damp from rain that had blown in and puddled on the porch. I picked up the paper, returned to the back door, and knocked again, this time hard enough to rattle the old wood in the doorframe. Nothing.

Panic jumped like loose springs in my stomach. I dumped the cantaloupe and newspaper in a tub of geraniums by the back door, ran home, and yanked the key to Thea's house off the hook by my own back door.

Kendra was just coming up the basement steps when I got back to Thea's house.

"Is something wrong?"

"I don't know. I can't seem to rouse Thea."

I unlocked the door and brushed past a hanging spider plant proliferating baby spiders. Kendra followed. We both stopped short in the kitchen. A cupboard door stood askew. A half-eaten Cup O' Noodles sat on the old plastic-topped counter. The microwave was open, light shining like a weak beacon. Thea would never leave the microwave like that, not unless . . .

I ran for the back bedroom, yelling Thea's name.

The bedroom door was open. I stared at the sheet covering the curled lump on the bed. Thea was not an insubstantial woman. Six inches taller and sixty pounds heavier than I am. But this lump looked so vulnerable and helpless . . .

Kendra pushed around me. Thea lay on her side, face turned toward the wall. Kendra's fingers found Thea's wrist, then moved up to her throat. I didn't need words to know what she didn't find.

"I'll call 911," I whispered.

"I don't think—" Kendra broke off. She tucked the sheet protectively around Thea's throat and nodded. "Yes. Call 911."

I made the call from the kitchen phone. Thea had never gotten around to having a phone installed in the bedroom. Then I pulled a chair up to the bed and sat there with my hands clasped between my knees to keep them from trembling. I didn't reach out to touch Thea. I was afraid of what a touch would tell me. A photo of Thea and me stood among the crowd of photos on the nightstand. We were smiling, our arms draped around each other.

"I'll make coffee," Kendra said.

Her voice startled me. I'd forgotten she was there. "Oh, that's okay. You don't need to stay. I know you have plans for this morning—"

"They can wait."

Kendra disappeared down the hallway. The sound of the microwave whirred in the kitchen. Thea, who had once prided herself on grinding French roast beans for the freshest coffee, now kept only instant in the house. Kendra brought back a steaming cup and handed it to me.

"Maybe she isn't dead," I said. "She has blackout spells, you know."

"No, I didn't know that."

"So maybe this is just a longer-than-usual blackout," I said hopefully. "Maybe even a temporary coma. They do all sorts of things to revive people these days."

"It shouldn't take the ambulance long to get here."

I wrapped my hands around the familiar cup and tried to

draw strength from it. It was from Thea's old Moss Rose set, remnant of careful scrimping and saving in her first year of marriage. Yet the mellow old cup now brought me no comfort, only a feeling of helplessness, of time slipping away. Sunday-best dishes gone to everyday and now to mismatched pieces. Like Thea and me.

And in my heart I knew there would be no high-tech revival for my best friend. The Lord had called Thea home.

I couldn't argue or question or berate his judgment. And yet . . . *Oh, Lord, are you sure it has to be now?*

How long had Thea and I been friends and neighbors? Thirty years? At least. We'd made strawberry preserves and watermelon pickles together in our younger years. Tried tofu together. Shared secrets and inside jokes. Cried and comforted each other when our husbands passed away. Sang in the choir at the old Madison Street church, taken a Prime Timers aerobics class, adventured on a trip to Branson to see Thea's favorite country singer, Loretta Lynn. Laughed about the idiosyncrasies of growing older and how time flew. "Why, just about the time I got used to being forty, there I was, fifty," Thea had once declared, righteously indignant.

The same with fifty turning to sixty. And now . . .

The ambulance came. A white-coated paramedic got out a small machine and hooked it up, but he shook his head and didn't use the paddles. Kendra and I, in Kendra's car, followed the ambulance to the hospital. The emergency room doctor told us what we already knew. I gave them the name of the Fleur & Fleur Funeral Home, where Thea had already made arrangements.

Then I started a frantic effort to contact Thea's only daughter, Molly, who with her husband was serving in a missionary outpost in Brazil. I couldn't get through for two days, and then it was a scratchy, patched-through phone and radio connection in which a despairing-sounding Molly said they were in the middle of some virus epidemic and there was no way they could get back to the States immediately. I assured her I'd take care of everything. Thea already had her cemetery plot next to Walter in Parkdale.

Kendra knocked on my back door the evening of the day I finally got hold of Molly. I was standing at the kitchen counter, looking at a tomato. It was a lovely, perfectly shaped, store-bought tomato, unlike many of the misshaped vegetables I grew. But I couldn't seem to rouse enough get-up-and-go to pick up a knife and whack the tomato with it. I kept thinking, *Thea loved a good bacon and tomato sandwich.*

"I just came over to see how you're doing," Kendra said. Today she was in red short-shorts that stopped below her belly button, and a gauzy white top that stopped above it. "This must be so difficult for you."

My put-up-a-strong-front response came automatically. "I'll be okay."

"Did you get hold of Thea's daughter?"

"Yes. But they can't get here for several weeks, maybe longer. She said to go ahead with the funeral."

"Oh, I'm so sorry . . . Are you sure you're okay?" Kendra put a hand on my arm. Twin lines of concern cut between her dark brows.

This time I opted for honesty. "Not really."

Kendra draped comforting arms around me. "I know how hard it is to lose someone you love."

"I feel so guilty. So responsible."

Kendra leaned back to peer at me. "Guilty?"

"I should've realized something was really wrong when we got home from the cemetery. I should've gone over to check on her. I thought about it during the storm. But she was so tired, and I thought it would be better if she slept through everything. I was wrong! If I'd gone over, maybe she'd still be here."

"Oh, Ivy, don't feel that way. She wouldn't want you to. I'm sure she went too quickly for anyone to do anything. You could see it in the way she was just lying there, the sheet not even mussed. It was just her . . . time."

I nodded and picked up a knife and whacked the tomato, barely missing my thumb because my eyes were blurry. "Would you like a glass of lemonade?" I asked.

"Oh, yes, please. The air-conditioning in our office still isn't working. And then I managed to lock my keys in the car when I was at the mall." Kendra leaned against the counter while I filled two glasses.

"Harley wired an extra key under the back bumper on the Thunderbird. I suppose it's still there, though I've never had to use it."

"My brother told me that's probably the first place a car thief would look, so mine's tucked into a little cavity where the front bumper fastens to the frame. I have to get down on the ground and practically turn myself into a pretzel to reach it. But I guess that means some car thief isn't apt to find it." She drank thirstily before cradling the cold glass against her bare midriff. "But I feel as if I sweated off five pounds today, so I guess I accomplished something."

I didn't think Kendra could afford to lose five pounds, but I didn't say anything.

"Can I drive you to the service on Friday?" she asked.

"I appreciate the offer, but . . . I think I'd like to go alone."

"I understand."

"I'm glad you're going to be there. I doubt there'll be many mourners. Not many of our friends are left around here now."

"Ivy, I hate to ask this . . . I don't like to be thinking about myself or bothering you with my troubles at a time like this. But I'm wondering about the apartment. Will Thea's daughter

29

want me to vacate it right away? I don't have a lease, and my rent is paid only through Monday."

"I told Molly I'd look after things here, and, as far as I'm concerned, you're most welcome to stay. Though I suppose Molly and her husband will put the house up for sale when they come."

"That's okay. I don't think I'll need the apartment for more than a few weeks longer anyway."

"You won't?" I was both surprised and sorry to hear that.

I thought she might offer some explanation, but she didn't. She just turned and set the empty glass on the counter. She'd tied her dark hair into a swingy ponytail, probably because of the heat. Then I spotted something I hadn't seen before. She'd missed a few strands behind her left ear when she'd colored her hair. Blond.

"Will you be getting another apartment? Or going back to California?" I asked.

"I'm just playing it by ear," Kendra said. "Thea didn't have any grandchildren?"

No solid information about her plans, and a smooth segue into a change of subject, I noted. "After five miscarriages, Molly and her husband gave up."

"Oh, that's sad. You don't have grandchildren either?"

"No. Our Colin was in the army. He was sent on a peace-keeping mission to Korea a long time ago. There was an accident and . . . he didn't come home." After all these years I could say it without overt emotion, but the pain would always be there. And never knowing what had happened to his body . . .

"Oh, my . . ." Kendra looked near tears, and I found myself in the unexpected position of giving her a comforting pat. I wondered about what Kendra had said just a few moments earlier about knowing what it was to lose someone you loved. Who had Kendra lost? Not her parents, because

30

she'd mentioned both of them. Had Thea been right about Kendra losing the love of her life?

"Life's so unfair!" Kendra suddenly burst out.

"But God is in control."

"You really believe that, don't you?"

"Of course."

"I wish I did. It might have made things easier when—"

"When?"

"Earlier." A stubborn note entered Kendra's voice, erecting a barrier around her loss as surely as if she'd thrown up a wall of concrete blocks.

I didn't prod further. "You can have God's comfort any time, child. Just—"

"Maybe I will. Later. But right now—"

"It isn't something that should be put off."

"Neither is what I have to do." Kendra swiped her left eye with a knuckle, smearing her mascara and smoky eye shadow into dark streaks. I was curious about what Kendra had to do, but I knew how far prying got with her. Like trying to read a book with the pages glued together.

"I'll see you at Fleur & Fleur on Friday, then," Kendra said. "But you call or come over if you need anything, or if I can do anything to help before then. Anything at all."

The short service at the funeral home was quiet and dignified. Closed coffin, as Thea had specified. "I don't want people looking down at me and telling each other how lifelike I look," she'd sniffed. The occasion had seemed far off when Thea said that. And now here it was.

I surreptitiously counted the people present. Including myself and Kendra, eighteen. More than I'd expected, actually. A few old Madison Street friends who lived in other parts of the city now. A man who used to do Thea's yard work, before he got too crippled up with arthritis. A few others were people I thought had worked with Walter in the county road department.

I didn't know the pastor who conducted the service. I'd requested one of the pastors from Riverview United, the big church that had absorbed our little one, but none had been available, so the funeral home had arranged for this serious, bespectacled young man. The music Thea had chosen a long time ago was recorded: "In The Garden" and "Standing on the Promises."

If I hadn't been convinced before that Thea was dead and gone, I truly knew it now. Thea had never been able to hear that old hymn without enthusiastically surging to her feet.

Afterward, when the few mourners had filed out, I went up to lay a hand on the casket. Kendra followed, standing a few feet behind me. I rubbed the smooth metal as I talked to Thea for the last time.

Well, I guess we always knew one of us would have to go first, didn't we? But that doesn't make it any easier. Say hi to Walter and Harley for me, will you? And Colin too. I'm going to miss you so much. I miss you so much already. Thanks for being a wonderful friend.

I gave the casket a final good-bye tap, secure, even though my tears flowed, in the knowledge that believers in our Lord never really had to say good-bye.

See ya later, alligator.

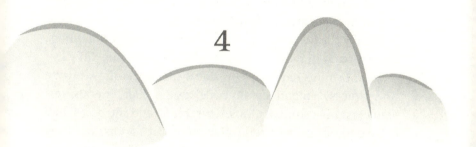

4

I felt at loose ends and drove out to Country Peace after the service. No more tombstones had been yanked out of the ground, but the air of serenity that had once lingered over the cemetery was missing now. I picked up the jar of withered marigolds beside the fallen tombstone on Aunt Maude's grave.

Today I had plenty of time, and I climbed to the top of the hill to look over the other side. The first thing that surprised me was that the road didn't end in the cemetery as I'd assumed. It wound back into the hills to a small house tucked into the woods, though on squinting I realized it was more tumbledown shack than house. The next surprise was how wild and untouched the wooded area looked, perhaps not much different than when settlers first arrived. Beautiful. But not for long, I supposed regretfully. The subdividers were on the move.

I called my niece in Arkansas that evening to tell her about Thea. DeeAnn Harrington, my dead sister's only child, and her family are my only living relatives, except for some distant cousins out in Idaho. Even though DeeAnn and I seldom chat more than once or twice a month, our relationship is warm and caring. I know I can always count on DeeAnn.

"Oh, Aunt Ivy, I'm so sorry to hear this. Your very best friend. And she was so sweet. I remember she brought me the most gorgeous fern one time when she came with you to visit. Look, why don't you come stay with us for a while? A long while, actually. We'd love to have you."

I knew the invitation wasn't merely obligatory politeness. DeeAnn and her family truly would welcome me. They live in an enormous old house outside a small Arkansas town, a noisy, messy, splendidly alive mélange of kids, friends, foreign exchange students, cats, dogs, birds, and the occasional baby possum or squirrel under temporary adoption. They are always finding homes for stray animals. DeeAnn's husband, Mike, is an executive with a roofing manufacturer, but he gives much time and energy to an active church youth group. I'd given all of Harley's fishing equipment to Mike when Harley died.

Their family consists of just-graduated twin boys, Rick and Rory, and daughter, Sandy, a lithe and limber teenager given to spinning into exuberant gymnastic back flips without warning.

"Thanks," I said, "but—"

"Now, Aunt Ivy, don't be so quick with your 'thanks, but,'" DeeAnn scolded. "The boys are heading off to college early because they both have jobs lined up. The house will be so empty. Sandy would love to teach you how to surf the Internet. It would be good for you. Us too, and we want you to consider living here permanently, either with us or in a place of your own nearby."

I had no intention of leaving my home, but I welcomed the invitation, finding comfort in the knowledge that a family haven awaited if I wanted it. My sister, Lily, DeeAnn's mother, had lost her battle with breast cancer just weeks after the twins were born, so I'd always been something of a surrogate grandma.

"Right now I have some loose ends to finish up." I didn't elaborate on what those loose ends were because I couldn't pinpoint them for myself. But it felt as if there were some. "How about if we plan on a few days around Thanksgiving?"

Thanksgiving would be a bad time to be alone. For years Thea and I had defied turkey tradition and made a ritual of eating out and trying something totally new and exotic for Thanksgiving dinner. Last year it was a Thai dish with tiny squid, which turned out to have way too many slippery appendages for comfortable consumption. But it supplied much happy laughter.

"Thanksgiving will be great, Aunt Ivy. We'll look forward to it. But if you get lonely or depressed or anything, you come anytime, okay?"

"Okay."

"We love you."

"I love you too, all of you."

I went for a walk before breakfast the following morning, for the first time since losing Thea. Thea hadn't accompanied me often in recent months, but now I was all too aware that she'd never walk on this earth with me again.

Yet in spite of my gloomy cloud of loss, I couldn't not be aware that this was a glorious morning. Even as shoddy and rundown as Madison Street had become, blue sky arched serenely over maples older than I am, and sunlight dappled the cracked and humped sidewalk. A hummingbird darted by, pausing momentarily to check out my red-flowered blouse.

A scent of fresh-watered grass hung like a promise in the air, and a bed of petunias in a nearby yard stretched into a purple carpet of bloom.

The Lord does mornings, I thought with unexpected joy. And Thea was no doubt having a morning so glorious that it put this one to shame, which also gave me joy.

I took a different route today, circling out past Wal-Mart and the new bowling alley, avoiding the section of Madison that had been taken over by taverns and something called the "Exotic Flower Club" that I was reasonably certain had nothing to do with growing orchids or African violets. I didn't see anyone I knew, which wasn't unusual these days.

I had no trouble passing the greasy-scented fast food places lined up beyond the bowling alley, but when I approached a portable stand called "Ella's Espresso" at the edge of the Thriftway parking lot, I paused and inhaled deeply. A magnetic scent, rich and lush and enticing. Coffee, surely fresh ground. Vanilla. Cinnamon. Thea and I had always intended to try one of the fancy espressos, but . . . *four dollars for a cup of coffee?* We'd also talked about saving up and taking a cruise to the Caribbean. And never had. We'd never tried a massage, rafting down the Grand Canyon, or going up in a hot-air balloon. A wind of regret, unexpectedly powerful, swept through me.

No more putting anything off, I decided fiercely. I patted the pocket of my walking shorts and found the emergency five-dollar bill securely pinned in place. I studied the menu posted by the drive-up window. Caffe latte. Cappuccino. Mocha. All of which were as unfamiliar as fancy liqueurs to me.

What'll it be, Thea? I know . . . let's go for that Mocha Mama!

I started around to the other side of the stand, where a green-and-white striped awning shaded a trio of diminutive metal tables and chairs. A bright red sports car pulled away from the drive-up window at the same time. But it didn't follow the directional arrows on the asphalt. Instead it whipped in the opposite direction, sweeping so close that the rearview mirror smacked my arm. I caught a glimpse of a middle-aged man behind the steering wheel, a horrified look on his face, as he only then realized he'd hit something. The car screeched to a stop.

He jumped out and helped me to a chair by the espresso stand. "Are you okay? I'm so sorry. I just didn't see you . . ."

My heart hopped like a crazed kangaroo as I plopped into the metal chair. If I'd been standing a foot to the left, the man would have flattened me like a pin struck down by a bowling ball.

"I can take you to the emergency room at the hospital," he offered anxiously.

By then, even though he was a nice and obviously responsible man, I suspected he was hearing siren alarms of liability and lawsuits. I ran a palm along my arm. It would no doubt bruise, but nothing was broken. "I'll be okay. I just need to sit here a moment and catch my breath."

"I just didn't *see* you," he repeated. He sounded bewildered.

"It's okay. I'm fine."

"I'll get you something . . ." He motioned toward the espresso stand.

Well, since he was offering . . . "I was just getting ready to order a Mocha Mama."

"Hot or cold?"

I hadn't realized there was a choice. "Cold, I think."

"One Mocha Mama, coming up." He sounded relieved to be getting off so easy.

He went over to the window and returned a minute later with a tall glass of frothy stuff. I again assured him I was fine, and he drove off, very slowly and carefully, as if afraid other elderly apparitions might suddenly leap up in front of him.

The Mocha Mama was rich, chilly, and delicious. I sipped it slowly, enjoying the spread of soothing coolness through my chest as it went down my throat. Thea would have loved a Mocha Mama.

I cut the walk short. My arm, although quickly beginning to swell into the shape of a bluish baseball, didn't really hurt. But I was feeling a little off-center, like the first time I got bifocals.

I rested a few minutes on the sofa in the living room and then spent the rest of the morning tying up string bean vines in my garden. I was over my nerves about the close call, but I was feeling a peculiar drift toward . . . something. Not truly depression. Just a kind of *down* feeling. Had the collision been more my fault than the driver's? Were my faculties fading, like yard-sale balloons cut adrift? Would it reach a point where I no longer felt safe going out for a walk?

I also was not, I realized unhappily as I wound a string around a stake, the greatest gardener in the world. That truth had been lurking in my subconscious for some time, but it really hit me now when I picked a couple of string beans to see how they were progressing. Harley grew string beans that were long and plump. They had an *attitude* and sounded like the crack of a miniature whip when snapped open.

My immature string beans were limp and anemic, with no more snap than an anorexic worm. Actual worms had invaded and devastated my green onions within weeks of when I planted them. My tomatoes, though still no larger than green marbles, were already showing bulbous lumps and protuberances.

I framed a particularly lumpy one with my fingers and held it at arm's length, squinting. *If you look at it just right, it bears an amazing resemblance to—*

I dropped the tomato. *No!*

I might find inkblot abstracts in a fingernail blister. I might flirt with a bit of whistle-blowing eccentricity. But I was not going to start seeing miniature Nixons in my tomatoes!

Maybe next year I won't even plant a garden, I thought. *I'll spend my time on something more productive and useful.*

Such as? that small voice chirped.

Oh, shut up, I answered.

I'd long ago given up on houseplants. Thea and my other good neighbor, Magnolia Margollin, enjoyed bountiful green thumbs, but mine seemed to carry an almost biblical scourge of death.

An appalling thought suddenly struck me. *Houseplants. Thea's houseplants!*

I rushed over to Thea's house. A scent of stale air, with an undertone of aging garbage, met me when I unlocked the door. I hastily carried the smelly plastic sack out to the garbage can at the back fence. From there I could see the small windows that opened into Kendra's basement apartment. I was surprised that the ugly curtains with bug-eyed fish that the last tenant had left still hung at the windows. Like some old picture of George Washington, the fish eyes seemed to follow you. I'd have thought Kendra would have put up something with a bit less of a fishy presence by now.

Back in Thea's kitchen, I filled a pitcher and carried it from room to room. The soil in the pots felt dry, although there didn't appear to be any fatalities among the plant population yet. But so many plants. Delicate coleus. Lush maidenhair ferns. Plump jade plants. Robust aloe vera. Whatever was I going to do with all of them?

I left a note on Kendra's door asking if she'd like to have some of the plants. Later, Kendra stuck her head in my back door just as I was slapping a slice of ham into a frying pan for supper.

"Would you like to join me?" I invited instantly. "I can

thaw out another slice of ham in the microwave. Won't take but a minute."

"Oh, thanks, no. I can't stay. I just wanted to give you this. It's a new Mary Higgins Clark, and I know how you like her mysteries. I thought it might . . . you know, help keep your mind off things."

"Why, Kendra, thank you." I accepted the book with surprise and gratitude for her thoughtfulness. "That's very generous of you. Please, won't you stay and eat with me?"

"I'd really like to, but I have a dinner engagement." Kendra made a little gesture toward her dress. It was ankle length but clingy, with exotic red flowers on a black background, a thigh-high slit up one side, and a back bare to the waistline. I couldn't see much except willpower holding it in place. "I can't go to church with you tomorrow, but maybe next Sunday, okay?"

"Great."

I couldn't help frowning, even though Kendra's tentative offer pleased me. Dinner engagement. Undoubtedly with her "friend." And in a come-hither dress like that. I was tempted to come right out and ask if he was married. The only reason I didn't was because I knew what kind of answer I'd get. Not a lie. I'd always sensed an innate honesty in Kendra that rejected lies. But she could also slither around a factual answer like one of those Thanksgiving squids slithering off a fork. So instead I merely said, "You saw my note about Thea's plants?"

"Yes, and I'd love to have some of them. But I think I'm almost through here, and I won't have room to take them with me in the car."

"You'll be quitting your job, then, and moving away?" The ham started to sizzle, and I covered it with a lid.

"The sooner I see the last of Bottom-Buck Barney's, the better."

I glanced up, surprised at the fervency in Kendra's voice. The words also had an edge I'd never heard from her before. "What about your . . . friend?"

"B—" Kendra cut off the name before she got past the first letter. She smiled. An oddly unpleasant smile, almost sly, nothing at all like her usual light-up-your-life flashes. "I think he may be going away somewhere too."

Kendra did not, I noted, sound brokenhearted. I felt as if I'd been hopscotched through some complicated detour. On impulse, I asked bluntly, "Kendra, are you up to something?"

I hadn't thought about how Kendra might react to the question, but, if I had, I'd have expected another devious sidestep, or teasing and laughter. *Oh, Ivy, what do you think? That I'm embezzling company funds?* What I'd never have expected was what happened. First Kendra's face paled, as if all the blood fled somewhere deep inside her. Her gaze made a squirrelly dart toward the door, as if she'd like to escape through it, and she touched her slender throat. Then the blood rushed back to her face in a heavy—guilty?—flush.

"Are you all right?" I asked.

"Fine. Just . . . the heat getting to me, I guess." She touched the back of her hand to her forehead.

"Would you like some lemonade?"

"Thanks, no. I have to be going."

It was obvious that my blunt question had touched a sensitive spot, and her reaction plainly showed she was up to something. But what? Just as plain was the fact that she wasn't going to enlighten me. Although what I suspected, of course, was what Thea had earlier suggested: romantic involvement with a married man. *Do she and he have plans for running off together, leaving wife and jobs, maybe even children behind?* I wondered in dismay. *Is that why she won't be needing the apartment much longer?*

Oh no, Lord, please keep her from that!

But what I also regretted was an instant feeling that my question had opened a gap between us, a gap that shut off any possible communication on this subject. I tried to close the gap and make a way for further communication. "I'll miss you when you leave the apartment. I hope you'll keep in touch."

"I'll worry about you, you know," Kendra said.

Yes, I thought, *maybe she will worry about me*. But Kendra's usual poise and control had now returned, and this was another of her non-answer detours.

I poured a cup of strong coffee into the ham drippings to make a bit of red-eye gravy to go with the meat. Not something those young doctors at the clinic would approve of, of course, but since most of them didn't even know my name until they picked up my file, I didn't feel obliged to give their opinions a high priority. And tonight, with my arm now starting to ache and my heart aching with missing Thea, I felt the need of some small indulgence.

Especially after I took a second bite of ham and crunched down on something that felt like a metallic boulder.

5

By Sunday morning, the missing filling wasn't causing pain, but my tongue wouldn't stay away from the pit. It explored the rough bottom, scraped over the broken edges, probed for some hidden pinpoint of sensitivity. Even while the choir was singing a lively but unfamiliar chorus and Pastor Elton was preaching on "Community Responsibilities of the Christian," this Mariana Trench of the mouth occupied most of my attention.

Thea and I had always come to church together, but only a couple of people had noticed the obituary and offered words of sympathy after the service. Several times Thea and I had talked about finding a smaller, more Christ-centered church, but a vague sense of loyalty to the little church on Madison Street that had been absorbed by this much larger congregation had kept us here. On the way out I paused by the bulletin board and saw a posted notice that a Sunday school teacher for the second and third graders was needed.

I'd always taught Sunday school at the little church on

Madison. I'd also run a children's story hour at the library every summer. *Oh, it would be so nice to have a connection with children again!* I picked up the pencil dangling beside the sign-up sheet. But . . .

I'd volunteered to teach Sunday school here at Riverview United once before. The youth pastor had been polite and tactful and so very earnest. "Our churches are losing the young people, you know, and that's a tragedy of our times. Who will take over when you stalwart warriors are gone? We want to pull in the young families and make our Sunday school and youth programs more attractive than Nintendo and PlayStation for the kids."

All very admirable. But what it boiled down to was that they didn't want old geezers teaching the Sunday school classes. I didn't fit the "youthful image" they wanted to project as a church.

Now I sighed and left the pencil dangling on its string and started toward the side door that opened onto the parking lot. Across an open space, a woman I recognized as president of the women's "Exploring Ourselves" group lifted her arms and beamed.

"There you are!" Rena Rasmussen exclaimed. "I've been looking for you! I wanted to ask—"

My spirits billowed with surprise and pleasure. Never before had I been greeted so enthusiastically here. I smiled as the woman rushed toward me.

And rushed right on by to throw her arms around a young woman in denim jumper and Birkenstocks. The two women chatted vivaciously, hands clasped.

I felt a bit dazed as I made my way out to the parking lot. If Rena Rasmussen had been equipped with a rearview mirror, I'd now be black and blue on the other arm.

Thea and I had often gone out to eat after church, and I promised myself I'd continue that routine soon. But not today. Today I just drove home. That vague *down* feeling had returned.

The Margollins were home, I noted as I passed their chain-link fenced yard. Their enormous whale of a motor home, rear wall covered with a huge mural of a bee hovering over a magnolia blossom, stood in the driveway. I was pleased to see the motor home. Whatever her flaws, Magnolia Margollin is one of the most cheerful and upbeat people I know. A marvelous idea now occurred to me, and I followed up on it after lunch.

I lifted the magnolia-shaped doorknocker beside the brass nameplate that said Magnolia House. It was really a very modest little house, though that fact was fairly well hidden by the camouflage of magnolia trees, dramatically larger and more lush than any others in the area. I could hear Magnolia's energetic tread bustle across the living room. When she opened the door, she wasn't wearing a silk magnolia in her hair, as she usually did. But her hair . . .

"Ivy, dear, how good to see you!"

My mouth fell open. Magnolia's hair had always been a red that rivaled any traffic light and, I'd always suspected, probably stopped traffic occasionally. But now . . .

Pink. Not shell pink, not carnation or rose pink. No, this was . . . It came to me. The color of that fuzzy fiberglass stuff that goes between walls. Insulation pink. It was also in an enormous new style. With a green bow that matched her gauzy green outfit. Magnolia has an impressive, dowager-type body, the top-heavy kind you see in drawings of elegant Victorian society ladies, and she wears clothes that have a life of their own, flowing and swirling giddily long after Magnolia herself stops moving.

Magnolia pushed the screen door open. "Come in! We've been unloading the motor home, and I'm ready for a break. Iced tea?"

Magnolia was, as usual, in full armor. Dramatic blue eye-shadow. Eyebrows swept out to bird-wing length. Blush like a tree-ripened peach. Also, as usual, her lipstick matched her hair. More insulation pink.

The total effect of hair, makeup, and floating attire was quite overwhelming, so much so that Magnolia was well into an animated account of their motor home adventures before I recovered enough to do more than nod.

"And in South Dakota we located this wonderful woman still living out on an old ranch all by herself. She is, as nearly as we can figure out, my great-great-grandfather's great-great-great-granddaughter by his first wife." She paused, reflecting. "Although I'm not positive I have all the 'greats' right."

From what I'd heard, most people do research into family genealogy on the Internet these days, but Magnolia prefers her research on the hoof and in the flesh.

I took a deep breath and interrupted. "I don't suppose you've heard yet, since you just got home . . . Thea passed away while you were gone."

Magnolia's genealogical mapping abruptly ended, and her hands flew to her cheeks. "Oh no."

Magnolia, for all her flamboyancy and a certain preten-tiousness in saturating her surroundings with magnolias to draw attention to her name, truly does possess a warm and caring heart. Last year, when I was hospitalized for gallblad-der surgery, she drove Thea over to the hospital to visit me every day. And even after I went home, she continued to visit my elderly roommate whom none of us had known before. Now she jumped up, then slumped back into her chair, her expression stricken.

"I can't believe it. Her heart?"

I nodded. "I found her dead in her bed last Sunday. We buried her on Friday."

"Oh my. Oh my. We should have been here." Magnolia's

heavy elbows dropped to the table. The green gauze fluttered around the drooping flesh. Her blue-shadowed eyelids quivered. Even her pink insulation hairdo seemed to wilt. "It—it won't be the same around here without Thea, will it?"

"No, not the same at all." Such an understatement that my throat swelled and constricted with the words.

"Was her funeral well attended?" Magnolia's voice suddenly bristled. Not attending a funeral was a major sin in Magnolia's book. When the time came, anyone who didn't attend Magnolia's funeral would suffer for it, I was certain.

"There weren't many there, no. But I think she went easy, and that's a blessing."

Magnolia's husband, Geoff, came in the back way with a big plastic garbage bag slung over his shoulder. Geoff is a short, wiry guy, though he is a bit taller than his hair, so a pink shine shows through. He always seems to be trailing in Magnolia's wake, although on rare occasions he puts his foot down and Magnolia meekly accedes. He is also the only person in the world who dares call her "Mag." Now Magnolia gave him the news.

Geoff echoed his wife. "Oh my," he said, and sat down. The plastic bag spilled dirty clothes at his feet. I would just as soon never have known that Geoff wore boxer shorts printed with miniature magnolias.

"Anyway, the reason I came over," I said with as much briskness as I could muster, "I'm wondering if you'd like to have Thea's plants. You know plants don't do well in my house—"

"They go down like the Titanic."

Yes. "So if you'd like to have them . . . ?"

Magnolia's bird-wing brows flew together in deliberation. "We're gone so much . . . But yes, of course. We'll take them." Her attitude was protective. *Keep those innocent plants out of Ivy's murderous hands!* And, even though they were gone a lot, Geoff had set up a drip-watering system so their house plants didn't suffer while they were away.

Magnolia instructed Geoff to get a wheelbarrow to transport the plants, and we all trooped over to the house. After the second wheelbarrowful Geoff went into one of his rare I'm-laying-down-the-law modes and said that was enough plants.

"I can probably give the rest of them to my niece, then," I said.

Magnolia kindly made no comment on the plants' chances of survival until I could pass them along to DeeAnn. Instead, eyeing the basement steps at Thea's house, she said, "Is that young woman still renting the apartment?"

"Kendra? Yes, she's still here, but I believe she may be leaving soon."

"Is she in some sort of trouble?"

The question startled me. "Why, I don't believe so. Why do you ask that?"

"Oh, just something I sensed about her. I'm very sensitive to the vibrations emanating from people, you know." Magnolia put a hand on her chest and breathed deeply, as if those vibrations came through her nose and she was inhaling fresh ones even now. "And there is just something about her that immediately put me on alert. An aura of darkness. Perhaps even danger."

I couldn't vouch for Magnolia's sensitivity. Her vibrations hadn't informed her that the young Beckett couple she invited to dinner last spring were strict vegetarians, and she'd blithely served them shrimp salad, big T-bones, and mashed potatoes laced with bacon bits. Nor had vibrations served her particularly well when she'd clasped a visiting baby to her breast with happy coos of family similarity, only to discover she was not holding her grand-niece after all.

But it had also been Magnolia who had recognized Effie

McKenzie's handsome new boyfriend as a con man even before he started trying to sell us all stock in some phony Montana mining company. Unfortunately, Effie had been late acknowledging the validity of Magnolia's vibrations about Roger, which was why her resulting financial situation forced her to move in with her daughter in Texas.

Now, after Geoff unloaded the last of the plants in my backyard, I considered Magnolia's question about Kendra. And the more I thought about it, the more I wondered if Magnolia could be right. Was Kendra in some sort of trouble, some danger even beyond her possible involvement with a married man?

I considered what I'd observed. Kendra's careful weighing before giving any information about her past. Her expertise at diverting questions about herself. Dyed eyebrows. Her lack of possessions. Her job at sleazy Barney's. Her odd pale-to-blush transformation when I asked if she was up to something. Those terrible, bug-eyed fish curtains that she'd never bothered to change.

Even I felt a hint of ominous vibrations.

I called the dental clinic the following morning. I'd been going there since old Dr. Sorenson retired. I requested the young dentist who'd filled my last cavity, but he was unavailable. *"But Dr. Griswold has a cancellation today, and if you could come in at 2:00 . . . ?"*

I wasn't surprised by the shift. They seemed to play musical dental chairs at the clinic. I said I'd be there. What I didn't say was that if this new man called me "young lady," as the ophthalmologist I'd tried out last year had done, I was going to kick him in the shins and stomp out.

Dr. Griswold did not do that. He politely called me Mrs.

Malone, gave the tooth a professional inspection, and told his cute young assistant to take me in the other room for X-rays.

The girl helped me climb into the chair and solicitously settled the protective lead shield over my chest and abdomen. She patted my shoulder. "You'll be okay now?"

"Of course." Why wouldn't I be okay? This was just an X-ray, not a rocket ride to the moon.

"I remember last time, how you got that terrible attack of claustrophobia, because the shield was so heavy on your chest."

This was news to me. "The shield's never bothered me."

The young woman frowned as if she thought I was stubbornly refusing to acknowledge something she well remembered. "And then, when your sister came in, she had the same problem—"

"No problems," I said. "No sister. Perhaps you have me mixed up with someone else?"

"Oh. Oh, I see. Oh, I'm so sorry. It's just that we have several elderly ladies among our patients, and you—" The girl put a hand to her mouth and broke off, flustered, but the unspoken ending was obvious: *You all look alike to me.*

The girl suddenly became very businesslike. She stuffed the uncomfortable little X-ray things in my mouth, zapped me a couple of times, and took me back to the other room. Her freckles pulled together in a concentrated frown all through the drilling and filling procedure. I could almost read her thoughts: *I've got to keep these old ladies straight.*

I stopped by the one-hour photo shop to drop my payment in the box the utility company had there, which saved me the expense of a stamp. I had the utility company's envelope in my hand and was just reaching to drop it in the proper slot when a young man pushed in ahead of me. No apology, not even acknowledgment of my existence when he knocked my envelope right out of my hand. He shoved his envelope in the slot, another envelope in the cable company's slot, and away he went to grab a carton of film off a shelf down the aisle.

I picked up my envelope, now decorated with a dark footprint, and stuffed it in the slot. I had to push his sloppily inserted envelope in also.

Well.

I don't want to be one of those doom-and-gloom senior citizens who believe the manners of the younger generation are careening the world toward a state of barbaric savagery, but sometimes you have to wonder.

Or maybe it wasn't just the younger generation. While I was in the little shopping center, I decided to go over to the drugstore. I was almost out of that pink hand cream I splurge on because the scent is so lovely. Two middle-aged clerks were stocking shelves and carrying on an animated conversation about someone named Destiny.

"Well, the thing is, she's just not in *touch* with herself," the woman in the purple T-shirt asserted as she climbed on a step stool to place bottles of blue shampoo on a top shelf. "Know what I mean?"

"There's this fantastic new psychic over on Madison Street. If you could just get her to go there . . ."

A psychic on Madison Street now. Just what we need.

I wandered up and down the aisles, looking for the hand cream, which was not where it had always been. I passed the women several times. Once I had to dodge the swing of the step stool as the clerk moved down the aisle.

"How about aromatherapy?" the woman in green pants suggested. "My cousin says—"

Finally I interrupted. "Excuse me, but I'm looking for some hand cream, and it's always been right over there." I pointed to a shelf loaded with a dizzying array of lotions and creams. "I don't remember the brand name right now, something about lace, I think. And it's pink. Oh, wait, I may have a coupon in my purse . . ."

It was a fairly long bit of conversation, from my point of view, but apparently it flitted right past the saleswoman. She looked through me to a leggy young creature studying a carton of hair coloring.

"May I help you find something?" the saleswoman asked with an eager air of concerned helpfulness. The other sales-clerk was already disappearing through the swinging doors into a rear storeroom.

I gave up on pink hand cream for today. My numb jaw now felt as if it was getting ready to burst into an ache. I wondered if, under the lingering effects of Novocain, I'd per-haps mumbled my request to the clerk. Or, heaven forbid, drooled over the numb lip.

Yet by the time I got home, a different and shocking new possibility rose up to confront me.

6

I'm invisible.

The proof was all there. The driver who hadn't seen me and almost ran me down with his car. Rena Rasmussen looking right through me at church. The young man pushing in front of me at the utility box, never seeing me. The dental assistant, seeing me but not *seeing* me. The salesclerks in the drugstore.

I stopped the Thunderbird in the driveway. At the moment I didn't feel up to putting it in the garage. I sat there with hands wrapped around the wheel.

Some of what I'd encountered could no doubt be attributed to simple carelessness. Or uncaring rudeness. People were busy, preoccupied, stressed. Manners were no longer a high priority. But was that all there was to it? No. People simply did not *see* me.

I jumped out of the car, rushed into the house and down the hallway to the bathroom. I stared at myself in the mirror over the bathroom sink. My stampeding heartbeat slowed, and my moment of panic felt like some foolish social gaffe. The mirror still reflected an image.

Of course it did. This was, after all, Madison Street, not the Twilight Zone.

Same possum-gray hair. Same hazel eyes. Same crow's feet, with deeper lines wrapped like half-moons around my mouth. My neck did look rather more scrawny than I remembered, but it hadn't disappeared.

So, technically, I wasn't truly invisible. I blinked. My image blinked back. All quite normal. And lots of people still saw me. Magnolia and Geoff and Kendra. The meter reader, who always waved. But still, for all practical purposes in the larger world of youth and beauty, rush and struggle, hype and hustle, I was indeed quite invisible.

It was, I must admit, a shocking discovery. I sat in Harley's old recliner and tried to assimilate this unexpected revelation of my new status in the world.

Invisible.

Actually, I reflected, this wasn't as new as it felt at the moment. As two little old ladies—LOLs, perhaps, in this era of timesaving acronyms for everything—Thea and I had been losing visibility for some time now. There was that time Kendra's young man almost ran over us near the back steps. It wasn't dark; the light over the steps had been on. Yet we'd been as invisible as radio waves to him until he actually bumped into us.

We'd also been at least temporarily invisible at the sheriff's office, a part of the lobby furniture, until my whistle demanded attention.

There were times further back too, now that I thought about it.

The department store downtown, where we'd gone to buy Thea a new pair of gloves. A pencil-slim, blond saleslady was strolling around with a tray, handing out samples of a new moisturizer. To everybody but us. Victorio's Seafood, the upscale restaurant where we'd gone to celebrate our three-days-apart birthdays. The waiter had hurried past our table near the swinging doors to the kitchen time and again, as if the space was occupied by only the salt and pepper shakers and an unlit candle.

"What do we have to do to get noticed here?" Thea had grumbled. "Jump up on the table and do a cancan?"

"I will if you will," I'd said boldly.

Then we'd looked at each other and giggled at visions of ourselves kicking our way across the polished table and flouncing our behinds at astonished diners.

The waiter had actually seemed startled to see us when I finally stuck out a stiff arm and snagged him. At the time I'd assumed it was a judgment call: *LOLs don't leave good tips. Ignore them.* Now I wasn't so certain. Maybe it was the encroaching invisibility.

So this had been creeping up unnoticed for some time, I had to acknowledge. It simply hadn't been so obvious when there were two of us. Or perhaps it hadn't really mattered, when Thea and I were laughing and enjoying life together, that we were becoming an island of invisibility in a bright sea of youth and energy.

Now Thea was gone, and life on Invisibility Isle was much less fun.

I sat in Harley's old chair so long that shadows of dusk crept through the old maples and into the windows. I felt as if they were settling into my heart.

I would, I supposed, become ever less visible as time went by. Like a figure in one of those old sepia photographs, I'd gradually become dimmer and dimmer until I completely faded away. Maybe my image in the mirror *would* eventually disappear.

Of course I didn't have to let the dimming happen. There

were actions I could take to snatch back visibility. I sat up straighter in the old recliner. Magnolia Margollin and I were of an age, and certainly no one would ever suggest she was invisible.

I could never duplicate Magnolia's imposing figure, but I too could color my hair stoplight red or insulation pink. I could do gold eyelids and rainbow cheeks, earrings that dangled to my elbows. Lime-green tights and T-shirts that said outrageous things. I could plant so much ivy that it would cover the house. Put up a sign proclaiming this was Ivy Mansion. Wear ivy jewelry, wind ivy in my hair, and get an ivy tattoo on my ankle.

I bounced my fists on the arms of the chair, warming to the subject.

I could write outrageous letters to the editor and sign them Poison Ivy. Call up radio talk shows and offer radical opinions. Poison Ivy would gain notoriety all over the city. Perhaps even the state. The world! I could become a one-woman Good Manners police force and blow my whistle whenever I spotted an infraction. Especially if it involved rudeness to some older person.

I could become so unconventional and flamboyant I couldn't possibly be invisible!

Yes. But . . .

I slumped back in the chair. Defeat washed over me. I might have some teensy leanings toward eccentricity. Perhaps a few quirks here and there. But I could never go the full route. Magnolia Margollin's flamboyancy came naturally to her. But it just wasn't in me. Even in younger years, I'd been small and quiet, not all that noticeable.

Apparently I had no choice, then, but to let the inevitable invisibility engulf me. *I'll probably get used to it,* I decided sadly. It might even have certain compensations. I could eavesdrop on conversations without being noticed. Wander stores without being pestered by overeager clerks. Go back a dozen times for some especially good sample being handed out at the supermarket.

Next day as I walked into the bank, the thought occurred to me that invisibility might even have a practical usefulness. Boldly testing this theory, I slid into the middle of the line rather than going to the end. No one noticed. The man behind me continued studying his bank statement. The young woman ahead gave an absentminded glance over my head and went back to appraising a good-looking bank teller.

Hey, how about this? All right!

I could probably use invisibility for even more nefarious purposes, it occurred to me as the line inched forward. Who'd see me if I walked into a movie theater without paying? Or I could drift into fancy get-togethers I hadn't been invited to—weddings would be good—and stuff myself with caviar canapés and shrimp on toothpicks.

Invisibility opened like a doorway into a spectacular new world.

I could shoplift whole jars of caviar and no one would notice! Treat myself to filet mignon and lobster tails from the meat counter. Pick pockets and melt away like a ghost. Rob banks, and no one would remember what I looked like. Smuggle jewels across international borders.

But that was a glittery world, I had to acknowledge only moments later, that I could never enter. Because even now guilt prickled me for grabbing this unwarranted place in line. With a sigh, I ducked out of the queue and circled around to the end, where I should have gone in the first place.

Flamboyancy was not in my makeup. Neither was a bent

toward criminality. What was left? Only that inevitable dimming toward invisibility.

Yet at 2:24 a.m.—I know the exact time because I looked at the red numbers on the digital clock above the bed—I woke with a fantastic revelation.

This newfound invisibility wasn't a curse of advancing years; it was a gift. A marvelous gift.

And I knew exactly how I was going to use it.

7

I planned carefully the following day. Black slacks, dark blouse, the stained sneakers I always wore for gardening. I didn't have dark socks, so I'd just go without. Isn't that what the kids did these days?

In the midst of my preparations, however, I paused to consider. *If I'm invisible, why all this camouflage?*

Because I'm basically a prudent person, and a prudent person, even an invisible one, doesn't take unnecessary chances. Besides, I was new at working this invisibility thing.

I laid out a dark scarf to cover my hair. Took off the diamond-chip earrings I always wore, a gift from Harley on our twenty-fifth anniversary. Starlight might glint on them. I was concerned about starlight also revealing my glasses, but that couldn't be helped. Without them I couldn't tell a vandal from a tombstone.

Just before dinner, I tried everything on. Great! A black cat had nothing on me. Except for those shoes . . .

I frowned at my reflection in the full-length mirror on the

closet door. Even dirty, the once-white sneakers stood out like a pair of untanned legs at the beach.

I was on the back porch smearing shoe polish on the dirty sneakers when Kendra cut across the yard behind Effie's vacant house.

"Ivy . . ." Kendra's smooth forehead wrinkled in concern after she watched me for a moment. "Did you know that's . . . um . . . brown polish you're putting on those white shoes?"

"That's because I don't have any black polish."

"Oh." Kendra hesitated but apparently decided not to question that line of logic. "I see."

I held up a sneaker. "But this is a really dark brown."

"Yes, it is. Really dark. Ummm . . . I think I have some white polish at the apartment. I could run over and get it."

I squatted back on my heels and scooped up another dab of polish. Sweet Kendra, thinking I may be slipping into senility, but rather than laughing or saying something hurtful, she offers a helpful way out.

"Oh, thanks, that's so nice of you. I appreciate it, but . . ."

But what? But I don't want white because I'm camouflaging the shoes for a midnight stakeout? Kendra would have a fit if she knew that. So I improvised with one of her own detour tricks. "They're really comfortable old shoes. I didn't want to throw them out."

Kendra knelt down beside me. "Look, I know how expensive shoes and polish and everything else is these days. How about if we go shopping together this weekend, and I'll get you a nice pair of shoes that are already black?"

More sweet Kendra. I was almost tempted to tell her what I was really doing. Instead I patted her hand with a finger, lightly, so I wouldn't get brown polish on her. "I'll see how these work out. So, how are things going over at Bottom-Buck Barney's?"

"Same as always." Kendra paused. "But if you ever decide you want a different car, don't patronize Barney's."

"The Thunderbird suits me just fine." This was a nice, safe topic. I smeared more brown polish on a toe and rubbed it in. "It has only sixty-two thousand miles on it, you know, even though it is a 1975 model. I don't drive much."

"Your husband bought it, I'll bet."

I heard a bit of curiosity in Kendra's voice. Maybe even a minuscule twinge of censure. *Your husband bought a Thunderbird . . . but didn't leave you enough to buy a pair of black shoes?*

"We happened to come into a bit of money," I explained. It was an unexpected share of a great-uncle's estate, the other shares going to those cousins in Idaho, although I didn't feel the need to supply Kendra with those details. "By rights I suppose we should've done something sensible with it. But whenever it came time to buy a car, Harley always looked at Thunderbirds and Cadillacs first. Then we'd settle on something smaller and more sedate and sensible. But this time, when we got the money, I said, 'Let's not be sensible. Let's just do it.' So we did."

"That's wonderful. Sometimes tendencies to be sensible need to be squashed."

"It's a great car. A wonderful ride, everyone says. Although," honesty forced me to admit, "it does get terrible gas mileage. I imagine you get wonderful mileage with your little car."

"It also doesn't hurt that my friend lets me use his charge card for gasoline." Kendra gave me a conspiratorial wink. "Next time the Thunderbird needs gas, let me know, and we'll sneak it through on the card too."

Again I saw that tiny facet of Kendra's personality that troubled me. It slipped through whenever mention of the "friend" came up. Something sly and scheming and . . . not quite nice.

"Well, I'd better be running along," Kendra said briskly. "I just wanted to drop over and say hi."

"I'm going to fix a nice shrimp salad for supper. Could you stay?"

"Oh, I'm sorry. Not tonight. I have some . . . papers I have to go over. But I'm definitely planning church with you this coming Sunday, if the invitation is still open."

"Always."

"And I'll give you the money for another month's rent then."

I watched the young woman cut across Effie's yard. A sudden thought occurred to me. How about asking Kendra to come along on this . . . what was this sort of thing called in those hard-boiled mysteries? A caper. Yes, this was a caper. Kendra was sharp, observant, nice company. She'd want to do this for Thea, just as I did. It would be good to have a partner on a caper.

"Kendra?" I called.

Kendra turned. "Yes?"

She was in white shorts, skimpy red top, and frivolous multicolored sandals, her dark hair piled on top of her head with a tangle of tendrils framing her face.

No, I decided regretfully. *Not a workable partnership for this endeavor. Leggy, beautiful Kendra is definitely not invisible.*

"Take care."

I didn't leave the house until almost 10:00. I felt reasonably certain the vandals wouldn't go into action before that hour. I timed the drive. Forty-five minutes. I drove slowly past the metal arch over the cemetery entrance and across the bridge where I'd watched the little boy fishing. This time I noticed there was a name sign by the bridge. Hangman's Creek. *Not*

a name to inspire confidence, I thought a bit uneasily. Was the person who had inspired the name now under a tombstone at Country Peace?

I turned around at the gravel driveway of a farm a mile or so down the road and made another pass by the cemetery.

The hillside was dark, only a faint glint here and there of starshine on tombstones. I braked and listened through the open window. No sounds beyond a chorus of crickets greeted my straining ears. The vandals wouldn't advertise their presence with lights or horns, of course, but I was reasonably certain the cemetery at this moment was quite deserted.

Now to find some place outside the cemetery grounds to park the car. I might be invisible, but the big white Thunderbird was not.

After two more passes, I finally found some old ruts taking off at an angle from the main road. They were about a quarter mile from the bridge and led into a thick grove of trees and brush. I cringed as branches scraped the sides of the 'bird—*Sorry, Harley*—but the flexible undergrowth closed behind the trunk like a concealing curtain slipping into place. A canopy of branches drooped overhead. Perfect.

But when I cut the engine, an unexpected uneasiness also closed around me. No starlight penetrated here. I had a peculiar feeling of being underwater, as if some predatory fish might drift by any moment. The thought also penetrated my brain that I was about to spend the night alone in a cemetery. *Isn't this the stuff of which creepy tales—and gruesome headlines—are born?*

I felt a breathless little giggle coming on, but it ended in my throat. *Oh, Thea, I wish you were here to giggle with me. It's so much harder to giggle alone.*

I slipped out of the car and pushed the door shut with no more than a barely audible click. Twigs and stickers snagged my blouse and hair as I pushed my way out to the road, and once I stepped on something that felt long and skinny and wiggly.

Just a fallen bough turning under my foot, I assured myself a little breathlessly. Not a snake. Maybe a root.

From the road, I was pleased to see that not a trace of the Thunderbird was visible. It was as hidden as if it was tucked away in the garage back home. I brushed my hands across the grass to hide evidence of exiting tire tracks where I'd pulled off the road.

I tied the dark scarf around my hair and kept to the shoulder, cautiously watching the road in both directions. When the lights of a car flashed over the hill, I ducked into the underbrush. It didn't cover me completely. I had a definite ostrich-with-its-head-in-the-sand feeling. But the car swept by without slowing.

Invisibility works!

Yet my confidence wavered when I had to step onto the exposed openness of the narrow bridge, and I rather wished I'd found a place for the car on the opposite side of the creek. What if the vandals arrived now, while I was right out here with no place to hide? I held my breath until I was safely on the other side.

No more headlights rose out of the darkness, and a minute later I was slipping under the metal arch. Inside the cemetery, I kept to the shelter of the tombstones, dashing across the open spaces between them, in case the vandals arrived before I reached my chosen station.

I hadn't brought a flashlight, but I had no trouble locating Aunt Maude and Uncle Romer's overturned tombstone by starlight. Individual as most of the gravestones were, none of the others approximated an overturned Volkswagen Bug.

I was also sweating from the climb up the hill as I settled into the protective shadows of the fallen tombstone. The night air was still and warm and humid, with a faint scent of swampy growth where stagnant water pooled along edges of the creek. Off in the distance a milky glow hung over the city, brighter sparkles of the city itself below. From this hillside spot I had an unobstructed view of tombstones, entryway, road, and bridge. No one was going to sneak up on me here.

I extracted a small notebook with attached pencil from my pocket. My plan was simple: When the vandals arrived and started their dirty work, I would, with my newfound invisibility, sneak up close enough to catch the license plate number on their vehicle and write it down. Then I'd have the goods on them and could go to the police again.

Headlights flared on the road. I eased deeper into the shadows, heart pounding, but the vehicle zoomed on by. After two more passing cars and another twenty minutes, I scooted around to rest my back on the tombstone.

With my head against the stone and my gaze turned to the stars, I found it impossible not to wander into philosophical contemplations. Had the Lord really made all this, stars as far as the eye could see? Yes. I had no problem with that concept. I could not, in fact, feature how anyone could think all this simply popped into existence by itself, without God.

But why all this, Lord? Why so many stars and so much space? Do you intend for your children here on earth to venture out there? Unanswerable questions. But one prominent truth. *Even in the midst of all this grandeur, you still care about each and every one of us, don't you? Yesterday, today, and tomorrow.*

I mentally fenced off a section of sky and tried to count the stars, but they seemed to wiggle and twist like so many celestial puppies. I let the count go. God knew how many there were and why they were there, and that was all that mattered.

The tombstone got harder. One bump felt like a headlight bulging into my back. A spot on my sneaker rubbed uncomfortably against my sockless foot. I suspected brown was migrating to my ankles. I peered at my digital watch with the oversized numbers I needed these days. Could it really be only 12:50? My stomach growled as if on a fast-track schedule for breakfast. Why hadn't I brought a snack? I stood up and stretched. A dog barked somewhere in the distance. The crickets had become white noise. I had to concentrate or I didn't even hear them now.

And in spite of the various physical discomforts, I was getting sleepy. Shouldn't I be wide awake, edgy about being alone here among the dead?

Well, I wasn't. I'd been a bit uneasy there in the car when I first arrived, but now I was just sleepy. I felt no ghostly presences, no restless souls. I was still nervous about encountering the vandals, but that didn't keep me from feeling as if I could pillow my head on the weedy ground and fall right to sleep.

I tried to remember some creepy ghost stories to scare myself awake. Banshees and ghouls, vampires and werewolves, satyrs and zombies. I conjured up the possibility that there were no living human vandals, that it was evil entities rising up from the graves to wreak havoc on the tombstones. But all that came to mind was a movie cartoon about a friendly ghost. Casper, wasn't that his name?

Actually, I found the cemetery considerably more peaceful and soothing than a trip to the crowded mall.

I tried mental exercises to stay awake. I recited memorized Bible verses. I counted to five hundred by increments of seventeen. I divided three thousand by twenty-two. I replayed memories. A vacation trip to Colorado with Harley and Colin, when we'd camped out under the stars like this. Backyard barbecuing with Thea and Walter, more stars. My first day of work at the Madison Street branch of the library. No stars there, but books and books and more books! I'd felt as if I'd fallen into a treasure trove. And the day, years later, when

I went over to watch the big wrecker swing its ball against the library's old brick walls . . .

No, no, no. Useless thoughts. Concentrate on the future. But there was so much more past than future in my life . . .

Ivy Malone, I chided myself sternly, *if you don't get off this gloomy track I'm going to sentence you to grits for breakfast.* And no matter if my mother was southern raised and spent years trying to promote grits to my father, sister, and me, I'd always thought buttered gravel would be preferable.

I stuck it out until 4:45 a.m. I didn't bother with conceal-ment as I trudged to the car. I backed the Thunderbird out of its hidey-hole and stopped for pancakes and sausage at a McDonalds on the edge of town, where they also give seniors a bargain deal on coffee.

Then I went home and slept until midafternoon.

The following night was a rerun. Only a handful of cars passed by on the rural road. No vandals interrupted the peace-ful silence of the cemetery. The only difference was that this time I remembered to bring a snack. I rationed out the Baby Ruth, allowing myself a bite every half hour.

The following night I added potato chips and a 7-Up. And finally, just after I popped the can of soda open . . . action! Headlights turned in at the arch and arced over the hill. I ducked around behind the tombstone, accidentally knocking over the can. 7 Up bubbled over my foot. I jumped out of the way, not wanting the brown polish to wash off my sneaker. I snatched the little notebook out of my pocket. *Okay, vandals, go to it! I've got you covered.*

The car stopped halfway up the hill. An undamaged tomb-stone stood nearby. A dark figure got out on the driver's side. Was he going around to the trunk to get a rope or cable?

Somehow I'd expected a boisterous group, not a lone vandal. And something larger and heavier for pulling purposes than this ordinary-looking little car.

I ducked low and dodged to the concealing shelter of another tombstone twenty feet down the hill. I'd have to get really close to get that license number. What kind of car was it? A sedan. Dark colored. I wished I was better at identifying makes of cars. I couldn't see the person now. He had apparently stopped on the far side of the car. I dashed to another tombstone.

A moment later the man came around the car. He was zipping up his trousers.

Then I realized in embarrassment what this midnight visitor had been doing while I tried to sneak up on him, and I was extremely grateful I hadn't gotten any closer.

And especially grateful that I was invisible.

I planned to skip Saturday night so I could get back on a normal time schedule for Sunday morning. I wasn't convinced Kendra would keep our date for church. I hadn't seen her since Wednesday when she came over while I was coloring the sneakers. But I didn't want to be too sleepy for church if Kendra did want to go.

But on second thought I decided that Saturday was surely the night most likely for partying and carousing and a little morbid fun with tombstones, and I'd better not miss it.

So I was at my usual spot by 10:30. I really expected something to happen. Tonight the vandals would howl. And I would nail them. I was too jazzed even to be sleepy.

Yet by 2:45 a.m. nothing had happened, and I was beginning to think the vandals had lost interest in ripping out tombstones and had gone on to other excitement. I gathered up my dark plastic sack holding a candy wrapper and Pepsi can. I was always careful to leave no trace of my presence in the cemetery.

I had just stepped onto the bridge when car lights arced over the hill. The vandals, arriving late? I ducked back, panicky. No time to make it to the brush, a good fifteen feet away. I crashed down alongside the bridge approach and flattened myself against the ground.

The car rolled smoothly onto the bridge.

And stopped.

8

I heard the car door open, but I didn't dare lift my head. At this moment, I felt anything but invisible. The headlights went off, but the engine was still running.

A click and crunch as someone stepped out of the vehicle. A popping noise. A trunk being opened?

A grunt. Rustles and thuds. A curse. More grunts. A splash.

A fairly good-sized splash. I remembered that refrigerator I'd seen dumped below the bridge. Trash collection charges big bucks if you put any kind of appliance out for pickup, so this scuzzbucket was apparently doing it the cheapo way.

An edgy minute of silence, as if he were watching to see what became of his deposit. Then a thump of trunk lid and a slam of door. A squeal of tires as if he was suddenly anxious to get away now that the deed was done.

I cautiously lifted my head when the sound of the engine receded down the road. I could feel the imprint of gravel on my cheek. I was just getting to my knees when I saw by the taillights that the car was doing what I'd done that first night, turning around at the farmhouse driveway. I slammed myself against the gravel and weeds again. This time my head was turned, and I got a look at the car.

Again my knowledge of makes and models was frustratingly deficient, but I could tell it was a big vehicle, long hooded, with a classy shape and shiny hubcaps. Definitely not a clunker. It went by too fast for me to read the license, although I was reasonably certain it was a Missouri plate. With maybe a seven as the first number.

More indignation zipped through me. With an expensive car like that, this cheapskate could surely afford to pay for proper disposition of his worn-out appliances.

When I was sure he was gone for good, I got stiffly to my feet and peered over the railing. I could see nothing down there, not even the old refrigerator. In the darkness, the area below the bridge was a bottomless pit.

Was what I'd seen important enough to report to the authorities? Probably not. If they hadn't manpower enough for investigation of tombstone vandalism, they were probably even less inclined to do anything about the illegal dumping of somebody's microwave or kitchen range.

I got back to the house in time for a nap before getting up to eat a Cheerios breakfast and dress for church. I dialed Kendra's number but got no answer. Nor was Kendra's little Corolla in the carport when I checked. I was disappointed but not surprised.

I went to church, but I didn't go back to Country Peace that night. Partly because I was feeling dragged out from keeping such odd hours, but even more because of an unexpected reluctance to return to the cemetery.

I couldn't pinpoint the reason. Not some newly awakened apprehension about ghosts or graves splitting open. Not some fresh fear of the vandals. But the encounter with the illegal dumper had left me feeling . . . jittery.

On Monday evening I determinedly ignored that feeling and was back at my usual spot beside Aunt Maude's fallen tombstone. I had taco chips, M&M's, and a can of Pepsi. I'd bought some dark socks, so my feet were more comfortable. No tombstones had been disturbed during my missing night. There was no reason the cemetery should feel different, yet somehow it did.

There were unfamiliar squeaks and rustles and thuds. Whining, bloodthirsty mosquitoes. Heretofore unnoticed shadows on the ground and in the trees. A vaguely unpleasant scent. Maybe the dumper had simply tossed a big bag of rotting garbage.

I'd seen an occasional bat chasing night bugs before, but now a whole flock of them swooped around the tombstones. But I didn't chicken out. I determinedly stayed until night turned to a pink dawn and it was light enough that when I paused on the bridge I could peer into the murky water below. Whatever the dumper had tossed was either heavy enough that it had sunk to the bottom or light enough to drift away, because all I could see was the same old refrigerator half submerged at the edge of the brush-covered bank.

Tuesday night's stakeout was also uneventful. I slept until noon on Wednesday, fixed a quick egg salad sandwich for lunch, and drove to the Palisades Nursing Home to visit my old friend Cecile Kettridge.

As usual, though Cecile's body was bent and painful with arthritis, her mind was bright and sharp, her conversation snapping with caustic humor. "Hey, have you heard this one going around?" she asked me in greeting. "Give a man a fish

72

and he'll eat for a day. Teach him how to fish and he'll sit in a boat with a fishing pole and drink beer all day."

"I'm glad to see you're in good humor."

Cecile had a friend who supplied her with these Internet tidbits. Some good, some not so good.

"I might as well be. It's the only thing that will keep anyone sane around here. How about this one: Time may be a great healer, but it's a lousy beautician." She inspected me critically. "Although you're looking pretty good."

I waited a while, letting her run through a few more lines, then told her about Thea's death. Cecile no longer read the newspaper, calling it too depressing, so I knew she hadn't seen the obituary. We reminisced a bit about Thea and the good ol' days on Madison Street, and shared a prayer. Then I kissed her on the cheek and repeated a line I'd read somewhere and had been saving for last. "Just remember, being young is nice, but being old is comfortable."

She tilted her head, considered that, and then smiled. "It is, isn't it? No more panty hose. No more curlers in the hair. No more worrying if your skirt length is out of style. And we're *expected* to be a little eccentric."

Back home, I intended to sleep a few more hours to prepare for another night at Country Peace, but Magnolia knocked before I could get to bed. I opened the door, and she swept in surrounded by Popsicle swirls of red and orange.

She twirled. "Isn't this gorgeous? My third cousin on Great-grandma Phillipe's side sent it to me from Hawaii, along with all sorts of information about that branch of the family."

Magnolia claimed ancestors from various bloodlines around the world, and, fortunately, most of the people she tracked down seemed willing to grant her relative status.

Now she steadied her balance with a grip on the sofa. The dress kept twirling. "That's the French side of the family, you know. I believe we're related to Marie Antoinette."

"Fantastic colors," I murmured, not wanting to get into French ancestry. "Lemonade?"

"Oh yes, lovely. And then I have a surprise for you."

Uh-oh. Magnolia had once surprised me with a vase in the shape of a purple mermaid playing a harp. Another time it was a book on the joys of genealogy. So I was a little wary now about the merits of this new surprise.

I poured two glasses of lemonade, and we went out to the backyard. Magnolia inspected Thea's plants.

"They don't look too bad so far."

"Thank you."

"Will you be taking them to DeeAnn soon?" Magnolia turned a leaf over and studied it as if estimating how long it might survive under my care.

"Probably not until Thanksgiving. I'm thinking I'll get some Miracle-Gro and give them a dose to hold them over."

"Good. You know, this is the third time I've been over to see you," she complained as she settled into a lawn chair that creaked under her bulk. I sat on the bench Harley had made years ago. It was oak, weathered now, but still solid, and I always felt the comfort of Harley's own solidity when I sat on it.

Now, with a hint of accusation, Magnolia added, "I pounded and pounded on the door, but you never answered. And your car was in the driveway."

"I . . . haven't been sleeping well at night," I said. Perhaps not total truth, but truth as far as it went. "So I've been napping during the day." Which I'd discovered went much better with earplugs to shut out sirens and meter readers. And, apparently, persistent door pounders.

"I could swear I saw a car pulling out of your driveway

late last night. I was afraid maybe something was wrong, and you were headed for the emergency room. But then I realized it was probably just someone turning around in your driveway. After a couple of hours at the bars, some of those guys don't know which way home is."

I decided a detour away from discussion of my daytime naps and nighttime excursions would be prudent. "Will you and Geoff be staying home now, or do you have another trip planned?"

"We may stay home for a while. Gas is so expensive now, you know. And the motor home guzzles it like an old drunkard bellied up to a bar. We had a rather unnerving experience too."

Magnolia waited expectantly for me to express alarm, and I obliged. "Oh, dear. What happened?"

"We broke down out in the middle of nowhere in Arizona. It was an eerie place, all these strange cactus standing around looking like people turned into statues." Magnolia raised her arms, making statue shapes. "Then out of nowhere comes this weird guy with a backpack, and he starts telling Geoff he's had a message that alien spacecraft are going to land in the area. And he kept looking at us, as if he thought maybe we were aliens in disguise."

"That does sound creepy."

"Actually, it all turned out okay," Magnolia admitted. "He showed Geoff what was wrong with the motor home, something about a loose spark plug wire."

"Perhaps he'll be able to help the flying saucer aliens, then, if they have mechanical problems," I suggested.

Magnolia rewarded the facetious comment with a righteous frown. "But he could have been a serial murderer, and we'd have wound up as a newspaper headline: 'Middle-aged Couple Found Decapitated in Luxury Motor Home in Arizona Desert.'"

Luxury motor home? Stretching it. Middle-aged couple? No way. Then I chided myself for this flippant attitude. Because desert decapitation was no doubt gruesomely possible.

"Of course, reading the newspaper or listening to the TV about things going on right around here is just about as scary," Magnolia declared. "Can you believe what's been happening?"

"I guess I haven't been keeping up with the news too well lately." My nighttime excursions and daytime naps didn't allow for much newspaper perusal. And I hadn't had the TV on in several days.

"Well, just awful things have been happening. That boy who took a gun to school and wounded three people. That girl's body found in the river. That shameful vandalism out at some old cemetery. That whole family selling drugs, even the kids. The man who—"

"Whoa. Back up. Vandalism at a cemetery?"

"It's out in the country somewhere. There were photos of several overturned tombstones. The police are asking anyone in that vicinity to keep an eye out."

Perhaps that trip to the sheriff's office had done some good after all.

"Has Thea's renter moved out?" Magnolia added, moving on with one of her rapid changes of subject. "I haven't seen her car for several days now."

"I don't think so. She said she was going to pay another month's rent. I don't think she'd just pick up and leave without saying good-bye." I hadn't been paying attention to Kendra's car.

"But she didn't pay the rent?"

"No, not yet." Actually, as of now, Kendra's rent was several days past due.

"Well, maybe she did leave then. If she didn't, I'd certainly hit her up for the rent and not let her get behind. She seemed nice, but you just can't depend on young people these days."

"I'm sure there are any number of thoroughly dependable young people around," I protested. "You just don't hear about them like you do the other kind."

Magnolia murmured a *humph* of doubt, set her empty glass on the grass, and stood up. "Oh, you almost let me forget my surprise."

Magnolia didn't appear to be carrying anything, which I took as a good sign. No more odd vases or books on genealogy. But her pleased-with-herself smile was not so good.

"Surprise?" I repeated warily.

"I want you to come over for a barbecue Saturday night. I'm inviting some people from our RV Roamers group."

I relaxed. A barbecue was fine. Geoff did a great job with chicken or hamburgers. And I didn't mind recreational vehicle people, though they did tend to spend an excessive amount of time discussing where good dump stations were located. "Can I bring something? A pie or cobbler, perhaps?"

"Yes, that would be lovely. I'm sure it will make a terrific impression on Mac."

I stopped relaxing. "Mac?"

Magnolia clapped her hands. "Mac is my surprise! He's this lovely man we met in Arizona. Not the weird, flying saucer one," she added hastily. "He travels the country in his motor home, and he'll be arriving here Saturday afternoon. I just know you two are going to hit it off."

As a surprise, I thought glumly, *I'd rather have had another mermaid vase after all.* Trying to be tactful, I said, "That's very nice of you, but I'm really not interested in—"

"That's the problem," Magnolia scolded. "You should be interested! You and Thea did everything together, and with her gone you're going to be sitting around here alone. You need companionship, and there aren't a lot of eligible men in our age group. And Mac is very eligible."

I couldn't argue with Magnolia's statement about men in our age group. Statistics always shout their scarcity. It is also a fact that their scarcity had never particularly concerned me. It's like pickled eel at the supermarket: If you don't want pickled eel, who cares if the store doesn't have any?

I searched for a polite way to wiggle out of the barbecue. Finally I settled for honesty. "Magnolia, I appreciate your concern about my being alone. And I've enjoyed meeting other RV people from across the country who've come to visit you. But I really don't want to get involved in a . . . matchmaking situation."

"Just meet him, Ivy." Magnolia's tone managed to reproach, cajole, and accuse. "You don't have to elope with him the next day, you know."

I sighed. Opposing Magnolia was like trying to stop a combination of charging bull and pleading kitten. I also knew she honestly cared. If I'd ever expressed interest in acquiring a man, she'd have been hauling them in by the truckload long before this.

"Where's his home?"

"I think he used to live in California." Magnolia airily waved a hand. "But the world is his home now. He lives in his motor home."

No rooted home? I found that difficult to comprehend. Harley and I had talked about traveling but never about giving up our home. I rubbed a row of itchy mosquito bites on my leg.

"Is he into genealogy?"

"Well, no . . ." Magnolia frowned at this flaw I'd so quickly uncovered. Then she brightened. "But he has a fabulous head of hair. And not a trace of potbelly. Every morning he

78

was out jogging around the RV park there in Arizona. And he reads a lot, just like you."

"Does he know you're planning to serve him up like an hors d'oeuvre to the widow down the street?"

"He's a writer, so you're going to have so much in common."

I noted that Magnolia had dodged my hors d'oeuvre question. The homeless but fabulously haired, non-potbellied Mac had no idea a booby trap was waiting for him. "I'm not a writer," I pointed out. "So I don't see the connection."

Magnolia dismissed that objection with another of her all-purpose airy waves. "Books, Ivy, books. No one knows more about words and books than you do, after all those years in the library. Mac does these fantastic articles about fabulous places for travel magazines. That's why he lives on the road and travels all the time. I'm sure he'll probably do a book one of these days."

"Thanks so much, but—"

"I'm simply not going to take no for an answer," Magnolia declared. She frowned, pulling insulation pink lips into a down-turned bow, and shot me a sideways glance. "This sleeping in the daytime is not a healthy sign, you know. I'm concerned."

I was not about to explain the reason behind my daytime sleeping. Magnolia would give the yelp-heard-round-the-world if she knew about those nighttime activities.

Okay, Mac had a couple of good points going for him, I conceded. One, he wasn't into genealogy. Two, if he was on the move in his motor home, he wouldn't be here long.

"Okay, barbecue on Saturday night. I'll be there."

"Wear something western. And be sure to bring that peach cobbler." Magnolia winked a blue-shadowed lid. "Who knows, maybe it'll be love at first sight and you'll *want* to elope with him the next day."

9

After Magnolia went home, I dug unread newspapers for the last several days out of the recycle stack on the back porch. I found the piece about the vandalism at Country Peace on an inside page in one of the papers. A photo showed two overturned tombstones. The caption said that eight of the thirty-six stones in the cemetery had been similarly desecrated. A bottom paragraph added that efforts to reach an officer in the Country Peace Association, which was the owner of record, had so far been unsuccessful. Responsibility for restoration and maintenance at the cemetery was at this point undetermined. A representative of a local mortuary was quoted as saying that Country Peace had been closed to new gravesites for many years, although at the moment he did not have information why.

"But it's a beautiful setting and certainly undeserving of this disrespectful treatment," the mortuary representative had added. "Perhaps a restoration fund could be set up."

The developer of one of the subdivisions between the cemetery and town was quoted as expressing concern that the vandalism might spread to the heavy construction equipment he had on the property and might even carry over to when houses were built and children were living in the area.

The tone of the article expressed indignation at the vandalism, but I didn't see anything to suggest increased patrols by the sheriff's department. I'd earlier thought about skipping tonight's stakeout but decided against it. In my bones I didn't feel the vandals were done yet. Maybe I could still nail them.

The people making drug-dealing a family enterprise were on Monday's front page. Inside was a piece Magnolia hadn't mentioned, about a dozen elderly people being scammed with a phony bank scheme. The discovery of the body of the young woman that she had mentioned got several paragraphs on page 3 of yesterday's paper.

The body had been found by children playing along the river and was as yet unidentified. There was a gunshot wound in the woman's chest, but further details were not available.

I shivered in spite of the muggy afternoon heat. Magnolia was right. Terrible things were happening.

There was more about the woman's body in that evening's newspaper. Now information was expanded to a specific description: approximately 22 to 28 years old, 5 feet 7 inches tall, 118 pounds, brown hair and blue eyes. The body was clad in a flowered red and black blouse or dress. It had probably been in the water for several days. The authorities were seeking help from the public in identifying her.

I folded the newspaper. A small frisson of uneasiness prickled my skin. Could the body possibly—

No. Unthinkable. Not even if Kendra did generically match the description and owned a black dress with exotic red flowers. Not even if I hadn't seen her for several days.

I went over after supper to pick up Thea's mail in the box by her front door. I carried the advertisement from AARP and a bill from a cardiologist around to the back, because that was the door to which I had a key. Kendra's car was not in the carport. Had it not been there for several days, as Magnolia had said?

Inside, the house already smelled musty and unused. I added the mail to the pile on the dining room table awaiting Molly's arrival. On the way out, I eyed the ring of keys hanging by the back door. A key to the apartment was undoubtedly among them.

I tapped the doorknob, undecided. I had no solid reason to believe anything was amiss, and Kendra, private person that she was, would surely be appalled if I snooped.

I went outside and peered at the basement windows. The dead-fish curtains were closed, and I couldn't see into the apartment.

Perhaps just a quick peek wouldn't hurt.

The third key on the ring unlocked the door. I peered inside, then pushed the door open wider.

I stared in astonishment. No pictures on the walls, no knickknacks, no pillows on the sofa, no magazines on the coffee table. I flicked the light switch, and a fluorescent fixture in the kitchen buzzed on. I opened a cupboard door above the bare counter. No food. No dishes. I opened the drawer below the oven of the kitchen range. No pots and pans. Empty refrigerator. I crossed over to the one tiny bedroom. No linens on the bed. No clothes in the closet.

So Kendra really had moved out without even bothering to say good-bye. Disappointment twanged me, even a twinge of betrayal. Not what I expected of Kendra. The phone was sitting on the nightstand by the bed. I picked up the receiver and heard a dial tone.

Kendra must have forgotten to have it disconnected. Perhaps because she'd left in such a big hurry. The apartment wasn't dirty, but neither was it spic and span. Crumpled tissues and bits of debris on the carpet, plastic clothes hangers scattered on the closet floor, overturned container of Comet in the bathroom. The empty medicine cabinet was open, as were the drawer of the nightstand and the bottom drawer of the mirrored vanity.

Now I also realized that all the furniture was fractionally askew. Not noticeably out of place, but not quite in place. The coffee table was off-center of the sofa. The nightstand stood at an awkward distance from the bed, and the vanity was angled against the wall. As if everything had been moved and then hastily shoved back into place.

My sense of order made me push the nightstand into proper position next to the bed and straighten the vanity against the wall. The movement revealed a snapshot lying on the floor, one corner bent, as if it had perhaps been tucked into the frame of the mirror and had fallen. A young man, tall, husky, clean-cut looking. Very blond. He was standing in a driveway beside a sporty bright red convertible, in jeans but shirtless and barefoot, as if he had just washed the car. I turned the photo over, but there was no identification on the back.

This was not the tall, lanky guy who'd bumped into Thea and me that night. That guy had been older, not nearly such an impressive hunk. Could this man in the photo be the central figure in Thea's speculation about a tragic romance in Kendra's past, the reason why Kendra had left California?

In any case, Kendra had now moved on, apparently in a hurry, considering the less-than-pristine state of the apartment.

Well, that was Molly's concern, not mine. I had a date with a stakeout.

The vandals, however, did not have a date with me. No activity in the cemetery. No illegal trash dumpers on the bridge.

Yet on this warm, moonless night, sleepiness was not a problem, even though I'd gotten only minimal sleep that day and had forgotten to bring snacks. Tonight nagging thoughts even more than mosquitoes kept me awake.

The thought that it simply was not like Kendra to leave without a word. Kendra had always been so thoughtful and kind, and this bordered on rude and inconsiderate.

I also thought about that eye-catching, black-and-red flowered dress in which I'd last seen her, the backless one with the plunging neckline and seductive slit up the side. The newspaper article hadn't said anything about a slit and had even indicated the item of clothing could be a blouse. But if the body had been sloshing in the river for several days . . .

No, it couldn't be Kendra. Kendra wasn't missing. She'd simply loaded everything she owned into her car and moved away.

Although there was a detail I decided it wouldn't hurt to check out.

I got home from the cemetery at 4:00 a.m. and set the alarm for 10:00. When it woke me, I looked up a phone number and dialed even before getting dressed.

"Bottom-Buck Barney's. Your credit is always good with Barney," a female voice piped in cheerful singsong.

"May I speak to Kendra Alexander, please?"

"Kendra doesn't work here anymore. This is Tiffany. May I help you?" Eagerness bubbled in the young voice. "Or would you like to talk to one of our salesmen?"

"What happened to Kendra?"

"She quit."

"Did she submit a letter of resignation?"

"A letter?" The girl sounded taken aback by mention of such a formality. "No, I don't think so. Usually people just tell Mr. Retzloff when they're quitting. Or don't show up."

"Mr. Retzloff is the manager?"

"Yeah."

"I understood Kendra was his assistant. Was he upset or angry that Kendra didn't give more notice?"

"Well, she could have given longer notice. I wouldn't know about that."

"I see. So you have Kendra's job now?"

"Oh no. Like you said, Kendra was Mr. Retzloff's assistant. Loans and titles and contracts and complicated computer stuff. I just do the, you know, receptionist stuff."

A couple of things to be said for forthright Tiffany. She didn't seem to mind being bombarded with questions, and she wasn't burdened with an oversized ego.

"So it's a real inconvenience there in the office with Kendra leaving so suddenly?"

"They're going to have to hire someone right away to do all the stuff she did, that's for sure."

Which told me that Kendra *had* left suddenly, without any standard length of notice, or they would have had someone competent lined up to replace her. "Is there any chance Kendra didn't actually quit, that she just hasn't been showing up for work?"

The girl giggled. "Well, that is quitting, isn't it?"

"Was Kendra a friend of yours?"

"Kind of. I mean, we didn't hang out together outside of work or anything, but she was always friendly. And she was really nice about helping when I couldn't figure something out. I've only been here a month."

"When did you see her last?"

"Umm, Saturday, I guess it was. Sometimes we have to work Sundays, but I didn't have to last Sunday. So I don't know if she worked then or not."

"Did she mention anything to you on Saturday, or any time before that, about another job or moving away or anything?"

"Not to me." Tiffany paused. "You know, I think maybe she did just stop coming to work without saying anything ahead of time. Because I remember Monday morning Mr. Retzloff asked where she was because he needed her to, you know, do stuff. But later he said she'd quit. I guess she must have called in or something."

"Okay. Thanks, Tiffany."

"Have a good day. And remember, Bottom-Buck Barney's wants your business!"

Okay, that was it. The fact that Kendra had abruptly quit her job in addition to removing everything from the apartment certainly said she'd simply moved on. Maybe she'd speeded things up so she wouldn't have to pay another month's rent.

Although there was the peculiarity of the security deposit. Even though she'd left the apartment a bit messy, I hadn't seen anything broken or damaged, so she could surely have expected to get most of the deposit back. Some of her clothes had looked rather expensive, but I doubted Kendra's finances were so bountiful that she could afford to ignore the deposit. I also guessed her "friend" had paid for some of those expensive things. So why hadn't she left an address so Molly could send her a refund on the security deposit?

No activity at the cemetery that night, except for the whine and chomp of mosquitoes. A broken bag of garbage lay on the bridge. Another night dumper or the same one with a fresh load?

The unidentified girl's body was still in the news that evening. Police were puzzled that no one matching her description had been reported missing. Speculation now was that she could be from outside the local area, and her killer may have dumped her body while passing through.

I debated calling the authorities. Kendra did match the description. What stopped me from marching to the phone was that all available facts indicated that Kendra had picked up and left of her own free will. Just like any other woman quitting a job and moving on. So all I had to go on was speculation and this uneasy feeling that the situation was not necessarily as it appeared on the surface. Rather like one of Magnolia's "vibes."

Okay, I'm going to call, I decided abruptly as I was eating lunch on Friday. Even if I came off looking like a meddlesome old lady who'd watched too many cop dramas and soap operas, I couldn't ignore these nagging worries.

A man who identified himself as Matt Dixon, detective with the city's major crimes unit, showed up that afternoon. He wasn't in police uniform, but his car in the driveway bore a police logo, and even in a plain tan suit he exuded an air of law-and-order authority, which was emphasized by the glimpse of a gun in a shoulder holster under the linen jacket. He also filled the doorway like a wrestler, young and blond, husky and handsome. He flipped out a badge and identification card.

"You called in to report that you believe a young woman in this area is missing?" His manner was courteous and respectful.

"Well, maybe missing. And she does match the description of that poor girl who was found in the river, so I'm concerned."

I invited him in. He sat on the sofa. I offered him iced tea. He declined. I perched on the edge of Harley's old recliner and explained my relationship to Kendra, then added, "We were supposed to attend church together last Sunday morning, but she didn't show up, and I haven't seen her since. And I just have a very bad feeling about all this."

"I see." Detective Dixon pulled a pen and small notebook out of an inside pocket. "And this woman's full name is . . . ?"

"Kendra Alexander. I don't know her middle name."

"Could you give me a description of her, please? In your own words."

"She looks about twenty-three or twenty-four, somewhere in there. She's several inches taller than I am—"

"Which would make her?"

"I'm five one. So that would make her about five foot six or seven, maybe even five eight. Slender, very attractive. Blue eyes and long brown hair. Except I'm almost certain brown isn't her natural color, that she's really blond."

He'd been writing down everything I said, but he glanced up when I mentioned the hair, as if he found this item of particular interest. He underlined something in the notebook.

"And just last week I saw her wearing a black dress with big red flowers on it."

"Do you remember what type of fabric it was?"

"Something slithery. Clingy. Rather expensive, I believe."

Those facts also seemed of special interest to Detective Dixon.

"I don't suppose you'd have a photo?"

"I'm sorry, no. Actually, I don't even have a camera anymore. I used one of those little disc cameras for several years, but then it got to where you couldn't buy disc film anymore. Anyway, I just never bothered to get another camera." I gave myself a mental kick, realizing this LOL rambling was not helping the credibility of my report.

"You went to church together often?"

"No, but she'd said she wanted to go that Sunday. At the

88

time, when she didn't show up, I assumed it was because she'd decided to do something with her friend instead—"

"Friend?"

"A man friend. Someone she was . . . seeing. I don't know his name. Thea and I called him Kendra's 'young man,' but he was actually somewhat older, I think."

"Have you tried to contact Kendra?"

"Oh, yes. I went to her apartment. Actually, I went inside." Hastily I explained my responsibility with the house.

"And it looked as if she hadn't been there for several days?"

"The apartment is empty. Everything, except the furniture that belonged to Thea, is gone." I squinted into the distance, picturing the apartment again and seeing a peculiarity. "Though now that I think about it, all the lamps are gone too, and I'm sure they belonged to Thea."

"So what you're saying is, it appeared as if this young woman had moved out."

"Yes . . ." Although I had difficulty imagining Kendra stealing lamps. And she wouldn't have had much room in the little car to put such bulky items.

"Was this woman employed?"

"She worked in the office at a used-car lot over on Sylvester Street. Bottom-Buck Barney's. They told me there that she'd quit her job."

"Did she have a car?" the officer asked.

"Yes. A red Corolla. I don't know what year."

"You wouldn't happen to know the license number?"

"No. But I'm sure it was a Missouri plate. So she must've bought it here instead of bringing it with her from California."

"She was from California?" he asked.

"That's what she said."

"And you haven't seen the car since she moved out?"

"No."

89

He politely asked more questions. Did I know where Kendra had lived before renting the apartment? What about family? Friends? Yet even as he wrote down my skimpy answers, I suspected the interview was basically over. Detective Dixon didn't see Kendra as a missing person, simply a young woman who'd quit her job and moved on. People did that all the time. He closed the notebook.

"Well, thank you, Mrs. Malone. We appreciate your help. If we need anything more, we'll be in touch."

That old line: Don't call us; we'll call you.

He stood up and glanced around the room. Suddenly I saw it through his eyes. Clean. Furniture out of date but dusted and polished. Everything turned toward the TV, as if it were a magnetic center of the universe. I saw myself through his eyes too. Nice little old lady trying to be helpful but making the proverbial mountain out of a molehill. I felt a flare of resentment at the polite dismissal.

"I know it looks as if she just moved away. But I don't think Kendra would leave without saying good-bye. Or without checking on her security deposit refund. And she wouldn't steal Thea's lamps! Maybe everything was set up to make it look as if she moved away. And she's really . . . dead. Because someone killed her."

Matt Dixon's head and shoulders reared back in surprise at the passion in my outburst. He studied me as if making a reassessment. "That's possible." His tone said unlikely, but possible.

"I'm really . . . very concerned."

"We'll run her name through the files and also check out her car and see if we come up with anything."

"Thank you."

The officer looked out the window. "My grandparents used to live here on Madison Street," he offered, as if he felt apologetic about his dismissal of my concerns and wanted to make amends. "The Polanskis. But that was a long time ago."

"But I remember the Polanskis! They were much older—" I felt a jolt. And embarrassment. "About the age I am now, I suppose. But I remember Mr. Polanski owned a meat market, and they had this great flock of towheaded grandchildren—"

"Yeah, I was one of 'em." Detective Dixon grinned. "On holidays we'd descend like a herd of hungry locusts. I broke my ankle jumping out of an upstairs window, playing Superman or something. But the house is gone. I think there's a Blockbuster Video there now."

"Yes, Madison Street has changed." I didn't add the obvious. *Not for the better.* "I don't suppose your grandparents are still alive?"

"They died about ten years ago. Within a few weeks of each other."

I put my hand out in silent sympathy, and he clasped it. Then, totally surprising me, he added a big hug.

"I don't really think the body in the morgue is your friend, but we'll check it out." He patted the shirt pocket where he'd put the notebook. "Then you won't need to be worrying about her."

I nodded. But now we were down to a final point I'd been considering.

10

"I think . . ." I paused and swallowed an uprising of squeamishness. "I think I could probably tell if it's Kendra if I saw the body. Unless, since it may have been in the water several days . . ."

Matt Dixon hesitated before speaking. "Actually, the body is in fairly good shape." Another pause, this one reflective. "Considering."

Considering. The squeamishness reared up again, but I didn't rescind the offer.

"But I'm not sure . . . Look, I'll check with my superiors and get back to you, okay? There's a couple from Philadelphia who thinks this may be their daughter who disappeared last month. They're flying in today. If they can identify the body or if we can determine that Kendra Alexander just moved in with her boyfriend or something, there won't be any need to put you through this. Identifying a body can be a . . . traumatic experience."

A new thought occurred to me, and I brightened. "I don't

know why I didn't think of this before, but there may have been a family emergency out in California, and that was why Kendra left so abruptly. Maybe I'll hear from her in a few days. Or today."

"Right. Good thinking. You let me know if that happens." He reached over and squeezed my shoulder. "Just don't let this prey on your mind now, okay?"

I hoped I'd hear good news from Detective Dixon by that evening. Kendra was alive and well somewhere. Or, tragic as it would be, that the Philadelphia couple had eliminated Kendra by identifying the body as their daughter. But the only time the phone rang was when Magnolia called. She small-talked for several minutes, obviously waiting for me to come up with an explanation about my afternoon visitor. I waited her out, and Magnolia eventually tired of the roundabout approach.

"I saw a police car in your driveway earlier. I've been wondering what it was doing there."

I had anticipated Magnolia's curiosity, so I had an answer ready. "It was just a little matter to do with Thea's place."

True. Although a rather narrow version of the truth.

"It hasn't been broken into, I hope? There's so much crime these days."

"Oh no. Just the police checking up on things."

Magnolia apparently hadn't yet made a possible connection between Thea's disappearing renter and the body in the river, and I saw no point in passing along speculations.

"I'm looking forward to the barbecue," I added brightly to dodge further questions.

I skipped the stakeout at the cemetery that night. Next evening I carried my warm peach cobbler over to Magnolia and Geoff's house. The city didn't allow long-term parking of recreational vehicles in driveways or on the street, so Geoff had taken their motor home to a storage lot, but a different motor home, apparently the fabulously haired Mac's, stood in the driveway now. It was smaller than the Margollins' boxy whale, but newer looking. A rack on back held a bicycle.

Cars were parked all along the street. The scent of barbecued chicken and sounds of country music and voices drifted from the backyard. I didn't own anything I considered "western" wear, but I'd done what I could to look cowgirlish with jeans, a plaid blouse, and a red scarf tied around my neck.

I paused outside the gate to the backyard, wishing now that I'd come earlier instead of waiting for the call that hadn't come from Detective Dixon. I had the uneasy feeling Magnolia would make a big entrance out of my attempt to slip in unnoticed. I was right.

"Ivy, there you are!" Magnolia swooped down on me like a hawk after a cowering mouse. She threw up her hands. "Oh, and you've brought one of your fabulous cobblers!" As if it were some big surprise.

Tonight Magnolia, who always did these elaborate themes for her get-togethers, had outdone everyone in her denim skirt, enormous squash-blossom necklace, and boots, complete with spurs. A cowboy hat rode her hair like a bronc buster caught in a sea of cotton candy. From an invisible tape deck, Hank Williams sang about a cheatin' heart. Magnolia grabbed my hand and held it up as if I were a victorious prizefighter.

"Hey, everybody, I think most of you know my neighbor, Ivy Malone. Ivy, you know the Dugans and the Roharities . . . and everybody."

Magnolia's wave took in the twenty or so people in the

yard, but she didn't give me time to acknowledge the few I did know among the RV Roamers group. "Mac, where are you?"

Subtlety was not Magnolia's strong point. She located her intended victim on the other side of the barbecue grill and, spurs jangling, dragged me along as if I were now a prize cow headed into the show ring. Beaming, she introduced us. Ivy Malone, Mac MacPherson.

"I'll just leave you two to get acquainted. And Mac, you absolutely must try some of Ivy's cobbler. Ivy is truly the most divine cook I know." Magnolia gave me a wiggle of eyebrows apparently meant to say, *There, I've done my part, it's up to you now*, and jangled off with an air of mission accomplished.

Mac stuck out a hand. The movement revealed a blue motorcycle tattooed on his forearm.

"I'm pleased to meet you," he said.

As Magnolia had earlier said, he had a fine head of hair. Nicely silver-white. Also an attractive tan, blue eyes, and an admirably flat belly. Sunglasses dangled from a clip on his blue polo shirt. His build was stocky, with sandy-haired, muscular legs below khaki shorts. Reeboks on his feet, no spurs.

His knees were on the knobby side, and I've never been a fan of the blue-tattoo school of body decoration, but, in total, he was a rather presentable package.

But if you aren't in the market for pickled eel . . .

We shook hands—good, solid handshake—and I murmured a repeat of the pleased to meet you. I still had my cobbler tucked under my left arm. I rejected an urge to thrust it at him—*Here, Magnolia says you have to eat this*—and beat a quick retreat.

"Let me set that on the table for you," he said.

I still suspected that Mac MacPherson had had no warning that under all this window dressing of people and food he was the hors d'oeuvre of the day. Yet I could also see that he was a quick study and was gamely prepared to live up to his duties as bachelor guest.

"Beautiful evening," he said when he returned. He made a gesture toward the crescent moon. No clouds tonight.

"Yes, isn't it? Too bad Magnolia's magnolias aren't in bloom now. They put on such an impressive display, unusual for this area, that the newspaper usually sends someone out to take photos in the spring."

"Yes, she's told me about her magnolias."

I liked the fact that he didn't make some sly joke about Magnolia and her magnolias. "I understand you and Magnolia and Geoff met out in Arizona?"

"Yes. Last winter. I was working on an article about a ghost town in the Bisbee area. Magnolia was checking out names on tombstones. Are you into genealogy too?"

"Much to Magnolia's annoyance, no."

Our smiles were mildly conspiratorial. We moved out of the ebb and flow of people milling around the tables and nibbling on chips and salsa. "Are you in this area looking for interesting travel article ideas?"

"I'm always on the lookout. But I prefer little-known places over the big tourist attractions everyone already knows about."

Would that include a country cemetery of unique tombstones? I wondered.

"Or sometimes I write about unusual celebrations. Such as the annual Rooster Crow Contest in southern Oregon. Or crab races on the California coast. The Junk Sculpture Festival in Texas. A turnip-eating contest . . . somewhere. Anyway, if you hear about a do-something-strange or eat-something-yucky contest, I'm interested." He smiled.

There was something gently self-deprecating about the comment, and I liked him for that too. He wasn't claiming

96

literary lion status with his travel articles. Not a guy who took himself too seriously.

"You stay on the road in your motor home full time because you're a travel writer?"

"I'd say it's more that I'm a travel writer because I'm on the road full time."

His slightly mysterious flip of my assumption interested me, but a female voice interrupted.

"Oh, Mac, I was hoping to get a chance to talk to you! You don't mind, do you?" The woman wagged a turquoise-ringed finger at me. "You mustn't monopolize our famous guest, you know."

I placed the woman as Willa somebody; her usually elegantly coiffed blond hair was now done in a farmer's-daughter style ponytail draped across the bare skin above a Daisy-Mae blouse. I vaguely remembered that Willa and her husband spent winters in Florida in their RV.

Willa turned her attention to Mac. "You see, I've written this fabulous children's story. It's all about these three kittens that live in the woods? And they talk to each other? My grandchildren just love it. I'm thinking you could take a look at it and tell me which publisher might be interested."

Mac took a small step backward. "I'm afraid children's books are out of my area of expertise. I'm strictly a travel writer."

"But you have grandchildren, don't you? Don't you read to them?"

"Well, yes, but—"

I felt half disappointed, half gleeful that Magnolia's match-making plans had been so quickly derailed. It was obvious, as I looked over the crowd, that Magnolia had invited only couples, so no predatory lone woman could sabotage her scheme and snatch up Mac MacPherson. Unfortunately, she hadn't counted on the wiles of would-be writer Willa.

97

Geoff gonged his bell to announce that the barbecued chicken was ready, but this did not deter Willa. She latched onto Mac's arm and herded him into the buffet line, her patient husband trailing behind. I heard her say, "And then I'd like to do a sequel in which the kittens take a trip in a canoe . . ."

I stepped into line a half dozen people behind them. My meals had been irregular lately, and I was hungry enough to chow down on anything that didn't move. Geoff forked a chicken leg and thigh onto my plate, and I added mounds of coleslaw, three-bean and potato salads, tomatoes, cucumbers, and warm cornbread. I found a seat at a picnic table beside the Roharities. They were a lively couple still going strong in their eighties, excited now about an RV caravan to Mexico this winter.

They were telling me about the calving area for whales that they planned to visit on the west coast of the Baja peninsula when I heard Magnolia's indignant hiss in my ear.

"Ivy Malone, what are you doing letting that woman cut in on you?"

"They're talking shop. Willa hopes Mac can give her some professional advice about the children's book she's written."

Magnolia frowned, apparently torn between a dilemma of conflicting loyalties and responsibilities. Help friend Willa with her book? Or help friend Ivy snare a man? She didn't settle it. She just wailed, "But Mac is only going to be here a few days. There's no time to waste!"

I hated to do it, but I had to point out that she had a rather lengthy streamer of toilet tissue trailing from one of the metal appendages attached to her boots.

Magnolia's aplomb was seldom rattled, and it wasn't rattled now. She picked up the streamer and rolled it into a ball while murmuring absentmindedly, "I wonder if cowboys find this a problem?"

"Magnolia, this is a wonderful barbecue. You went to so much trouble, making your special cornbread and everything, and I really appreciate it. I also appreciate your trying to set me up with Mac. But—"

"No buts. I want you to get over there and talk to him. Turn on some charm. Scintillate. I'm worried about you now that Thea is gone. You never used to sleep all day," she added darkly, as if this were an ominous vice I'd developed.

Agreeing seemed easier than arguing, and I wasn't ready to explain my nighttime sleep deprivation just yet. Also, Mac seemed personable and pleasant. I doubted if I was up to *scintillating*, but it wasn't as if talking to him would be a hardship. I also caught him looking at me once, and I thought I detected an appeal for rescue.

Okay, when it came time for dessert, I'd do it, I decided. But before then another guest came around with a digital camera. One of those jokesters who delight in catching people at un-flattering moments. He snapped me gnawing on a drumstick, not exactly as I want to be remembered for posterity, but that concern vanished as another thought struck me.

Photographs!

I'd told Detective Dixon I didn't have a photo of Kendra, and that was true. But I was almost certain there *was* a photo.

11

I hesitated, momentarily uneasy at the thought of digging around in Thea's things. I banished that qualm by reminding myself that Molly had told me to do whatever needed doing around the place. And Thea certainly wouldn't mind my poking around.

Another hesitation. I'd promised Magnolia I'd talk to Mac again . . .

I didn't have to search for the photo tonight, of course. I could do it after church tomorrow.

Yet now that I'd thought about the possibility of the photo, I was excited about checking it out. It wouldn't take long. I could be back to the barbecue in plenty of time to do my duty by both Magnolia and Mac. I might even try to scintillate. No one would even know I'd been gone.

My nerves prickled when I let myself into the back door at Thea's house. I hadn't been here at night since Thea was gone, and the house felt . . . different.

I also felt a certain dismay as I made a quick tour of the living and dining rooms. This might take longer than I'd anticipated. I was so accustomed to seeing Thea's clutter of photos that I'd forgotten how many there were. Except for bare spots where plants had been removed, photos covered every available surface, lined every windowsill, crowded bookshelves and an antique walnut hutch. Square frames, oblong frames, oval frames. Hinged frames, chains of frames, silver frames, gold-tone frames. Many snapshots were simply leaned against other photos, sometimes two or three deep.

I peered at the faces, like a parade from the past. Our old Madison Street friends, Thea's husband, daughter Molly and friends from kindergarten to college, Harley and me and Colin too.

Thea had not, unfortunately, felt any need to organize the photos according to date or relationship. Portraits of long gone relatives, stiff and formal, were mixed with friends and later generations of relatives, many of whom I was certain Thea had never met. Graduation and wedding photos. Informal snapshots of unnamed babies, children, and animals. Unidentified celebrations, events, and occasions.

I was rubbing my back, stiff from bending over, by the time I concluded the photos I was looking for were not on display. Which did not mean they didn't exist. I cautiously opened a bureau drawer in the bedroom. Photo albums filled it to the top, like fossils stacked in a museum. Another drawer held loose snapshots. I poked hopefully at the upper layer, thinking that newer snapshots would surely be on top.

Wrong. The first photos I picked up were of a grade-school birthday party for Molly and friends. Near that was a photo of a one-eyed cat that had died years ago.

I was about to give up when a fresh thought occurred to me. Was it possible Thea had never had that recent roll of film developed? I'd never actually seen the photo I thought existed. I opened more drawers and finally found the camera among a haphazard clutter of old eyeglasses, binoculars, and Walter's electric razors.

I opened the leather case and checked the window on the back of the camera. It showed film still inside, twenty-two photos taken.

This had to be it! I'd get the film developed tomorrow afternoon at that one-hour photo developing place. Having to wait that long was frustrating, but right now it meant I could go back to the barbecue.

Unexpectedly, as I conscientiously wrote a note for whom-ever it might concern that I had the camera, I now found myself looking forward to talking to Mac again. An interesting and, yes, an attractive man.

Yet when I got outside I was surprised to see that cars no longer lined the street. The Margollin's house was dark, only a faint light still showing in Mac's motor home. Surely I hadn't been at Thea's that long . . .

Yes, apparently I had. My watch, when I held it up to the dim streetlight, showed almost midnight.

Oh, dear. Magnolia was not going to be happy about my disappearing act. I also felt a huge rush of guilt. Maybe I hadn't particularly wanted Magnolia's matchmaking, but she'd done it out of love and concern for me, and I'd been appallingly rude to both her and her guest.

Too late to do anything about it tonight, but tomorrow I'd make amends, I vowed. I'd invite Magnolia and Geoff and Mac MacPherson over for dinner, and I'd do it up right with those ham roll-ups Magnolia was so fond of.

It was also long past time for my stakeout at the cemetery. I was briefly tempted to skip tonight. But I hadn't been there last night, and I didn't want to miss two nights in a row. This was also Saturday night, the night I thought most likely for the vandals to come out and do their dirty work.

Muggy clouds had moved in, and the night was sultry and sticky. I yawned from my now familiar hiding place behind Aunt Maude's fallen tombstone. In spite of the excitement of finding the undeveloped film and an attack of the Killer Mosquitoes, I was having difficulty staying awake.

I tried my usual mind games. Naming the books of the Bible backwards. Counting by fourteens. But thoughts of Mac intruded. Was he divorced or widowed? He'd acknowledged grandchildren. How many? Where were they? Had he liked my cobbler? Why did he have a tattoo of a motorcycle on his arm? Did this suggest other colorful body decorations, perhaps a fire-breathing dragon or talon-baring eagle hiding in some less visible area?

Yet neither mosquitoes, numbers, or mild curiosity about Mac MacPherson had any effect on my sleepiness level, and I finally resorted to physical movement to stay awake. Can I still touch my toes? After a half dozen tries, yes indeed. Squats. Lunges. I tacked one hand on top my head and did eight side leg raises. Now jumping jacks. Oops. Not so good. My left knee twisted, and I had to grab for Aunt Maude's tombstone to catch my balance again.

And a good thing, because at that moment a vehicle that looked as if it was driving past the cemetery suddenly cut its lights and turned under the arch. I ducked behind the tombstone and carefully lifted my head so only my eyes cleared the rounded surface.

The cloudy night was too dark to make out the vehicle clearly, but it didn't appear to be car shaped. A pickup or van? It paused about halfway up the hill, lights off but engine still running.

Now the vehicle was turning around. I didn't rush to the next tombstone. I didn't want to find myself sneaking up on someone making a pit stop, like that other night. More movement. No, this was no emergency pit stop. The engine growled and tires crunched on rough ground as the vehicle backed off the cemetery road.

This was it. The real thing. Lights, camera, action!

I ducked low and scooted down the hill to the cover of the next tombstone. It was too dark to see figures getting out of the vehicle, but I heard the muffled slam of a door. Another dash, and I was two tombstones closer. A big pickup, I could see now. Engine still running. I paused to catch my breath and consider strategy. They'd backed onto the hillside, so they must be planning to attach chain or cable to the rear of the vehicle to do their dirty work. Missouri vehicles had plates on both front and back, so I wouldn't have to sneak up to the end of the pickup where they were working. I could circle to the front and grab numbers off that plate while they were busy around back.

Yet I could already see a big flaw in my amateur stakeout technique. With a night this dark and all the vehicle lights out, including the ones that illuminated the license plates, I couldn't possibly see the plate well enough to read the numbers and letters. Defeat, after all these nights waiting for this?

No, I decided determinedly. *I'm going to get those numbers if I have to crawl close enough to do it by feeling the license plate with my fingers.*

Another dash and I was within forty feet of the pickup.

Now I could make out shadowy movement. Two figures of indeterminate size. A scrape and rattle. Yes, they were wrapping something around one of the tombstones!

Another sprint and I was crouched directly opposite the wheels of the pickup. Just the narrow road and fifteen or so feet of hillside separated me from the license plate. But now there was nothing more to hide behind between here and there.

I flattened myself on the ground as a shadowy figure came around the side of the pickup. The door opened and the engine revved.

"Hold it!" A high-pitched, excited sounding voice. More movement at the back of the pickup. "Okay, go!"

Rumble . . . screech of straining metal . . . tires digging deep. Then a crash as the tombstone burst loose, and the pickup surged forward.

More shadowy movement, the rustle of cable being removed from the fallen stone. Then the pickup moved backward again, lining up to connect the cable with another tombstone.

Who *were* these vandals? All along I'd assumed they were kids, partying teenagers out having a malicious, beer-guzzling version of a good time. Yet there didn't seem to be any good times involved here. No cheering each other on, no joking or drinking or carousing. Just methodical, determined destruction. Up to now I'd been too busy dodging from tombstone to tombstone to be really scared. But with throat-tightening clarity I suddenly recognized real danger here. These guys weren't playing games. What if they saw me?

I had a sudden, ghastly vision of *me* dragging on the end of that cable.

I swallowed, flexed my hands, and wiped out the vision. I couldn't let fear paralyze me now. And now was my chance, while the two men were busy fastening the cable around the next tombstone.

I darted forward, across the road.

And plunged headfirst into a shallow ditch I'd never noticed on the far side of the road. To my own ears the crash sounded louder than the tombstone ripping from the earth.

Stars that had never known sky reeled across my vision. My heart rabbit hopped.

I hunched my shoulders, bracing myself for a hand reaching down, plucking me up, and dangling me like a fish on a hook.

I saw a flare of lights. I wanted to lift my head, but it felt like a sack of cement on the end of my neck. No way could they miss seeing me in the glare of their lights.

No, the flaring lights were from some other vehicle turning around under the arch at the entryway.

"Let's get outta here!" It was the high-pitched voice again.

I pressed myself flat against the bottom of the shallow ditch. Weeds and gravel bit into my hands and cheek with unpleasant familiarity. The pickup growled forward, lights still off. I heard the sound of something dragging on the ground when it reached the road—

"You forgot the cable, you idiot!" A deeper voice, with a note of angry authority.

Pickup door opening. Shadow running around to the rear of the pickup. Curses. Apparently the dragging cable was fastened to something at the rear of the pickup, and the guy who'd gotten out couldn't get it loose. With a curse the driver joined him. The two men weren't more than two or three yards away from me now. I could see that one of them was big and beefy, the other small and wiry. I could hear their grunts and hard breathing. If one of them so much as glanced toward the shallow ditch—

Invisibility, don't fail me now!

"Get a flashlight." The hard voice from the big guy, commanding, no panic.

"We can't use a light!"

"Get the—" I cringed at the expletive, "flashlight!"

The smaller figure ran to the passenger's side door. The glove compartment rattled as he dug into it. Light flared when he aimed the flashlight beam on something at the rear of the pickup where the cable was attached. A scraping sound.

"Okay," the harsh voice muttered. "Got it."

A split-second flare of beam upward into the face of the big, rough-talking man. Then a clunk as he threw the cable in the back of the pickup. Slam of doors. Out-of-gear coast down the hill. Momentary flare of red taillights under the arch, then headlights turning on as the pickup wheeled onto the main road and drove away.

I sat up. I felt like one of those cartoon characters slowly reassembling itself after being flattened by a steamroller. I filled my lungs with a deep breath. My neck felt crinked, as if my head had made a 180-degree swivel. I had a pain in my right elbow and blood trickling from a cut on my chin.

I ignored pain and blood, closed my eyes, and concentrated on branding that face into my memory. A square face. Beefy. Flab around the eyes, making them look small and piggish. Wide nose and broad forehead, heavy jaw. Thick neck. Hair? I wasn't certain. He'd been wearing some kind of cap.

But I can remember that face. I'll never forget that face. I'd know that face if I ever saw it again.

Yet what good did that do? I had no license number. No description of the vehicle other than it was a pickup, maybe dark colored, and had something on the rear to fasten a cable to. The high-pitched voice of the smaller man was a little unusual, but was that his usual voice? Under less-stressful conditions, he might have a perfectly normal sounding voice.

I drove home feeling more discouraged than I had on nights I'd seen nothing. The vandals had come and gone, and all I had was the floating vision of a heavy-set face and body. I couldn't even put a definite age to it, although I knew he was no teenager. Forties, maybe.

I caught a few hours sleep before church the next morning, where, since jumping jacks were hardly appropriate, I resorted to pinching the web of flesh between thumb and forefinger to stay awake during the sermon on the empowerment of self-reliance.

Afterward I drove directly to a little shopping center, the one where I'd almost gotten run down, and rushed into the one-hour photo developing shop. I wasn't certain how to take the film out of the camera, but the pleasant young woman at the counter did it for me. I killed time eating a taco salad and milk shake until I could pick up the photos. I was so eager I opened the envelope right there at the counter.

I held my breath as I flipped through the glossy photos. Dismay was my first reaction. Flowers? Thea's petunias and geraniums and marigolds. Ferns. Was that all there was on this roll? A dark shadow . . . Thea's thumb? She'd taken a number of thumb pictures over the years.

Then there we were, Thea and me posed on the back steps, all dressed up for our once-a-year birthday splurge on lobster at Victorio's Seafood. Kendra had come dashing up the basement steps on her way somewhere, saying, "Oh, don't you two look grand! We should have a picture."

Thea had beamed, saying, "I'll go get my camera!"

"Smile!" Kendra had said gaily as she aimed the camera at us. "Pretend you just won a million dollars!"

I shoved that photo aside. Nice to know my image hadn't yet become too invisible to show up in photos. But underneath was the important photo, the one I was hoping for. After Kendra had taken our picture, she'd handed the camera back to Thea, and Thea had playfully aimed it at Kendra.

Kendra hadn't wanted her photo taken. She'd raised her hands in startled protest. "Oh, don't do that! I hate having my picture taken."

I'd thought at the time how odd that was. A beautiful girl not wanting her photo taken? Kendra hadn't managed to cover her entire face, although one hand did hide her chin.

One thing about the circumstances of the photo I hadn't remembered.

Kendra had been wearing that clingy, backless dress that evening, the black one with exotic red flowers. The slit exposed her leg to the upper thigh, long and slim.

The other thing about the photo was something that had apparently happened so briefly that I hadn't noticed it at the time. But the camera can catch a frozen split second.

And what the camera had caught on Kendra's lovely face was a stark panic of fear.

Fear.

Was it an eerie prophecy? Because now a young woman in a black-and-red dress lay dead in the morgue.

But surely Kendra couldn't have been afraid of Thea and me! So what was this about? Why had she feared having her photo taken?

It was almost 3:00 in the afternoon by the time I got home. I headed for the bedroom and a nap but then remembered my plan to invite the Margollins and Mac MacPherson to dinner. I was tired from the long night and little sleep, but I very much wanted to make amends for last night.

I dialed Magnolia's number and, not giving her a chance to jump on me, did a hasty apology about last night and an invitation for dinner tonight all rolled into one. "Or if you can't make it tonight, tomorrow will be fine." As a token of appreciation for Magnolia's matchmaking efforts, I added brightly, "I really would like to get to know Mac better."

"I'm afraid it's a little late for that." A definite up-on-her-high-horse note there. It might take more than ham roll-ups to appease her.

"What do you mean?" I asked cautiously.

"Mac picked up and left this morning."

"Already? Where did he go?"

"I don't know. South, I think."

"Is he coming back?"

"Not that I know of."

"But I thought he was staying for several days—"

"Apparently something changed his mind." That statement was so heavily weighted with meaning it could have sunk a battleship.

"You mean just because I—"

"He was really looking forward to meeting you."

"He was?" I was astonished. Mac hadn't come into this as a happy wanderer ambushed into an unwanted widow trap? He'd really wanted to meet me?

"Yes, he was. I'd told him all about you, and he was very interested. And then you sneaked out like a deadbeat avoiding a bill collector."

I was briefly baffled by what Magnolia could have told Mac to arouse his interest. She'd embroidered a bit, I suspected. I tried to use that to make myself feel less guilty about letting her down, but it didn't work.

"I'm sorry, Magnolia, I really am."

And it wasn't just guilt. I was sorry. I'd missed out on something that might have been very good.

Mac MacPherson was not pickled eel.

12

Detective Dixon called Monday morning.

"We're going to have to ask you to come in and take a look at the body after all. The couple from Philadelphia said she isn't their daughter."

"And you haven't determined that Kendra is safe somewhere?"

"I'm afraid not. There seem to be some . . . discrepancies about Kendra. You've never heard from her?"

"No."

I told him about the photograph and that in it Kendra was wearing the dress that matched the description of clothing on the body. I guess I was hoping he'd say they could use that to make identification, and they wouldn't need me at the morgue.

No such luck.

"The photograph may be helpful, but we need a visual ID."

I swallowed. Kendra's body. With a gunshot in the chest. In the water for several days.

"But what you may be able to give us, of course, is a negative identification, that the body isn't your friend Kendra. In that case, if she's actually missing, the photo may be helpful in finding her."

I knew he was trying to put an upbeat spin on this, and I appreciated the effort. Although on second consideration, it made me feel only a smidgen better. Because I'd still be looking at some murdered young woman, whoever she was.

Lord, help me to do this.

"It's quarter of nine now," Detective Dixon said. "How about I pick you up at 11:00?"

So soon?

"Or this afternoon, if you prefer," he added, as if he'd heard my thoughts.

"No, 11:00 will be fine."

I spent the time before that hour reading some comforting verses in Proverbs and Psalms and trying not to let morbid imagination get out of hand. I didn't wait for Detective Dixon to come to the door when I heard the car in the driveway. I picked up the photo and my purse and went out to meet him. He opened the passenger's side door for me. He still looked more like a wrestler posing as a businessman than a police investigator. Except for that gun under his jacket.

"You're sure you're okay with this?" he asked.

"Whether I'm okay with it or not, you need me to do it, don't you?"

"Yes."

Inside the car I handed him the photo. "This is Kendra. It was taken about six weeks ago, just outside her apartment."

I didn't point out the dress, but I knew Detective Dixon noted it. He gave no indication, however, whether or not Kendra resembled the body that had been pulled from the

112

river. Being careful not to influence my identification one way or the other, of course.

What he did say was, "It looks as if she didn't want her photo taken."

"She was quite distressed about it, actually."

"Any idea why?"

"No. Except that she was, in general, a rather . . . secretive person. But she was nice, very sweet and considerate. A responsible renter."

He turned the snapshot over. "May we keep the photo?"

"Yes. Of course." It occurred to me that I'd still have the negative, though I didn't know what use I'd have for it.

And then we went to the morgue.

There were a few formalities. Detective Dixon introduced me to a woman in charge, tall and lean, wearing white pants and lab jacket and thick-soled shoes. I showed my identification and signed my name in a logbook.

I'd read enough detective and mystery novels to know a little of what to expect, so I wasn't horrified by the sound of laughter behind a closed door as the woman led us down a long hallway, her shoes squeaking as she walked. Life goes on in the midst of death. Maybe someone was telling a good morgue or corpse joke.

I also wasn't surprised by the formidable double doors at the end of the hallway, or the glaring fluorescent lights, surfaces of stainless steel, chilled air, and antiseptic scent. I expected the impersonal aura of the room. I wasn't shocked by the big refrigerated unit with individual pull-out compartments that held remains of the dead.

Yet none of that prepared me for when the woman rolled one of the compartments out and I saw a body draped in a green sheet. Or for the moment when she pulled the sheet back just far enough to expose the face of the dead woman.

Kendra.

Not an instant of doubt in my mind, even though I felt a reeling moment of blackness. I heard a gasp and realized it was my own. Detective Dixon's hand was already on my arm to steady me, and I was grateful for the support. The top of my head felt as if it might float away.

Not because the body was in a dreadful state. I couldn't see the horror of the fatal gunshot wound. Marks of an autopsy, which I knew must have been performed, were not visible. In spite of the fact that she hadn't been treated to cosmetic touches by an undertaker, Kendra's face was still delicately beautiful. Her skin was pale and bloodless, a single abrasion on her temple, her dark hair tangled but not matted.

Yet there was a horror here that had been absent at the many funerals I'd attended. Because here was no impartial disease or accident or old age. Here was murder.

"Did they find a bullet when they did the autopsy?" I whispered.

"Yes. It may be helpful at some point. Can you identify her?" Detective Dixon asked gently, although I'm sure he already knew my answer. He pulled the sheet up an inch and tucked it around Kendra's chin, an almost protective gesture that touched me.

"Yes. It's my neighbor. Thea's renter. Kendra Alexander."

I signed something confirming my identification, but I have no memory of going out the double doors or walking down the long hallway. I blinked at the sudden blaze of summer sunshine. We were outside, standing above wide concrete steps leading down to the sidewalk.

"You have guts, Mrs. Malone," Detective Dixon said.

I didn't feel as if I had "guts." I felt drained, a bit woozy

and disoriented. A faint scent of antiseptic and other uniden-
tifiable chemicals lingered, more in my head than nostrils. I
grasped the metal railing and breathed deeply, trying to bring
in fresh clean air and expel the tainted.

Back in the police car, I propped my purse in my lap and
wrapped my fingers around the clasp to keep them from
trembling. "Now what?"

"Now we pour a big cup of coffee into you."

That wasn't what I'd meant, but even in the heat of the
summer day it was exactly what I needed.

Detective Dixon pulled into the drive-through window
at a McDonald's. He ordered two large coffees. Black. I was
so rattled I didn't even think to tell him mine should get a
senior discount. Then he drove the police car around the
building and parked in shade on the far side of the lot. He
took off his tan jacket. I wondered when, if ever, he took off
the shoulder holster and gun.

After several minutes of sipping strong coffee, I repeated
the question. "Now what happens?"

"Now we try to find out more about your friend so we
can notify her next of kin. And we figure out who did this
to her and nail him."

"I think I told you her family is out in California. She
never talked much about them, although I don't think there
was any family estrangement. I never did know why she left
California and came here."

"We'll check into all that."

"Will you investigate the man she'd been seeing?"

"Oh yes. Now that we have positive identification, he's definitely a person of interest. You have no idea who he is?"

"Not a clue. I saw him once, but all I can say is that he's
tall and lanky. An angular face. Walks with a swagger. He
seldom came to the apartment, and he was very skittish the

one time Thea and I bumped into him there. Kendra usually met him somewhere."

"You mean as if they were . . . sneaking around?"

I didn't like to get into this, because it made Kendra look sleazy, but there was no avoiding it. "Thea and I suspected he might be married."

"Sounds possible."

"Have you found out anything about her?"

"Not having positive identification of the body, we've done only some preliminary investigation so far. We ran the name through the files and didn't find any criminal records. Not even a traffic ticket. But now we'll dig much deeper, of course. The photo you furnished will help."

"Bottom-Buck Barney's should have some information. Kendra must have filled out a job application and listed references." I felt sudden embarrassment. "But who am I to be telling you how to investigate?"

Detective Dixon grinned, apparently not offended by my unsolicited suggestions. "I think we can use all the help we can get on this one."

"There's another case I'd like to ask you about."

He lifted blond eyebrows. "Not another murder, I hope?"

"Oh no, nothing like that. But there's been this vandalism out at a little rural cemetery called Country Peace. Maybe you've heard about it?"

"I'm with the city's major crimes unit, so that would be out of my jurisdiction. But I do remember seeing photos in the newspaper. Makes you wonder what's wrong with people, that they get their kicks doing something like that."

"My friend Thea's aunt and uncle are buried there, and their tombstone was overturned. Thea was so upset about it that after her passing I decided to . . . do something about it."

"You contacted the authorities?"

"Yes. But it didn't sound as if the county sheriff's office

116

could do much. So I've been going out there almost every night to watch for the vandals. And Saturday night—"

Detective Dixon turned in the seat so rapidly that his coffee tidal-waved over the edge of the cup. "You've been doing what?"

"Watching for the vandals. I stash my car down the road a ways, and then hide behind Aunt Maude's tombstone and—"

"Let me get this straight. You, just you alone, you're sitting out there in the dark, in the middle of the night, all alone in a cemetery?"

"You're repeating yourself."

"I'm having a hard time picturing it." He paused. "I'm not sure I want to picture it."

"Picture a tombstone resembling a Volkswagen Bug. Yours truly swigging 7-Up and doing jumping jacks to stay awake. But I wasn't alone. God was right there with me, just as he always is."

Detective Dixon shook his head. "You've got guts, Mrs. Malone," he said again.

More guts than brains, I suspected he was thinking.

"You don't happen to have an unmarried granddaughter stashed away somewhere, do you?" he added.

The disconnected question momentarily befuddled me. "Granddaughter?" I repeated. Then I realized what he was getting at and felt a nice glow at the roundabout compliment. "Unfortunately, no."

"Shucks."

"You don't happen to have an attractive unmarried grandpa stashed somewhere?" I challenged.

"No."

"Shucks. Now to get back to my stakeout at the cemetery—"

"Mrs. Malone, I really have to ask you not to do that anymore. It could be dangerous. Kids get out like that, drinking and partying, you can't tell what—"

"They weren't kids. And I don't think they were drinking."

"No?"

"No. It was two grown men. I'm not sure how old, the big one maybe in his forties, but definitely neither of them teenagers. They were driving a pickup, probably four-wheel drive, with something on back to fasten a cable to."

"Probably a trailer hitch."

"They'd wrap the cable around a tombstone, fasten it to the pickup, and pull."

"You could see all this from a distance, in the dark?"

"It was dark, but I wasn't far away. I sneaked up to within a few yards of them. But then I fell in a ditch, so I didn't get close enough to the license plate to feel the numbers, and I know that's what you need."

Detective Dixon groaned. "Mrs. Malone, you shouldn't . . . you can't—"

"One man I didn't see clearly. I just heard him speak. He had a high-pitched, almost squeaky voice. But the flashlight accidentally lit up the other one's face. It was broad, not exactly fat, but kind of beefy. He was the boss."

"Look, Mrs. Malone, you have to promise me you won't go out there again."

"But somebody has to do something about what's going on, and if the sheriff's office doesn't have time or man-power—"

"This is out of my jurisdiction, but I'll talk to the sheriff's office. But you have to promise me—"

I jiggled my almost empty coffee cup, reluctant to make promises. But I didn't mind bargaining. "If I promise you this, will you promise to tell me what you find out about Kendra?"

"Some information is confidential, for departmental use only."

"Just promise you'll tell me anything that isn't confidential. I'd like to express my sympathy to her family, once you find out who they are. And maybe I'll be able to think of something more that would be helpful. For example, if you'd like to look around her apartment, I have a key."

"A key? Great! We'll need to get into the apartment. Okay, we have a deal. You don't go out to this cemetery anymore, and I'll tell you what I can as the investigation on Kendra progresses."

"Okay. Now, I've been wondering about Kendra's car. I assume she must have driven it to wherever she disappeared from."

Detective Dixon filtered that question through some mental strainer and apparently decided this wasn't confidential information. "We ran the name through vehicle registrations, and now we'll distribute the license plate number and VIN, that's vehicle identification number, nationwide. My guess is that it'll turn up abandoned somewhere. But not necessarily around here. Her killer may have driven halfway across the country by now. She may have been killed during a theft of the car, in fact."

I shuddered to think that someone would kill for that mundane little car. "I've also been wondering what happened to all her personal belongings that were in the apartment. It looks as if she loaded up everything intending to leave, and then someone killed her."

"Are you saying the killer could be someone who didn't want her to leave? Like the boyfriend?"

"I'm not sure what I'm saying," I admitted. "I guess I'm just thinking out loud. Although I still can't imagine Kendra taking Thea's lamps when she left."

"Which means whoever killed her may not have been after

the car. That the killer may have been someone she knew, and that person came back and emptied the apartment to make it look as if she'd left on her own—" He broke off as if he realized he was also thinking out loud, and he'd rather I didn't hear his thoughts.

Could someone have done that without anyone in the neighborhood seeing it happen? Yes, under cover of darkness, there would have been no problem. Most nights I hadn't been around, and Magnolia, though certainly inquisitive and observant, slept with plugs in her ears and an anti-wrinkle mask over her face. And this was no longer an area where neighbors in general looked out for each other or paid much attention to what anyone else was doing.

"Do you know where her body was put into the river?" I asked.

"Probably tossed from one of the bridges, although it'll be tough to pin down, unless someone comes forward who saw it happen. Or she could have been dumped into a smaller tributary and then the body floated on down to the river."

"You mentioned 'discrepancies' about Kendra," I said.

"Nothing I can tell you about at the moment."

"Kendra had mentioned to me once that she had something to do here, and another time said she was almost through here. I asked her if she was up to something, and she reacted very strangely. I've wondered what all that meant."

"I'll keep it in mind."

Detective Dixon took me home. He insisted on walking me to the door, even though I told him I was fine. I could see Magnolia watching from the side gate to her backyard. If she craned her head any further, she'd have a neck like that weird little alien in the *ET* movie.

The police car was barely out of the driveway when Magnolia barreled over to my backyard. I told her about identifying Kendra's body, and she plopped down on Harley's bench. I was glad it was good and sturdy. She fanned herself with a handkerchief from the pocket of her caftan.

"I can't believe it," she said. Though she did believe it, of course. Her horrified expression said so. It was just one of those things people say. "I gave her my recipe for vegetarian lasagna," she added, as if that somehow should have protected Kendra.

I couldn't think of anything comforting to say. Especially when a totally new thought suddenly roared into my mind.

Detective Dixon had said the body could have been dumped into a tributary and floated on down to the river.

A tributary. A creek.

Splash.

13

Detective Dixon had asked me to contact him if I thought of anything more. He'd given me a card, adding his unlisted home number in ballpoint pen on the back.

Now I'd definitely thought of something. But was it of value or just my imagination spinning wheelies? I decided I'd let him decide and called him that evening. I was a little surprised to find him home. I briefly wondered where "home" was. And what did a police detective do in his spare time?

"I hope I didn't interrupt anything?" I said. "Or wake you?"

"I'm just getting some supplies together for a course I'm taking at the community college."

"Course in what?"

"Flower photography." He sounded defensive, as if flower photography was somehow un-detectiveish. "I find it relaxing."

And a nice change from people offing each other with guns, knives, baseball bats, et cetera, I suspected.

I told him why I was calling, about Hangman's Creek and someone throwing something off the bridge that night. "Although I didn't actually see it happen. I was lying on the ground, and my face was turned the other way. But I heard the trunk lid of the car open and then a splash."

Detective Dixon groaned. "Mrs. Malone—"

I hurried on before he could dive into another lecture. "There's an old refrigerator on the bank down below the bridge, so when I heard this splash I figured it was someone dumping trash or some other old appliance. But you'd said Kendra's body could have been thrown into a tributary, and now I'm wondering if this was when and where it happened."

He asked what night this was, something I should have figured out before I called him, of course. But after looking at the calendar by the phone, and mumbling to myself about what snacks I'd had on which nights and the guy making the pit stop—all of which, I suspected, made it look as if my memory was about as stable as melting ice cream—I finally got it pinned down.

"I did get a look at the car when it turned around and came by again. I don't know the make, but it was big, long, and expensive looking. Again, I didn't get a license plate number—"

Another groan.

"But it was definitely a Missouri plate, and the first number may have been a seven."

"We'll check it out," Detective Dixon said.

"And tell me what you find out?"

"I'll see. We're also going to have to check out the apartment. Can you let us in tomorrow afternoon?"

"I'll be here."

"And you're remembering your promise about not going out to the cemetery anymore by yourself, right?"

"Right."

But there was something else I hadn't promised, and it wasn't dangerous anyway.

I picked up Thea's mail right after breakfast next morning. The pile on her kitchen table was growing. I hadn't heard anything more from her daughter, Molly. Then I stood there with mental dust motes of guilt dancing around in my head. Because this snoop I was planning was much more personal than just going through Thea's photos.

Yet since it might help find Kendra's killer, I could almost hear Thea saying, "Go for it, girl."

What I was looking for turned out to be not all that difficult to find. Thea's photos might be a jungle of disorganization, but her business affairs were not. She'd turned one corner of the bedroom down the hall into a neat little office, and there was Walter's old rolltop desk, a goose-necked lamp, an ancient Underwood typewriter, and a two-drawer filing cabinet. A manila folder in the bottom drawer was labeled Rental Agreements.

The agreement with Kendra was right on top, a standard, office-supply form with Thea's and Kendra's signatures. Kendra's handwriting had a strong back slant, letters nicely formed, name easily readable. Attached to the agreement was what I was looking for: the list of references Kendra had given.

I didn't want to make long-distance calls from Thea's phone, so I took the list over to my house. I started with the number for a Richard Lehman, who was listed as a former landlord. I got a recording saying the number was no longer in use. I was reluctant to try Information for a current number. They charge some exorbitant amount for such calls.

I went to the next name: Anne Morgan, also a former land-lord. The woman who answered said, "Lenninger's Carpets." After some confusion on both sides, it seemed I did have the number I'd dialed, but this person had never heard of either an Anne Morgan or Kendra Alexander. A yell to someone else in the office confirmed that neither had ever worked for Lenninger's Carpets, and no one there was a landlord.

Two down. Two to go.

I took time out for a glass of iced tea and to consider whether or not I should be doing this. I had a feeling Detective Dixon wouldn't approve. Yet I didn't see how I could be doing their investigation any harm. I might, in fact, be saving Detective Dixon investigative time by finding out where in California Kendra was from. And he'd said they could use any help they could get. I decided not to delve into whether he'd meant that literally, at least concerning help from me.

The next name was Judy Ortemo, a character reference. Judy Ortemo was unknown by the person who picked up the phone at a noisy Taco Bell. Ditto for Kendra Alexander. "Which Taco Bell?" I inquired. The one on 163rd Street, the girl answered impatiently. The city was to remain anonymous, because she hung up without telling me.

The last name on Kendra's list was Pastor E. R. Bremer-ton, at Rio Bravo Community Church in a California town of the same name. Thea had mentioned this reference. Again I thought a ministerial reference seemed odd, given that Kendra had never shown any indications of having a church affiliation. But an actual letter from Pastor Bremer-ton was attached. In glowing terms, it assured "To Whom It May Concern" that Kendra was a conscientious, trustworthy person, of exemplary moral character, and that the writer had known the Alexander family for years. A fancy, unread-able signature looked like the jagged lines on a graph made

125

by one of those machines when I was in the hospital for gallbladder surgery.

I dialed the number. This time I got a slightly deaf, irate man who called me an unsavory name, said he wasn't buying anything and to take his name off my list or he'd sue me.

I was a little bewildered, given that I hadn't tried to sell him anything, but I assured him he was definitely off my list.

This time I invested in Information and learned that there was no E. R. Bremerton in Rio Bravo, California, because there was no Rio Bravo. It occurred to me that Rio Bravo was, in fact, the name of an old John Wayne movie.

But there was that lovely letterhead on which the recommendation was written, complete with a drawing of a stream running by a little country church . . .

Which proved nothing, of course. Computer expertise begins in first grade these days, doesn't it? By high school, any devious sophomore could probably turn out a decent letterhead for anything from his father's company to NASA. Bright, competent Kendra could certainly do so.

I looked back through the list of references. One name not panning out probably didn't mean anything. People moved, phone numbers changed. Kendra might have gotten one digit wrong, throwing everything off.

Even two unverifiable references wasn't beyond reason.

But all four? No. Sweet, friendly, considerate Kendra had pulled her references out of thin air, every one of them as phony as plastic fruit. Maybe even played a sly little game with that Rio Bravo name. I remembered her saying once that she really liked John Wayne's old movies.

Hadn't she worried about getting caught in her deception? Apparently not. Or, more likely, she was simply willing to take a chance that Thea wouldn't check the out-of-state references. A safe bet, actually, and one without consequences if it didn't work. If Thea had confronted her about false

126

references, she'd simply have gone elsewhere to rent an apartment to fulfill her agenda. Because she had an agenda, I was certain now.

But what was that agenda? Why the deception?

Was there some awful secret lurking in Kendra's background? Bank embezzlement, apartment fire arson, insurance fraud? Was she even from California?

I thought about the dyed hair and eyebrows. The evasiveness about her past. What appeared to be a sleazy affair.

Not good.

I also thought about how she'd run errands for Thea, driven her out to Country Peace and other places, given us matching boxes of chocolates after she realized we were celebrating birthdays. Her teasing cheerfulness with both of us, her caring concern about me after Thea's death.

I just couldn't believe Kendra had done something awful before she showed up to rent Thea's apartment. Yet she'd obviously been far more devious than we'd ever suspected.

But, given her fate, perhaps not devious enough.

Which meant . . . what?

That she was running away from someone in her past? Someone she was afraid of and disguising herself to hide from? Someone who had found and murdered her?

That photo I'd found in her apartment. Was he the murderer?

I located the photo where I'd placed it on top of the chest of drawers in my bedroom. I'd give it to Detective Dixon when they came to look at the apartment.

But then I wouldn't have it anymore . . .

I couldn't give myself any good reason that should matter, but I made a quick trip to the one-hour photo shop to have it copied anyway. Turned out that making a copy without the negative to work from cost more than I felt comfortable paying, so I did it el cheapo. Three dimes plunked into the photocopy machine got me three copies of the photo. They weren't in color, but they were reasonably sharp. I did get a color print made of the negative I still had of Kendra's photo, which cost only twenty-four cents.

I'd had visions of a team of experts arriving with a van of technical equipment to collect evidence from the apartment, so I was a little disappointed when only Detective Dixon and another man whom he introduced as Detective Harmon arrived at about 3:00.

I let them in with Thea's key. They looked around, not much differently, I thought, than if they were considering renting the apartment themselves. I was a bit disappointed in that too. I wanted to see some real Sherlock Holmes–style detective work, some fingerprint powder and evidence-gathering with tweezers. I told them that I'd straightened the furniture and showed them where I thought I'd touched it.

"So maybe you'll need to take my fingerprints?" I could hear the hopeful sound in my own voice. I'd never been fingerprinted and was interested in how it was done.

"Maybe we will," Detective Dixon agreed. "We'll send someone from the crime scene unit around within the next day or two to dust for fingerprints and see if they can pick up anything useful in the way of hair or fibers. But you say the man she was seeing seldom came to the apartment?"

"That's right."

"Did she have other visitors?" Detective Harmon asked. This was the first time he'd spoken; he'd merely nodded when Detective Dixon introduced us. He was taller than stocky-bodied Detective Dixon, with a deeply tanned face, thinning dark hair, and mirrored sunglasses. Which seemed just a bit pretentious, considering he was merely inspecting a basement apartment, not running down terrorists on a sunlit freeway. He'd opened and slammed doors in the apartment with an air of impatience, and I got the impression he thought being here was a waste of time.

"No other visitors that I know of. But there is this." I whipped out the photo, feeling rather like a magician rescuing a trick for a bored audience.

"Who is it?" Detective Dixon turned the photo over, same as I'd done when I first picked it up.

"I don't know." I explained how I'd found it. "I'm wondering if Kendra was hiding out here. Maybe hiding from this man. And he found her."

"Women don't usually keep a photo of a stalker as if it were a precious memento," Detective Harmon pointed out.

True, I thought, feeling dumb.

"But it may be useful," Detective Dixon said. I could see he was trying to be diplomatic and not downgrade my evidence, which Detective Harmon had already dismissed. "Maybe he's an old boyfriend, one she still had feelings for."

"Old boyfriends sometimes stalk and murder their old girlfriends," I said, and I could see Detective Harmon give a mental roll of eyes.

"We'll be in touch," Detective Dixon said when we went back outside. He locked the door and handed me the key. "Don't let anyone else in."

"By the way, is anything happening on finding out who's been vandalizing the Country Peace cemetery?" I asked.

"Not that I've heard."

"I was thinking maybe the public would come up with something helpful after the sheriff's office gave the information to the newspaper."

"They've had a lot of calls, but just from people outraged about the destruction. Actually, it wasn't the sheriff's office that contacted the newspaper. It was that land developer who's worried about his heavy equipment getting vandalized."

"With good reason," I agreed. I had one more question. "Have you contacted the car lot where Kendra worked?"

"We have. No one there seemed to know her very well, but we picked up a copy of her employment application and will be checking the references."

I didn't say it, but I was pretty sure they'd be as phony as the references on the apartment rental application. I decided not to mention that list. It couldn't help the investigation, and I'd rather not let Detective Harmon roll his eyes at how nosy I'd been.

"Did you ask about that man Kendra's been seeing?" I asked.

Detective Harmon answered my question. "We did, but no one at Barney's knows anything about him."

"Or at least they weren't telling us anything," Detective Dixon added.

Which left me wondering if Detective Dixon thought someone there wasn't telling all he or she knew, or if he was just trying to make up for Detective Harmon's polite rudeness.

I knew I'd have a visitor as soon as the detectives were gone, and I was right. Magnolia rushed over. She was disappointed in how little I could tell her about the investigation of both the cemetery vandalism and Kendra's murder. I was disappointed too.

So we sat there and commiserated about where the world was headed in a handbasket, and I was glad I still had the sturdy comfort of Harley's bench.

14

Next morning I visited Cecile in the nursing home. She was feeling glum, and she didn't even have a new joke when she insisted on giving me her prized necklace consisting of five blue ceramic starfish strung together. I protested, for several reasons, one of them aesthetic . . . but she said she couldn't take it with her and I might as well have it.

"Cecile, you're not going anywhere you can't take the necklace for a long time yet."

"I feel like I could go next week. Or tomorrow. Maybe in the next ten minutes." She looked up at the ceiling as if expecting to spot a transporting angel waiting for her, but the sole occupant of the ceiling plaster was a scurrying daddy longlegs.

By the time we ate lunch in the dining room she'd perked up and decided to get a perm the next day. She said it was so she'd look nice at her funeral, but I suspected the fact that some interested glances from a rather attractive guy visiting Ellen Hooper may have had something to do with it. I looped the necklace around her throat, hoping she'd decide to keep it, and she did.

"I always feel so bohemian in this." She fingered a blue star-fish fondly. "I wonder what a group of starfish is called?"

"How about a constellation?" I suggested.

"A constellation of starfish. Perfect." She spun her wheel-chair expertly. "Now let's go see who that guy was who was visiting Ellen, and if he's single."

Afterward I drove out to Parkdale Heights cemetery. The oblong of grass had been replaced over Thea's grave, but the flat bronze marker wasn't in place yet. I left a bouquet of snapdragons I'd picked from her flower garden. I gave Harley some snapdragons too, and then took a circuitous path to acknowledge some old Madison Street friends and a co-worker at the library.

It was beginning to feel as if I knew more people residing in cemeteries than in houses these days, and I left feeling a little glum myself.

I figure hard work is the best cure for glumness, so I tackled weeds and bugs in the garden when I got home. My thoughts were more on Kendra than on vegetables, however, so I guess it was no wonder that when Magnolia came over she asked why I was spraying my tomatoes with Pledge instead of bug spray.

"We have to keep our minds open to new ideas," I said on a virtuous note. I started rubbing tomatoes, some looking as if they might ripen soon, and they did take on a lovely gloss.

I wasn't fooling Magnolia, however. I hadn't purposely set out to shine my tomatoes with furniture polish. It was one of those senior moment things.

"Are you still sleeping in the daytime?" she asked, her tone severe. Today she was wearing an enormous floppy-brimmed straw hat with a long pink ribbon that swirled like confetti around her knees.

"No, I'm not doing that anymore."

"Good. If we start doing too many things like daytime sleeping and spraying our tomatoes with Pledge, people may start thinking we're drifting toward the S word."

The S word. Magnolia did a lot of crossword puzzles. I didn't. The only S word I could think of was Saskatchewan, which didn't seem particularly relevant here.

"Senility," she said meaningfully.

Oh. That S word.

"Just think," she said, "if you'd been nicer to Mac, he might have hung around. And right now he'd be sitting in this chair instead of me, and you'd be talking about books and travel and doing the salsa together."

"Salsa?" I repeated doubtfully. I thought salsa was something you ate, not something you did.

"Haven't you heard? It's the latest dance since the Macarena."

No, I hadn't heard. And since I was about ten dances behind the Macarena, I wasn't really interested. "If Mac is big on salsa dancing, I'm afraid he'd have been disappointed in me anyway."

"I don't know if he salsa dances or not," she said, annoyed. "Don't be so literal, Ivy. You know what I mean. You'd be talking about doing exciting things together. You'd be doing exciting things together."

"Have you heard anything from him?"

"He sent a nice thank-you card for our hospitality. And I don't believe I've showed you the lovely vase he brought as a gift when he arrived."

A very proper and thoughtful guest, she was telling me.

A treasure I'd let slip through my fingers like melting Jell-O. "Where is he now?"

"He didn't say. And the postmark was blurred even when I looked at it with a magnifying glass."

I wondered if he'd mentioned me, but I wasn't about to ask. Magnolia told me anyway.

"He didn't say anything about you," she said, obviously still miffed about my miserable showing in her matchmaking scheme.

Detective Dixon in a police car and three people in a white van from the crime scene unit showed up the following day. The detective came over to pick up the key to the apartment. He returned and said the crew would bring the key back to me when they were finished. I took the hint. I wasn't supposed to run over and watch like a puppy hoping for a bone.

"You won't be sticking around?" I asked.

"No, they don't need me," he said, although he seemed in no hurry to leave. "Though I wouldn't mind having a glass of that iced tea you offered me one time."

I went in the house for the iced tea. When I came back he was inspecting my tomatoes.

"These are exceptionally shiny tomatoes," he said.

I didn't explain my secret. Instead I asked, "Do you have a garden?"

"No, I live in an apartment. No place for a garden."

"You could grow tomatoes in tubs."

He went back to a lawn chair and sipped tea, and I could see he had something other than tomatoes on his mind. I sat beside him, letting silence do its work, and finally he came out with it. "I probably shouldn't be telling you this,

134

but it is puzzling. And I figure you're a person who can hold information in confidence . . . ?"

"Like a hacksaw buried in a chocolate cake."

"None of Kendra Alexander's references panned out. The employment references were from California jobs, and the companies don't exist. Neither do her named next of kin. She also never went to the business college she listed."

No surprise there, but I felt a kind of sinking in the pit of my stomach anyway. "Bottom-Buck Barney's didn't check on any of this when they hired her?"

"No. The manager, a Mr. Retzloff, said they tried her out on their computer, she knew what she was doing, and they hired her on the spot. With their pay schedule, I think their help changes as fast as flipping hotcakes, and they probably don't do much reference checking. Although it may have helped that she'd just bought that Corolla from them and paid cash."

I hadn't known either of those facts, and the statement about cash surprised me. Although, on reflection, I decided it shouldn't. She was new in Missouri. She needed a car. Why not Bottom-Buck Barney's? And then why not inquire about a job? It was also reasonable that she'd brought cash from California to help her get started in a new place. Although California was definitely looking questionable.

"They promoted her to be Mr. Retzloff's assistant, so she must have had good training and experience even if what she said on her employment application was . . . misleading," I pointed out.

Whatever her shortcomings in the references department, I still felt defensive about Kendra. And it still struck me as odd that someone with her obvious competence was willing to work for low pay at a place like Bottom-Buck Barney's.

"There's more," he said. He lifted the glass and jiggled the ice cubes. "Although all her references showed a California

135

background, her place of birth on the application was given as Clancy, Arkansas. Arkansas records confirm that Kendra Kay Alexander was born in Clancy on October 26, 1980, to Alvin and Marcy Alexander."

I was glad to hear something about Kendra checked out.

"Except there's a peculiarity. Kendra Kay Alexander has been dead for two years. She died of leukemia, according to the death certificate. She's buried there in Clancy."

It took a moment for that information to hit bottom. It landed like a cast-iron skillet slamming a cockroach.

"You mean our Kendra was using someone else's identity?" Our Kendra had *stolen* someone else's identity? I was horrified, yet, by now, not surprised even by this.

"She acquired a copy of the Arkansas birth certificate and used that to get a driver's license here in Missouri."

"Wouldn't they have asked about a license in some other state, maybe say she had to give up the old one?" I asked.

"She took care of that by claiming she'd never had a license before. She took the written and driving tests, passed, then bought the car under the Kendra Alexander name."

"She seems to have thought this through rather thoroughly," I said. "How about a Social Security number?"

"She had that too. The real Kendra Alexander's real Social Security number. But we had the authorities down in Arkansas show the photo you gave us to the parents, and they have no idea who this girl was."

"Do you think she just picked a name at random? Maybe visited cemeteries until she found dates that looked suitable and then went after the documentation?"

"It's certainly been done that way. But the fact that she had the right Social Security number suggests inside information."

"So you have no idea who she really is?"

"Not yet. Her fingerprints aren't on file. So she's not in

the criminal system, has never been in the military, and has never held any of various jobs that require fingerprints and would get into the FBI system."

This certainly explained why Kendra—I'd always think of her as Kendra, I suspected, even though I now knew she was someone else—was so secretive about herself and her past. Why she didn't want her photo taken. Again I came back to the idea that she must have been hiding from someone. Unsuccessfully.

"Has anyone checked out the bridge over Hangman's Creek where I heard someone toss something over?"

"A county sheriff's deputy and I went out there. We didn't find anything."

Not surprising. A splash doesn't leave a trail to follow.

"I did drive through the cemetery. Not a pretty sight." Detective Dixon sat there silently for several minutes, while we both digested his revelations. Then he unexpectedly changed the subject. "You go to church, don't you?"

I was momentarily pleased that my Christian foundation showed. Then I remembered that I'd told him about church and God being with me in the cemetery. "Yes. As I'd mentioned, Kendra was planning to go with me, just before she disappeared."

"Yeah, that's right." He gave me a thoughtful appraisal. "But I think I'd have known even if you hadn't told me that."

"I'm glad to hear that. I accepted Christ as my Savior when I was ten years old, and the Lord has been my guide, companion, and comforter ever since." I also had to add regretfully, "Not that I've always lived a perfect Christian life."

"It's what I saw in your guts, maybe, that told me something. As if you have a strength beyond your own to draw on." He squirmed in the lawn chair, as if he was uncomfortable with this line of conversation. Not usual cop talk. "Anyway, I've been thinking maybe I'd start going to church."

That was a much more pleasant surprise than the others I'd received today. "I'm pleased to hear that."

Then I realized he'd ended on an expectant note and was waiting for me to invite him to my church. I dragged my feet, uneasy with that. "Have you ever been?"

"To church? Well, of course I have." He straightened in the lawn chair, as if I'd implied he was an unwashed heathen and wouldn't know a hymn from a haiku. "Whenever we visited, Grandma and Grandpa took us to a Sunday school around here somewhere. I even remember memorizing some Bible verses."

"That church is gone now. The freeway off-ramp goes across where it was."

"And I've been a few times since. For a while I had a girlfriend who belonged to a church near the community college, and I went with her sometimes."

"Often?"

"Well, like . . . once or twice, maybe."

"That church might be a good place to go again, then."

"Our breakup was a bit . . . hostile. I don't think I'd feel comfortable there."

Okay, here it was. Time for me to jump in and say brightly, "Why don't you come to my church, then? We'd love to have you."

And Riverview United would love to have him. They'd jump on young, personable, good-looking Detective Matt Dixon like a Bottom-Buck Barney's salesman jumping on a guy waving an inheritance check from a rich uncle.

I could say some good things about Riverview United. That it had a magnificent building, with enough stained-glass flowers and doves to impress Michelangelo. A terrific choir, lots of young people and activities from bowling to barbecues.

A senior pastor, several associate and youth pastors, and a nursery run by a registered nurse.

But not a cross in sight, and Christ-centered messages scarce as pennies in the collection plate. At my church, Detective Dixon might learn about getting empowered through self-reliance, but he wasn't going to learn much about salvation and the eternal consequences of not having it.

Then it hit me. If I was reluctant to invite Detective Dixon to my church because of its deficiencies in leading a newcomer to Christ, what was I doing there? The thought that had been lurking in the depths of my mind, like a knitting needle in a mattress, rose up to jab me.

"Actually, I've been a bit . . . dissatisfied with the church I've been attending. I've been thinking about trying to find a different one. Maybe smaller. Maybe one not quite so . . . busy."

"There's a little brick church out on the other side of town, beyond my apartment building. I don't know what kind. I jogged by there one Sunday morning and heard them singing. One guy was really off key, but they sounded enthusiastic."

Harley used to be as off-key as a garage-sale piano. But no one ever sang more enthusiastically. "I doubt the Lord subtracts points for being off-key."

The detective gave me a sideways glance. "Want to give it a try?"

It took me a moment to realize he was suggesting we go together. And even if I hadn't just realized I wanted to find a different church, I'd have said yes. There's something to be said about the character—and potential—of a young man who's willing to tackle a churchful of strangers with a faux grandma in tow. I suddenly wished I did have a granddaughter to introduce him to.

"I think I would," I said.

We agreed on this coming Sunday. He offered to come pick me up, but I said going to a new church wasn't quite like visiting a morgue, and I could make it there on my own.

I gave him several tomatoes before he left, advising him to put them in a paper sack to help them ripen. I didn't point out that one had an amazing resemblance to Barbra Streisand's profile. But I did tell him he'd better wash them thoroughly before he ate them. I was uncertain about both the taste and nutritional properties of Pledge.

After a woman from the crime scene unit returned the key, I figured I'd save Magnolia a trip and went over to her place.

Geoff was off somewhere getting a valve fixed on the motor home, and Magnolia was writing a letter to a Scottish man who might be a descendant of her great-great-grandfather's second cousin. Neither geographical nor relationship distances ever dampened Magnolia's enthusiasm for possible genealogical connections. I spotted what was apparently Mac MacPherson's gift vase on the sideboard. Very nice. Decorated with the obligatory magnolias, but discreetly so.

I gave her the not-surprising news that the evidence-collecting crew hadn't informed me if they'd found anything helpful in Kendra's apartment. "Of course, they probably don't know anything yet," I added. "Everything has to go to a lab."

I didn't pass along the information Detective Dixon had given me about Kendra not being Kendra, since that was confidential. Magnolia tapped her chin with her old Parker pen filled with turquoise ink.

"You know, I've been getting some vibes about this situation," she said.

Considering that before we knew Kendra had been murdered, Magnolia had expressed the view that Kendra might be in some sort of trouble, I couldn't totally discount her vibes. "About Kendra?"

"About her car."

This was a new one. Even Magnolia had never come up with vehicle vibes before.

"What about the car?"

"Well, I'm not sure." She squeezed her eyes shut, which apparently helped connect her to the vibe world. "She had the hood of her car up one time when we were walking by. She was leaning over as if she was looking for something in the engine. Geoff asked if anything was wrong, and she said the engine sounded funny, and she was wondering if the spark plugs were in backwards."

This struck me as more peculiar than enlightening. I don't know much about cars, but I doubt an engine would even run if the spark plugs were in backwards. Or if it was even possible to put them in backwards. I also recalled seeing Kendra competently change a flat on the car herself one time, which suggested she probably wasn't totally ignorant about the workings of other parts of the vehicle.

But one word jumped out at me.

Backwards.

I got a peculiar little vibe of my own that had nothing to do with spark plugs.

Had I been looking at Kendra's reason for being here backwards?

15

What if Kendra had not been running away, as I'd been thinking, but had instead been running *to* someone?

From what Detective Dixon had said, it looked as if she'd headed for Bottom-Buck Barney's like me racing for a dollar sale on Sara Lee cheesecake at the supermarket. Thinking back, I again remembered Kendra saying she had something to do here, something that should be finished within a few days or weeks.

Could she, rather than hiding from the man in the photo, have been searching for him? A lost love and a foolish quarrel or misunderstanding she wanted to rectify?

But if that was the situation, why was she using a phony name and background and dyed hair? Why would searching for this man get her killed?

Magnolia reached over and shook my arm. "Ivy, are you okay? You look as if you drifted off to some other world."

The S-word world, no doubt. "I'm fine," I assured her. I

stood up. "I was just thinking about some things I should be doing."

I wasn't exactly sure what they were, but I did feel a sudden urgency. Kendra was dead, her killer was still out there somewhere, time was flying, and I was sitting here looking at Mac's magnolia vase.

On the way across the street, a different and more chilling twist on the possibility that Kendra was searching for the guy in the photo occurred to me. What if she'd wanted to find him not because he was someone dear to her but because he'd done something unscrupulous, even horrific, to her or her family? Had she been trying to run him down and bring him to justice? But when she found him, he killed her?

Yes, that fit with a phony name and dyed hair and eyebrows.

I intended to go over to Bottom-Buck Barney's the next morning, but Detective Dixon called and said they did want my fingerprints. He met me at the station, and we took care of the interesting process of rolling my fingers in ink and pressing them on a little card. Then he gave me a map he'd drawn so I could find the church on Sunday.

"Did they find many different fingerprints in the apartment?" I asked as I tucked the map into my purse.

"Actually, no. Lots of Kendra's prints, of course. Plus some blurry smudges. But only one other clear set, which I suspect will turn out to be yours."

"Which means that Kendra either removed the apartment's contents herself, or whoever did it was wearing gloves."

"Right."

We didn't have to exchange more words to know we both leaned toward the glove theory. So where was all that stuff from her apartment? And where was her car?

I walked over to Bottom-Buck Barney's about midmorning on Saturday. The used cars gleamed brighter than my Pledgeenhanced tomatoes. Flags waved, balloons bounced in the breeze, and a banner draped over the entrance read a tongue-boggling "Bottom-Buck Barney's Blow-Your-Mind Blowout Sale!" A scent of chili drifted from a big pot simmering over a gas stove set up along one side of the building. Behind the paper-covered counter a young guy in a white chef's hat stirred the pot, and two girls in short skirts vivaciously handed out soft drinks. A four-dinosaur merry-go-round for the kids tinkled carnival music. Very festive.

The lot wasn't crowded with customers, but a few were wandering around. As soon as a car pulled into the parking area, a salesman would break out of the vulture congregation around the main door and rush to greet the occupants. The salesmen, a couple of whom I tardily realized were women, wore identical dark pants, white shirts, spiffy little straw hats, and big smiles.

I tried to think of something appropriate I could say if one of the salesmen cornered me. I wasn't even sure what I was doing here, except that Kendra and Bottom-Buck Barney's somehow seemed ominously intertwined. I finally settled on the old "I'm just looking" standby, although I suspected Barney's salesmen were experts at transforming lookers into buyers. I reminded myself that no matter how convincing they were, I was not going to become the new owner of a '92 Buick.

I needn't have worried, however. No salesman rushed to greet me. No one asked if I was looking for some specific vehicle. No one inquired if I'd like to take a test drive. They were, so far as I could determine from a stroll past one sales-man studying his fingernails, totally unaware of my existence. LOL Ivy Malone was not even a blip on the screen of their potential buyer radar.

I resisted an urge to stick my fingers in the corners of my mouth and cross my eyes to see if I could even make myself visible to them. Instead, I reminded myself to enjoy my freedom as I wandered unnoticed among the bright rows of cars and pickups. Yet after some fifteen minutes of this, I still didn't know why I was here. The day was also getting uncomfortably hot, and I decided with some frustration that I might as well just pick up a bowl of free chili and head for home. It was then I spotted the car. I stopped short.

It was a Corolla. Red. Exactly like Kendra's car. A double take assured me it was Kendra's car. Same gray upholstery. Same rearview mirrors. Same radio antenna.

But then I also realized that I was surrounded by Corollas; it was as if a wagon train of them had moved in and circled up for the night. And, except for color, I couldn't see a smidgen of difference among them.

So perhaps this wasn't Kendra's car. Maybe it was just another red Corolla.

But then, maybe it *was* her car.

An easy way to find out. Detective Dixon could check the license plate numbers.

Except the red Corolla had no license plates. The metal-rimmed oblong squares were empty.

This was definitely a situation for Detective Dixon, but I was reluctant to bother him with something totally off the wall. He was a generous-minded young man. He thought I had guts. But I also suspected he viewed my spending nights in a cemetery of overturned tombstones as borderline eccentric, and I didn't want to cross over that border by coming up with some goofball idea about a look-alike red Corolla.

Then I remembered. The key! Kendra had said she always kept a spare key in a really out-of-the-way space behind the front bumper. Someone could have found and removed it, of course. But if the key was there, I'd know this was Kendra's car.

I got down on my knees and felt around the metallic

underpinnings of the car. No luck. I couldn't even find the hiding space Kendra had mentioned. I scrunched lower, until I was lying on my side half under the bumper. Now my arms wouldn't bend right for the search. I turned over on my back and scooted further under.

And that was when I learned that while I might in total be invisible, the lower half of my body sticking out from under a Corolla was not.

"Hey, what're you doing under there?" a male voice yelled.

While I was trying to figure out an appropriate answer to that question, another even more excited female voice yelled, "You idiot! Maybe she fell and broke something. Maybe she's had a heart attack! Get an ambulance."

With a screaming ambulance a complication I definitely did not want, I hooked my elbows in the asphalt and shoved. I shot out from under the car like an oiled pig.

So there I was, flat on my back on the asphalt at Bottom-Buck Barney's, with my derrière feeling like shredded cheese and a flower-petal arrangement of salesmen and curious customers peering down at me. "I'm fine," I croaked hastily. "I don't need an ambulance. I was just . . ."

Just what? In the mystery and detective books I read, the clever characters have no problem with blithe lies or pretenses to gain information or get out of awkward situations. But I'd always had a squeamish relationship with untruths.

"Just looking for a lost key," I finished on a surge of mild elation for holding to my standards. No need to be specific about what key or where I was looking for it.

Although, when I tried to get up, I had to admit I'd stretched the truth about how I was feeling. Definitely not as fine as before I'd started squirming around on hot asphalt.

The saleswoman rushed to help me to my feet. She brushed

my backside. I scraped at what felt like permanently embedded asphalt in my elbows.

"You'd better come inside and rest for a few minutes," she said.

I started to decline the offer but changed my mind. Perhaps a few minutes with Tiffany, the eager young woman I'd talked to who did "receptionist stuff," could prove profitable.

The saleswoman solicitously walked me inside and handed me over to a young woman with exuberant blond hair and curves. This was a Tiffany if ever I saw one.

"Oh my, are you okay?" The young woman guided me to a chair by her desk. "My grandma fell like that once and broke her hip, and it was just awful. Oh, and it looks as if you have a stain on your pretty blouse."

With unexpected efficiency she produced a spray can of something and worked on the back of my blouse with a paper towel. "Would you like a Mountain Dew or bottle of spring water? I can get one from the machine right over there."

"A plain glass of water would be nice." Do young people know plain old tap water exists anymore?

She brought a paper cup of water she'd located somewhere. "Do you feel faint or anything?" Little furrows of concern appeared between her baby-blue eyes.

"No, I'm fine."

"You know, your voice sounds so familiar," she said. She perched on the corner of her desk, her short skirt revealing unexpectedly sturdy legs, and studied me. "I'm very sensitive to voices. I'm taking acting lessons, so I try to listen to everyone I hear to catch the nuances of voices so I can use them myself."

I was surprised that she knew what a nuance was. And then I felt guilty for making a prejudgment about her just because she was young and cute and bubbly. "That's very interesting."

147

"This is my southern voice." She slid off the desk and draped her hand on a jutted hip. "'Ah don't mind makin' a fool of ma-self ovuh you, Brick.' That's Maggie the Cat. You know, from *Cat on a Hot Tin Roof*?"

I recognized the title, if not the quotation. A word I thought might be appropriate came to mind. "Awesome."

"Hey, now I remember where I heard your voice. You're Kendra's friend. You called up and asked about her when she quit!"

I was astonished. And impressed. This really was rather awesome. Also a bit unnerving. I've never been inclined toward anonymous crank calls, but I'll certainly think twice before making one if my voice is that identifiable. Although probably few people shared this voice-sensitive talent of Tiffany's.

"Ummm . . ." I demurred.

Tiffany didn't wait for me to confirm or deny her identification. "I'm the one you talked to that day, Tiffany, remember? And now Kendra's dead," she said. "Isn't it terrible? That anyone could *do* something like that to her? Or to anyone. I suppose her body has been sent to her family somewhere for a funeral?"

"I believe there's been some . . . delay there." I thought about mentioning that the Corolla on the lot looked like Kendra's, but I decided to be more circumspect. "I was looking at a nice little Corolla out there when I had my . . . incident. I notice it has no license plates. I was wondering what that meant."

"Oh, some of our cars come from wholesalers in other states, but when they're sold here they have to have new license plates from this state."

If this was Kendra's car, it shouldn't be lacking Missouri plates. But still, it looked so much like Kendra's car. "Could you find out where this particular car came from?"

148

"Kendra probably could have done it on the computer. She knew how to do all that stuff. But I don't."

"Has someone taken Kendra's place now?"

"Jessica Holt is Mr. Retzloff's assistant now. She's no Kendra," Tiffany added with a roll of eyes.

"You mean she isn't as competent?"

"Oh, I'm sure she's competent enough. She's been working at some big new car dealership on the other side of town. I think we're just a bunch of used-car peasants to her."

I stood up and thanked Tiffany for the water and the clean-up on my blouse. Then I remembered something. I dug in my purse and pulled out one of the photocopies of the snapshot I'd found in Kendra's apartment.

"Is this anyone you know?"

Tiffany studied the black-and-white copy. "No, but I wish I did. He looks . . . nice."

The word was generic, but the hint of wistfulness in her voice impressed me. No oohs and aahs about the guy's hunky good looks or the snazzy convertible. I could appreciate a young woman attracted to a man because he looked *nice.*

"Is there some reason I should know him?" she asked.

"I'm not sure. Maybe. Kendra may have known him."

"I could make a copy of this and show it around." Tiffany motioned to a copy machine in the corner. "I haven't been here long, and maybe somebody else will recognize him if he used to work here."

"You can keep this one. And give me a call if you find out anything." I scribbled my phone number on the back side of the photo.

Tiffany put the photocopy in her desk. "Did you come in a car?"

"No, but—"

"You shouldn't be walking in this heat. How about if I drive you home?"

"Mr. Retzloff would just let you leave?"

She gave me a conspiratorial wink. "I'm entitled to a coffee break."

I declined the offer, but again I was impressed with Tiffany. Willing to use her coffee break to take me home. A very nice young woman. It was none of my business, but I asked her where she lived.

"I'm still at home with my folks. My sister was killed in a car accident last year, and I think they need me at home for a while yet."

Yes. A very nice young woman.

It wasn't until I was back home that it occurred to me that putting my phone number on the back of the photocopy wasn't a wise idea. If this guy had put a bullet in Kendra because she'd found him, how would he react if he realized I was on his trail?

Too late to do anything about it now, however. And probably nothing to be concerned about anyway. The guy obviously wasn't working at Barney's now, so there was no reason to think he'd find out I was asking about him.

That evening, the newspaper reported a surprising development in the vandalism case at Country Peace. The subdivision developer who was worried about vandalism spreading to his equipment, a man named Drake Braxton of Braxton Building and Development Corporation, had offered his construction crew to dig up each of the graves, all thirty-six of them. He'd then donate a quarter-acre on the back edge of his subdivision in which to have the bodies reinterred, and he'd supply a secure fence as well. The cemetery could then be turned over to some appropriate organization for maintenance, and donations could be accepted to furnish a bronze headstone for each grave.

"I think we all want to see these loved ones where they will be safe," the reporter quoted him as saying. There were two photos, one of the desecrated cemetery and another of the proposed new site on the far side of his subdivision.

An expensive undertaking, and a most generous offer to rectify an unpleasant situation. Mr. Braxton was surely to be commended.

Yet I didn't really like the idea of scrunching all the graves into a quarter acre of ground. The spaciousness of Country Peace was part of its charm, as if each gravesite had a country place of its own. And it would be a shame if all those wonderful, individualistic headstones were replaced by flat look-alikes.

On impulse I sat down and wrote a letter to the editor thanking Mr. Braxton for his generous offer but suggesting that some local organization take over restoration and maintenance of the cemetery where it was now located. I pledged a hundred dollar donation toward the project.

That evening I scrubbed more asphalt stains out of my elbows and set out clothes for church with Detective Dixon the following morning. Navy blue skirt and matching heels, pale blue, bow-at-the-neckline blouse, diamond stud earrings Harley had given me.

But church with Detective Dixon was not to be.

16

Actually, I did go to church.

The location was in the triangle of a three-point intersection, and the sign stuck on a minuscule plot of grass identified this modest brick building as Tri-Corners Community Church. People clasped my hand and asked my name, and the congregation claimed an eclectic mixture of young and old, suits and jeans, pearls and funky earrings.

The music was a mixture too, old hymns and lively praise choruses, and yes, one voice definitely boomed off-key. Made me feel wonderfully at home. The message, delivered by a lean young pastor who looked as if he might run marathons in his spare time, was from Ephesians 10:9. As I listened to the sermon, I noted the image of Christ centered on the lone stained glass window behind the pulpit.

I also made mental excuses for Detective Dixon all through the service. Car trouble. Sudden illness. Police emergency. But by the time I was back in the Thunderbird, my ears still tingling with invitations to return, it was obvious he wasn't coming.

I sat there with disappointment puddling around me. Some of the puddle was simply because he'd stood me up, of course. I'd looked forward to this morning with him. In spite of murder being our connection, he lifted my spirits. The bigger disappointment, however, was for Officer Dixon himself. Apparently his interest in church was merely a passing impulse. I pictured him sleeping late, snoring off a late night out, and thought of the conversation Magnolia and I had shared about where the world was headed in a handbasket, young people leading the pack.

Detective Dixon called that evening, and in thirty seconds I was mentally thrashing myself for being negative, judgmental, ageist, and unfair. And for jumping to conclusions with more agility than my grandniece Sandy doing backflips.

"I'd have called earlier," he added, "but it took a long time for the anesthetic to wear off after the surgery this morning. And then they've kept me dopey on pain pills all day. I hope you didn't have problems finding the church. And that it didn't turn out to be unpleasant or weird?"

Here he was, lying in a hospital bed, leg smashed by a bullet, and he was apologizing for not meeting me at the church, worried that it might have been unpleasant for *me*.

If Detective Dixon was any example of the younger generation, put that handbasket in reverse.

I discarded an irrelevant point I'd wondered before—*What is a handbasket, anyway?*—and said, "Tell me again so I'm sure I have this straight. You went to this house about a murder—" A dismaying thought occurred to me. "Did this have something to do with Kendra?"

"Oh no. This was a stabbing in a bar. But when we got to the house we discovered an illegal meth lab, and the guy running it tried to escape out the back way."

"But this wasn't the guy you were looking for? This was another crook?"

153

"Right."

My head felt like the spinning light on a police car, going round and round with stabbings and shootings and drugs. To me, Kendra's murder was a once-in-a-lifetime horror, but Detective Dixon dealt with killings every day.

"Fortunately he stumbled just before he pulled the trigger," Detective Dixon added.

Or he'd have hit what he was no doubt aiming for, Detective Dixon's head or heart. A cold shudder shot down my back. "Is your leg going to be okay?"

"They got the bullet out. Now the doctors are having committee meetings about what to do next." He sounded disgruntled.

"I'll pray about it."

"Couldn't hurt, I suppose," he muttered.

"How about if I come visit you?"

He consulted with someone and then came back to say he could have a visitor the following afternoon. "I'll tell the guard you're coming, but you'll have to bring identification."

"You have a guard?"

"Just a precaution for a day or two, until they nab this guy."

I had second thoughts. "Do you want me to come?" I didn't want to barge in on a room full of family and friends.

"Well, yeah, I do want you to come, Mrs. M. I really do."

Mrs. M. I liked that. I knelt and said a prayer for Detective Dixon and his leg right then and there.

I didn't know if they were restricting what Detective Dixon ate, but I figured a homemade oatmeal cookie never hurt anyone, so I baked up a batch and took them along.

The guard at the hospital checked my ID and patted me down. Me, I got patted down! I felt rather flattered that he thought I could have an AK-47 concealed in my pants leg or a bomb strapped to my Wal-Mart bra. He wouldn't accept a cookie, but Detective Dixon grabbed one as soon as I held out the paper plate.

He was in a hospital gown, no gun. No machines were attached to him, which I figured was a good sign. I didn't know exactly what to talk to him about, so told him about the friendly people at the church, the strong message, and the invitations to return. I asked him about family and learned his parents were divorced and lived on opposite coasts, and his brother, in the navy, was in the Middle East. Which meant he wasn't going to be overloaded with family visitors.

I wondered about a girlfriend. Or girlfriends, considering his eligible-male attractiveness. Asking seemed a little nosy, however, so I didn't. He made an effort at cheerfulness, but his blue eyes looked uncharacteristically bleak.

I didn't intend to say anything about the red Corolla at Bottom-Buck Barney's, figuring police matters were the least of his worries now, but he brought up the subject of Kendra's car himself.

"It would be a real lead if we could find that car. We need to know if she was killed in it or elsewhere. I'm also thinking about making a trip down to see the real Kendra's parents in Arkansas."

Did that mean he'd be back on the job shortly? Or was he just talking to keep his hopes up? I told him about the red Corolla I'd seen at Barney's, prudently leaving out the part about my skidding around under the vehicle. "Though I don't see how it could possibly be Kendra's. I mean, if it's hers, how could it have gotten there?"

"Good question."

"I suppose the killer could have sold or traded it in there, and it's just a strange coincidence he picked the place where Kendra had worked," I suggested.

"Or someone at Bottom-Buck Barney's could be involved in the murder."

"But then it wouldn't make sense to stick the car right out there under everyone's noses!"

"Putting something out in the open is sometimes the best way to hide it."

I couldn't see any reason anyone at Bottom-Buck Barney's would want to murder Kendra, but I felt a little frisson of excitement that Detective Dixon wasn't dismissing my suspicions as totally off the wall. "Is there any way to trace a car other than the license plates?"

He told me about every car having a VIN—vehicle identification number—listed on the title and also located where it could be seen through the windshield. "An easy place for a cop to check. But every car thief knows about that identification, so it's the first thing they change. But there are also numbers located in various other places on a vehicle, and it's difficult for a criminal to catch and change every one of them. Most often they just figure on the quick buck and don't even try. But they do have to come up with the paperwork to make everything look legal on the surface."

"You're saying that even if the car on Barney's lot has a different VIN than Kendra's Corolla, it could still be her car?"

"Not a strong possibility, but a possibility."

I remembered Magnolia telling about Kendra's peculiar story about her spark plugs being in backwards. Had she been looking for numbers? But there'd have been no need for phony numbers on her car then, before the murder. "I could go back to Bottom-Buck Barney's and look through the windshield to check the VIN on the car—"

"Mrs. M., I do not want you prowling around Bottom-Buck Barney's! Or anywhere else. As soon as I get out of here—"

156

He broke off as Detective Harmon strode through the hospital room door, mirrored sunglasses glittering, oversized smile spread across overtanned face.

The two men shook hands, and Detective Harmon said jovially, "Hey, I wish I could just lay around and take it easy."

"The trick is knowing exactly when to step in front of a bullet," Detective Dixon said.

All very teasing and friendly, but a certain wariness in Detective Dixon's attitude made me think they weren't best buddies. I didn't offer Detective Harmon a cookie.

"You remember Mrs. Malone?" Detective Dixon added, motioning toward me. I gave the mirrored sunglasses a fingertip wave.

Detective Harmon's head jerked as if he was startled to see a live person standing there. I guess until then I'd blended into the hospital equipment. But his "Of course" was hearty, and he shook my hand too.

Officer Harmon's big news was that the stabbing victim had died, but they had the guy who'd shot Detective Dixon in custody. The men went on to chitchat, but we all knew Detective Harmon hadn't come here just for police department gossip. Finally he got to the good news/bad news.

The bad news was that the police chief had talked to Detective Dixon's doctor, and they understood he'd be off work a minimum of several weeks, possibly even several months. The good news was that Detective Dixon needn't worry about the Kendra Alexander murder; Detective Harmon had been assigned to take over the case.

Detective Dixon's face looked like someone had dropped a hammer on his leg, but, good cop that he was, he passed along the information about the red Corolla I'd spotted on Bottom-Buck Barney's lot.

Detective Harmon was not impressed. "The plate numbers

on the victim's Corolla are spread all over the country," he scoffed. "No killer would be dumb enough to sell or trade it in right here in town."

"The license plates are missing," I put in.

"One Corolla looks a lot like another," he said loftily, his tone suggesting I couldn't tell an eighteen-wheeler from a skateboard.

"It wouldn't hurt to at least check out the VIN on the Corolla on the lot." A stubborn note had crept into Detective Dixon's voice. "Find out where the vehicle came from and who shows as the last owner."

Detective Harmon shrugged. A big, put-upon shrug. "Sure. Why not? It isn't as if I'm busy or anything."

He left a minute later, grabbing two cookies off the paper plate on the metal cabinet by the bed. I didn't know what to say to Detective Dixon. His fists were clenched, muscle twitching in his jaw.

"I'm sure there'll be plenty of other murders," I murmured finally.

Surprisingly, Detective Dixon blinked and then laughed. The clenched fists relaxed. "Yeah, I'm sure you're right, Mrs. M. There will always be more murders."

"Well, I'd better be going. Perhaps we could share a prayer?"

"Mrs. M. . . ."

"Yes?"

"I decided it was time to get in touch with God. Start going to church and all. I even bought a Bible."

"I'm glad to hear that."

"After messing up my life several times, I felt I was finally heading in the right direction. So what happens? Does God applaud my efforts?" He grimaced and answered his own question. "No way. I get zapped. Before I can even show up at church, a bullet rips into my leg and here I am in the hospital."

"Detective Dixon—"

"You can call me Dix if you want. Some people do."

I noticed he didn't say "Everybody does," and even though he sounded grumpy, I got the impression this wasn't a familiarity offered to everyone.

"Dix—"

"If this is how God rewards efforts to get in touch with him, I don't think I'm interested after all."

"You're blaming God for this, then?"

"Well, not exactly *blaming*. I don't suppose it was up to him to look after me, considering I've never been one of his people. But it seems as if he might have offered a little more encouragement when I show some interest."

"There's a verse in Isaiah that says the Lord's ways are not our ways. There's another saying that isn't a biblical quote, but one I've sometimes found helpful when I don't understand things: God works in mysterious ways."

Dix lifted the blanket, rearranging it over his leg. "Maybe his ways are too mysterious. Because if he's trying to make a point here, I'm not getting it. What I'm seeing right now is 'Make a move toward God, get zapped.'"

"There's also plain old evil to consider. Evil people doing evil things."

He scowled lightly. "I can't argue with that. I see evil all the time."

"But no matter how it looks sometimes, God loves each and every one of us. Including you."

"I remember that old song of Grandma's." He sang it in a surprisingly boyish voice. "Jesus loves me, this I know, because . . ." He had the tune right. Does any child who's ever sung that little song forget the tune? "Because . . . because something," he muttered.

I sang the next line for him. "'For the Bible tells me so.' I'll bring my Bible next time, and we can consider a few things together."

He tapped his fingertips together in an oddly old-mannish gesture of considered thoughtfulness. "No, I don't think so. I don't mean I don't want you to come," he added hastily, reaching for my arm. "Just . . . skip the Bible."

I was disappointed, but then, you have to start somewhere. "Okay. Tomorrow afternoon again?"

"That'd be nice."

There was a piece in that evening's newspaper about Detective Matt Dixon—Dix—getting shot. It said something he hadn't bothered to mention, that he'd shoved a toddler to safety before taking the bullet in his leg.

I went back the next afternoon. A couple of police officers had been visiting him, but they were leaving as I arrived. Dix didn't have much to say, so I filled in with white noise about my garden, Harley's fishing, and how I used to tie flies for him. I stayed away from murder and depressing subjects.

Dix didn't say anything about his leg, but his occasional grit of teeth as I babbled told me it was hurting. "Would you like me to tell the nurse you need a pain pill?" I finally asked.

"No. I hate pain pills. They make my body feel like a slug and my head as if it's full of fog." Somehow the gritty resistance to relieving the pain didn't surprise me. "I don't want to be in a fog. I need to think."

"About . . . ?"

"They have to do another surgery to put a metal plate and a bunch of screws in there. I may wind up being disabled and stuck on a desk job for the rest of my life." He smiled without humor. "To say nothing of never making it through an airport without setting off alarms."

"God can help."

"Do you really trust God in everything?"

"'Cast all your anxiety on him because he cares for you,'" I quoted from 1 Peter.

"Without Bible quotations," he growled with uncharacteristic surliness. "Just tell me about you and God personally. How believing affects you when things go wrong."

"Like if I got a bullet in the leg?"

"That's not too likely. But like when your husband died."

"Harley's death, and my son's death too, were like . . ." Like my heart had been shredded and ripped out. Like sunshine had disappeared into a bottomless pit. Like tomorrow had no meaning. But I didn't want to be melodramatic, so I simply said, "They were more painful than I could have believed possible."

Dix looked up sharply. "I didn't know you'd had a son."

I didn't want to elaborate at the moment. "A bullet that changed my life would be a big jolt too. But Harley and Colin's deaths didn't shatter my faith, and neither would a bullet."

"No?"

"No. I know they're with him. And God took care of me yesterday, he's taking care of me today, and he'll take care of me tomorrow."

"That doesn't mean you won't suffer."

"No, it doesn't. But if God doesn't shield me from troubles, or even tragedy, then he gives me his strength to see me through it. He never deserts me. I could give you a biblical quote—but I won't," I added hastily.

"Thank you."

"I also believe God can bring good out of evil circumstances. Although, in the end, eternal life with him is all that really matters, and Jesus died on the cross to make that possible for us."

He stared out the window. "I wish I had your faith."

"I wish you did too."

Dix might not want to share prayers, but that didn't keep me from silently offering one right there.

I wondered if I was his only visitor other than police force friends. I changed my mind about a question I'd rejected earlier. LOLs can get by with nosiness, right? "Do you have a girlfriend coming to visit you?"

"No. I don't have a girlfriend."

I'd never been a matchmaker, but a big ol' light went on in my head right then and there. This was too good an opportunity to miss.

17

I called Tiffany at Bottom-Buck Barney's the following morning. I told her I had a friend I'd like her to meet. "He's very nice. Good-looking too."

"So how come he's not taken?" she asked with a suspiciousness I hadn't anticipated. A suspiciousness that suggested some unhappy experience. I sighed. Being young isn't easy.

"Why don't you check him out and decide for yourself?"

Tiffany ran that through some bad-experience filter and finally said, "He's not weird or anything?"

"Tiffany, if he was weird, would I be recommending him to you?" I came down heavy on the reproach.

"I guess not."

"One thing I probably should tell you, he's a cop. Also something of a hero," I added, since this situation seemed to call for a sales pitch.

"Aren't they all, to hear them tell it," she muttered. But even if Tiffany was a bit jaded, she was still hopeful. We arranged to meet at the front doors of the hospital at 7:00 that evening.

"Oh, I showed that picture to several people," Tiffany added. "None of them know the guy."

Dix had suggested a rapid turnover in employees at Bottom-Buck Barney's, and this guy's connection with the car lot, if any, may have been before any of the current employees worked there. Although there was the boss . . .

"Including Mr. Retzloff?" I asked.

"I was kind of scared to ask Mr. Retzloff, since he's . . . uh, you know, unpredictable," Tiffany said. An understatement, I suspected. Not a man with a "Favorite Boss" plaque on his wall. "But I caught him in a good mood right after we'd just sold three cars. I thought for a minute maybe he did recognize the guy. He leaned over and really looked at the picture. But all he was interested in was the car. He called it a classic, a Mustang from back in the sixties."

"The sixties?" This put a slant on the photo that had never occurred to me. Could it be a very old photo, maybe even of Kendra's father when he was young? Nothing to do with her murder?

"Mr. Retzloff collects old cars. Can you imagine? I have a hard time keeping up the payments on my one car. And he *collects* cars, has some enormous, temperature-controlled garage to keep them in. I've also heard he's kind of a letch, though he's never hit on me."

Altogether, way more than I really wanted to know about Mr. Retzloff. Although, on second thought, I wondered if he'd acted like a letch toward Kendra. Was it even possible he was her on-the-sly boyfriend? "Is Mr. Retzloff married?"

"Oh, yeah. I know when his wife comes in by the perfume. She must buy White Diamonds by the gallon."

"What does Mr. Retzloff look like?"

"Well, uh, short and kind of paunchy. Moustache. He

thinks no one knows, but he's had those little hair plug-in implants. It's kind of like a hairy garden sprouting on his head."

Again, more than I wanted to know. But Mr. Retzloff was definitely not the lanky, no-moustache guy Thea and I had bumped into. But one more question. "Was anyone curious about where you'd gotten the picture?"

"Mr. Retzloff was. Probably because he'd like to own that car. But I figured you wouldn't want your name connected with any of this, so I just told him I'd found the picture fallen down behind a drawer in my desk."

"Thanks, Tiffany, I appreciate your efforts. See you to-night."

I called Dix to tell him I'd visit this evening instead of this afternoon, and that I'd be bringing a friend. I suppose he assumed the friend was someone my age, because he straightened up in bed as if an electric prod had hit him when Tiffany and I walked in through the now-unguarded door. Tiffany was wearing hip-huggers . . . or are they called low-riders now? Whatever, they were definitely living up to the name, with lots of swing.

Dix didn't have a lot to say, but Tiffany chattered with bubbly animation. She had all these stories about odd people she'd encountered at Bottom-Buck Barney's, and she acted them out with verve. The woman who was all set to buy a little Nissan, until her poodle didn't like it. (Demonstration of poodle yips and growls from Tiffany.) The woman who traded in an old Oldsmobile, then came back to tell them her conscience was bothering her. "You see, that cah is haunted." Tiffany was speaking in her southern voice now as she imitated the customer. "Mah Aunt Elsie, who's been dead a dozen years now, is in there, and I wouldn't mind, 'cause she was a sweet thang, but she just won't quit singin' them old Elvis Presley songs."

Tiffany had Dix laughing, and the laughter circled my heart with a nice warmth.

Before we left, Tiffany said tentatively, "I could come back again tomorrow night," and Dix said, "Yeah, that'd be great."

Outside in the hallway she gave me a grin and a thumbs-up sign, and I mentally preened. *Magnolia, let me show you how a real matchmaker does it.*

The next evening was also successful. Wanting to give Dix and Tiffany time alone to get acquainted, I tactfully said I couldn't make it the following night. When Tiffany left, Dix asked me to stay a minute. I thought he wanted to thank me for introducing them, but what he told me was that Detective Harmon had called.

"He checked out the VIN on the red Corolla at Bottom-Buck Barney's. The car came from Colorado and was traded in on a new car at one of the big dealerships here in town. It was older and had a lot of miles on it, so they wholesaled it to Bottom-Buck Barney's. Detective Harmon said he confirmed this with the former owners themselves, a retired couple who moved here to be near their daughter."

"Oh. Definitely not Kendra's car then." I was half relieved, half disappointed.

"Like Detective Harmon said, one red Corolla looks a lot like another red Corolla."

So much for my car identification skills.

Dix didn't say it in so many words, but I had the impression Detective Harmon had been smugly superior that the red Corolla on Bottom-Buck Barney's lot had been totally legit. He hadn't wanted to bother checking it out, and he'd been right. No connection with Kendra. Then I remembered I had something to show Dix, something totally unrelated to the case. I dug the newspaper clipping out of my purse and handed it to him.

"Hey, all right!" Dix said after he read my letter to the editor. "Very well done. Do you suppose some church would take on the cemetery restoration as a project?"

Riverview United? A possibility, of course. They were always raising money for something. Country Peace looked to me like a more worthwhile cause than another stained-glass window, although I doubted the idea would "climb the steeple and ring the bell," an expression I'd heard applied to the consideration of another project. But Tri-Corners Community? Hmmm.

They did Dix's surgery on Friday morning, putting the leg back together with metal plate and screws. Tiffany had to work, but I went to see him that evening. He was back in his room by then, more alert than I expected. He wasn't the kind of guy to want to make lengthy conversation about his operation, so I asked if he'd heard any more from Detective Harmon about Kendra's case.

"No. It's his case now. He won't be reporting to me."

Which meant my private line into the workings of the police department was also cut off. All I'd know now would be what I read in the newspaper.

My phone was ringing when I got home from the hospital. "Aunt Ivy, where've you been?" my niece DeeAnn exclaimed. "I've been calling all evening. I was getting worried. I didn't think you went out much at night anymore."

"Just visiting a friend at the hospital."

"I wanted to find out how you're doing."

"Fine, just great." I'd never told her about Kendra, not wanting to worry her about such a terrible thing happening in the neighborhood.

"We really want you to come down for a visit. And this time we won't take no for an answer. Sandy's suddenly into crocheting, and I can't help her with that purl two stuff—"

"That's knitting, not crocheting."

"See? We need you. We'll take the boat out on the lake and go yard-saleing and barbecue some ribs and play Go Fish. It'll be great! And we're starving for some of your fried chicken."

I dredged up excuses. My garden. This friend in the hospital. Although basically I dragged my feet because it just didn't seem right to dash off and enjoy myself with Kendra still in the morgue and her murder hanging out there unsolved. I also didn't want to run off and abandon Dix. Then another thought surfaced.

DeeAnn lives near a small town called Woodston, in the Ozarks area of Arkansas.

And Clancy, home of the real Kendra Alexander, is also down in Arkansas . . .

18

I could discuss this with Dix and see what he thinks . . .

I kicked that idea into the trash bin. I knew what Dix would say. *No way, Mrs. M., keep away from Clancy. Stay out of this.*

But it wasn't Dix's case anymore . . .

So I could discuss it with Detective Harmon. Yeah, right. I could also offer my skills in military strategy to the Pentagon. The proposals would undoubtedly be met with equal enthusiasm.

Which didn't necessarily mean the idea of further investigation in Clancy was without merit . . .

Yet what would be the point of my prowling around there? The real Kendra's family had already told the authorities they couldn't identify the girl in the photo claiming to be Kendra.

"Aunt Ivy, are you still there?"

Out of the corner of my eye I could see the pot of Thea's ferns that I'd moved in from the backyard because the fronds were curling like toes on little elf shoes. This was one of several I'd been hiding from Magnolia. Thea's plants desperately needed the safety umbrella of DeeAnn's green thumb.

The thought also occurred to me that Dix was in good hands with Tiffany. They'd discovered they both liked Goldie Hawn movies and Szechuan Chinese food, and they both wanted to learn to scuba dive. She also occasionally went with her parents to South Hill Baptist. I'd hardly be abandoning Dix if I left him in her hands for a few days.

With the support of those two virtuous thoughts, I yanked the Clancy idea out of the trash bin. Who knew what an investigation might produce until that investigation was actually made?

"Yes, I'd love to come visit you. Would tomorrow be too soon?"

"Tomorrow?" I suspected DeeAnn was a bit taken aback by the early date, but she rose to the occasion. "Tomorrow'd be just great! I'll go get your usual bed ready right now."

"I'll bring some plants Thea left. Some of them could use a little TLC." Right. Some of them could use CPR and life support.

"TLC we've got," she assured me. "For both the plants and you."

Believing a good guest should also offer a departure date, I added, "I can stay until Thursday."

I was, I noted to myself, careful not to say I'd be coming *home* on Thursday.

I called Dix at the hospital. He thought my going to visit my niece was a great idea. I packed my old Montgomery Ward suitcase and cosmetics case and called Magnolia the next morning to ask her to pick up both my and Thea's mail while I was gone. She insisted she and Geoff come over to help load the plants. Concern for my back, or concern I might leave some poor, helpless plant behind? No matter. It was Magnolia's good heart that counted.

The backseat of the Thunderbird looked like a Noah's ark of vegetation by the time we were done. Magnolia gave me a big hug, her floating caftan enveloping me like a parachute.

"I'm so glad you're doing this. It'll do you good to get away from everything here for a while."

"Everything," as it turned out, included an event far outside my wildest imagination.

It began as a wonderfully enjoyable mini-vacation. I loved the wooded, mountainous area of northwest Arkansas. Rick and Rory hadn't left for their college jobs yet, and on Sunday, we all— DeeAnn, her husband, Mike, daughter Sandy, and the twins, whose college-age bodies had caught up nicely with the size of their feet— went to church together. Afterward we crowded into two little boats, theirs and a borrowed one, and rowed to the far end of the sun-sparkled lake for a picnic of the fried chicken I'd cooked up the night before. The twins made a chair of linked hands and carried me from boat to picnic table as if I were an exotic princess. On Monday I gave Sandy crocheting lessons, and we turned out a handful of snowflake Christmas tree decorations in psychedelic colors. DeeAnn kept bringing up the subject of my coming there to live with them permanently. I kept demurring.

But by then I'd reluctantly decided I had to tell them about my plans for Clancy. I couldn't in good conscience just drive off without informing them that I wasn't headed straight home.

But before I got around to saying anything, Magnolia called.

"Oh, Ivy, it's just awful! I hardly know where to begin!"

"It can't be that awful if you're in good enough shape to call me," I assured her. Magnolia did tend to go melodramatic occasionally. When Geoff had to cut down one of her magnolia trees that died, she wrote a eulogy for it.

"I went over to pick up your mail a few minutes ago. I hadn't gone earlier because I was getting my hair done. I found the back door wide open. Somebody's been in there. Ivy, it's a disaster—"

"You mean a burglar broke in and stole things?"

"It's such a mess that I can't tell if anything's been stolen or not. Broken dishes, slashed furniture, smashed television—" She broke off on a big sob.

I tried to maintain my own calm and not push Magnolia over into hysterics. "It's okay," I soothed. "It's just stuff."

"I feel so to blame. We should have been watching more closely."

"It must have happened at night, and you can't watch things twenty-four hours a day. Do you have any idea when it did happen?"

"I picked up the mail on Monday morning, and everything was fine then. So it was sometime between then and now. I've called the police, but no one has come yet."

I should have put timer lights on a couple of lamps so the house wouldn't look dark and empty, of course, but I just hadn't thought about it. Too often I neglect the fact that Madison Street is no longer a genteel residential neighborhood.

"Okay, when the police get there, you tell them I'll be home by tomorrow evening. And don't let this upset you. These things happen. Vandals just saw a dark house and decided to go on a wrecking spree."

But after I got home late Wednesday afternoon, I wasn't so sure about that.

Magnolia had been watching for me, and she and Geoff

rushed over as soon as I turned into the driveway. Magnolia's hair had ripened from insulation pink to rich raspberry.

"Go in the front door," Magnolia said. "They broke a hinge on the back door, and Geoff nailed a board over it."

Hearing from Magnolia that the house was a disaster was one thing; actually seeing it was something else. I walked slowly through the rooms. Harley's old chair slashed, stuffing sticking out like a furry tongue. Sofa crisscrossed with Xs. Shards of colored glass like sharpened confetti on the carpet. Drawers of papers dumped out. Phone smashed through the TV screen. Broken dishes in the kitchen, including the old Meito china platter my mother had treasured. Blankets of flour and sugar from canisters dumped on the floor. Bottle of shampoo squirted around the bathroom. Mother's old kerosene lamp smashed.

I'd assured Magnolia that it was just stuff. Even now I could remind myself that whatever had happened here was trivial in the eternal scheme of things. But some of it was stuff that held memories and couldn't be replaced, and the loss left a little hollow in my heart. The prospect of cleaning up the mess also made my stomach feel as if those confetti shards were churning around in it.

The vandals had been upstairs too. Bedspread ripped, feathers from slashed pillows everywhere. Scent of my smashed bottle of faux Eternity, a gift from Thea, hanging in the air. More dumped drawers. And a crude lipstick scrawl on the full-length mirror on the closet door.

I got a big cramp in my stomach as I studied it. Stick drawing of a woman—identifiable by the triangular shape of a skirt—with a noose pulled tight around her neck. Her eyes were bulging circles, her tongue was hanging out the side of the wobbly line of her mouth. Below the drawing was a crudely printed message: *Old busybodies die!*

Did they mean me?

"Artists they're not," I muttered. There was a certain cartoonish silliness to the drawing. But it wasn't funny.

Magnolia twisted her hands together. "Who would do such a terrible thing?"

I shook my head and tried to look on the bright side. The drawing had been done with a scarlet lipstick I'd bought on magazine advice that bright red gives an older woman's face pizzazz. All it had given me was the look of an over-the-hill strumpet, but I'd been too thrifty to throw it out almost unused. It was certainly used up now, the plastic carton crushed in a garish smear on the carpet.

"I'm just glad you weren't here," she declared. "Who knows what might have happened if you'd been home?" Downstairs, she pounced on a scattering of purple shards. "Oh, and look, they broke that lovely vase I gave you!" she wailed.

The harp-playing mermaid had indeed been a casualty of the vandals' attack. I decided this was not a good time to philosophize about clouds having silver linings, good coming out of evil, etc.

Geoff had been quiet, but now he said, "Your homeowner's insurance will probably pay for cleanup and replacement of what's broken or ruined," and I blessed his practical heart for reminding me of that.

Geoff went around the back way to remove the board he'd nailed across the door. Magnolia and I waded across the kitchen, flour billowing around our ankles and sugar crunching under our shoes.

When I looked in the backyard I knew for certain that this was not random destruction. My house had been targeted.

19

Harley's heavy wooden bench had been yanked off the oblong of concrete where it had stood for so many years. Then
dragged across the yard until it smashed to smithereens
against an old maple tree.

Uprooted and dragged just as the tombstones at Country
Peace had been uprooted and dragged . . .

The similarity was unmistakable. There was a phrase for it,
I remembered from my mystery novels. An MO. Method of
Operation. An MO used both here and at Country Peace. This
and the crude drawing and threat upstairs said the vandals
were well aware of who occupied the house.

But why would the Country Peace vandals be after me?
I was positive the two men hadn't seen me that night. Even
if they had, they had no way to identify me and target my
house. Except . . .

Old busybody.

It had never occurred to me that vandals might be readers. Was it possible they had read my letter to the editor . . .

and not liked what they read? Connecting the name in the newspaper with an address would be as simple as looking in the phone book.

I remembered the beefy face of the man I'd seen there that night, the squeaky voice of the other man in the shadows. I shivered at the possibility they'd been in my house, my bedroom.

I stared again at the broken pieces of the bench, the rope still tangled in the wreckage. The old bench, too, was just "stuff," but it had comforted me when I sat on it. The solidity of the oak always reminded me of Harley's strength, the curve between seat and back a reminder of the curve of his body spooned around mine at night. I felt a sick plunge of loss.

"The police came?" I asked.

"Yes, an officer was here this morning."

"Did he have any comments?"

"Only that it's been a busy season for vandals."

I called DeeAnn that night to tell her the house was indeed a mess but that everything was under control. I didn't tell her about the threat on the bedroom mirror. I decided not to worry Dix about that either, at least not right now.

The officer had left a card with Magnolia, and I called him next morning. Officer Larson was sympathetic and polite but not optimistic about apprehending the villains. "Have you had time yet to determine if anything was stolen?"

"I don't see anything missing. Just destroyed."

"Too bad. Sometimes stolen items turn up in a pawnshop or secondhand store and give us a lead."

"I think they must have used a vehicle to drag the bench across the yard. Wouldn't there be tracks?"

"We checked, but your driveway is gravel, and there were no identifiable tread marks."

Okay, shot down there. "I'm concerned about the message on my bedroom mirror. It sounds like a threat."

"I don't think you need take it personally. It's just another vandal thing. I see graffiti showing everything from heads chopped off with machetes to concrete weights attached to feet. Terrorizing is part of their 'fun.'"

I outlined the similarity between what was done with the bench in my yard and the uprooting and dragging of gravestones at Country Peace, plus the possible connection to my letter to the editor. "I think there's at least the possibility that both the threat and damage here are quite personal."

Big empty silence. I could almost hear myself being shuffled into the PLOL category. Paranoid Little Old Lady afraid the boogeyman is out to get her.

"We'll keep the possibility of the cemetery connection in mind as we continue our investigation," he said finally. "And you let us know if you have any further problems."

I got in touch with the insurance agent who had replaced the agent I'd dealt with for years. Margo Halenstack was young and blond, and both her pale blue suit and figure were trim, her manner brisk, sympathetic, and helpful. Together we itemized damages. As a longtime saver of bits of paper, I still had receipts filed away on the larger items. I hadn't realized it until then, but the vandals had rummaged around in the box where I kept such papers, along with other old records and income tax returns.

Margo told me I could purchase replacements for the destroyed furniture and gave me the name of a cleaning service. I called, and they said they could do the work but not until the following Monday. I cleaned up the flour and sugar myself so I could use the kitchen. I also Windexed the closet mirror. I didn't feel comfortable in the same room with the figure of a woman dangling on the end of a rope.

I called the hospital Friday morning and found that Dix had been released. When I dialed the apartment he sounded bored and depressed. I baked chocolate chip cookies and went to visit him that afternoon.

We sat in webbed chairs on his tiny balcony, his cast-covered leg stretched out in front of him, a metal walker beside the chair. I was surprised they were letting him walk already, but he said they were insisting on it, so his muscles wouldn't atrophy. He gave the walker a look as if he'd like to toss it off the balcony. I put off telling him about the vandalism and instead chattered about my nice visit with DeeAnn and family. I rivaled Tiffany for bubbliness.

"Tiffany still coming to see you?" I asked finally, since he hadn't mentioned her and my bubbles were fizzling.

"No. Well, actually she and Ronnie did come one time."

"Ronnie?"

"Ronnie Hilderman. New guy on the force. He and Tiffany met in my hospital room last week. They kind of hit it off."

"But I thought you and Tiffany hit it off."

"She's a great girl, Mrs. M. She really is. But Goldie Hawn and Szechuan Chinese food really aren't enough to base a relationship on." He smiled and patted my hand. "Don't worry. I'm not heartbroken. And Ronnie's a very nice guy."

I wasn't heartbroken either, but I was definitely disappointed with the negative results of my matchmaking. Although relieved that I hadn't already crowed to Magnolia about my skills in that area.

"So, what have you been doing since you got home?" he asked. Before I could answer, he suddenly straightened and leaned toward the metal railing.

My gaze followed his. A young woman, her dark hair tied back in a ponytail and her slim body in khaki shorts and a T-shirt with printing, had just wheeled into the parking lot on a bicycle. She dismounted and removed a big paper sack from a basket behind the seat.

"Someone you know?" I asked, since he seemed so interested.

Dix leaned back in the webbed lounge chair. I sensed pretended indifference. "Haley McAndrews."

"Does she live here in the apartment building?"

"No. We . . . used to know each other. She saw in the newspaper that I'd been shot. I guess she figured it was her Christian duty to come see me." He sounded grumpy about it.

I made the connection. The woman he'd been to church with a "time or two," the one with whom the breakup had been hostile. A minute later the doorbell rang.

"Come on in," Dix yelled. He sounded as welcoming as if she were delivering a sack of overdue bills.

The young woman set the groceries on the kitchen counter and came out to the balcony. Now I could see what her T-shirt said: "God believes in you even if you don't believe in him." The words were written over a rainbow. Dix made introductions. He scowled at the T-shirt.

"Dix has told me about you," Haley said. She offered her hand and a nice smile. To Dix she added, "Chicken tonight. With rice and salad."

Dix just muttered an ungracious, "Whatever." To me he added, "My car is stick shift, and I can't drive it with one leg in a cast. So Haley thinks it's her duty to chauffeur and feed me."

"Her Christian duty."

"Whatever."

"That's very nice of you, Haley," I said.

179

We were both standing behind Dix, and Haley rolled her eyes as if she'd like to pick up that sack of groceries and smash it over his head. "I'd just lend him an automatic car if I had one. But I won't have a car until I get my student loans paid off."

I was impressed. A very responsible attitude.

"Would you like to stay and eat with us?" she added.

My first instinct was to back off. The tension here felt like the atmosphere in a deadlocked jury room. Then I decided maybe I should stay and act as go-between before they started throwing chicken and rice at each other. "May I help with dinner?"

"Sure."

We left Dix on the balcony. Haley started putting the groceries away. I said, "Dix seems a little . . ." I paused, trying to think of a suitable word. Ungrateful grump, although accurate, felt a little harsh, so I tried, "Edgy."

"His appetite is okay."

She pounded the chicken breasts thin and rolled them around slices of ham and Swiss cheese. I made salad and started some biscuits.

I told her about trying out this different church. She gave me a surprised glance, which told me Dix hadn't mentioned my Christianity, and said she'd heard good things about Tri-Corners Community. She told me she'd been reading that series of books about the end times, and I said I'd been meaning to start them as soon as I finished the C. S. Lewis book. We smiled at each other in the way of kindred souls who've just recognized each other.

"You work, or go to school . . . ?"

"I work at the community college where Dix has been taking classes. I'm assistant librarian at the college library."

Oh yes. Kindred souls.

"So that's how you met Dix?" I asked.

180

She nodded. I hesitated about asking more questions, but then I went with the theory that people expect LOLs to be nosy. "Why did you break up?"

"We had . . . philosophical differences."

I didn't need diagrams. She was a Christian, he wasn't.

"And you're visiting and helping Dix strictly as a Christian duty?"

Frown. "I'm not sure."

I offered the blessing before dinner. Dix didn't comment, but I got the impression he'd waited for it. At least he hadn't grabbed for food the minute we sat down. Haley and I, in unspoken agreement not to gang up on him, detoured talk about God and church and discussed an upcoming bond election for the community college.

Eventually I told Dix about the vandalism and the words and drawing on my bedroom mirror. "I mentioned to Officer Larson that all this might be connected to the vandalism at Country Peace, because of the similarity in MO with the bench, but he seemed doubtful. He also said I shouldn't take the drawing as a personal threat, that vandals often leave threatening graffiti. What do you think?"

"I can't say that I've dealt with graffiti or vandalism much. But a threat is . . . a threat. You should take precautions."

"I've contacted a repairman about installing a new back door with a dead-bolt lock."

"Good. You said earlier that you'd seen one of the vandals at Country Peace, a big, brawny guy?"

"Yes."

"Could you describe him more thoroughly?"

I looked off into the evening dusk over the balcony, and I didn't have to dig deep to remember that beefy face. I described it slowly. Broad forehead, wide nose, eyes made piggish by folds of flab over the corners. Heavy jaw, thick neck.

"Shape of face?" Dix asked.

"Squarish."

"Hair?"

"I don't know. He was wearing a cap with a visor."

I hadn't realized it while I was describing the face, but Dix had been sketching it with a ballpoint pen as I talked. He handed me the paper napkin, and I stared at it in disbelief. Dix had caught the man as if he'd been right there in the ditch with me.

"That's him! Is he someone you've seen? Career criminal or something?"

"No. I just drew what you described."

"You learned this in a class?"

"No. It's just something I've always been able to do."

Haley spoke up. "He'd never met my mother, but one time he was picking her up at the airport for me. I described her to him so he could recognize her, and he drew her perfectly."

A natural talent for turning words into pictures. "Did you ever think this is something you might do—" I started to say "if you can't go back to detective work," but amended it to "in addition to your regular police work? Don't they often need an artist to sketch a suspect from someone's description?"

Dix didn't respond, though he looked thoughtful, and we went on to dessert.

After cookies and pecan-fudge ice cream, Haley rinsed dishes and I put them in the dishwasher. Just before leaving, I got bold and said to Dix, "Since we missed our 'date' for going to Tri-Corners Community together, how about making it this Sunday? I can pick you up. There's plenty of room in the car for your cast and walker."

After a scowl from Dix, Haley said, "The only way you're going to get this man into a church is whop him over the head with that walker and drag him."

"Shows how much you know," Dix retorted. To me he added, "Sure, let's go."

20

Considering Dix's current attitude, I was undecided whether to anticipate or dread church with him, but I found a nice surprise in another area when I settled down with the newspaper at home.

The letters to the editor section held a letter from an older gentleman named Will Arleigh. He, too, thanked Mr. Braxton for the offer of a new cemetery site, but he concurred with my suggestion for setting up a fund for restoring the current cemetery. His wife was buried there, and he didn't want to see her moved. He backed up his preference with the offer of a thousand dollars to whatever organization was willing to take charge.

A thousand dollars! Now if only some organization *was* in charge . . .

I picked Dix up a half hour early on Sunday morning to allow time for maneuvering him from apartment to car to church pew. He sat on the pew like a frowning stump for most of the service, leg stretched out and one hand curled around the walker in the aisle beside him, but I could see he was paying attention to the message about why even strong Christians sometimes have doubts. Afterwards I talked with one of the deacons about Country Peace, and he expressed real interest in it as a church project and said he'd look into it further. "Although these things move slowly," he warned. I was just grateful he hadn't suggested running it up the steeple to see if it rang the bell.

Dix was silent on the subject of both church and message on the drive home. I suggested dinner out, but he said Haley had come by and put a roast in the oven before she went to church.

On Monday and Tuesday, the cleaning people came, along with the repairman to replace the back door. I left them to their noisy work and went shopping for new furniture and television. I'd been thinking I might save the pieces of the old bench and try to glue them together, but when I came home that afternoon the cleaning people had taken them. I felt a pang—another tie with Harley lost—but a little later I decided I'd rather keep my memories whole and unbroken than tie them into a cobbled-together bench.

By Wednesday the house was back in order, smelling of freshly shampooed carpets and new furniture. With my life more or less back in order, I made a decision.

A decision that at 7:45 the following evening put me on the edge of Clancy, Arkansas. Clancy was some 150 miles beyond where DeeAnn lived, and it had taken me considerably longer to drive there. My back felt stiff, my bottom numb, and my joints stuck in a bent position. I was looking forward to a hot shower and early bedtime in a motel.

I'd expected a sleepy town rolling up its sidewalks for the

night, so I was surprised to find the stores open, sidewalks jammed with people, bluegrass music blasting from an unseen loudspeaker, and the wide main street crowded with cars. A scent of barbecue drifted in the dusty air, and an espresso stand was doing big business. Honking horns combined with friendly yells and whistles when a convertible with three pretty girls sitting above the backseat inched by.

Off to the left of downtown the upper curve of a Ferris wheel circled lazily, and beyond it another carnival ride whipped a bullet-shaped capsule back and forth as if intent on slinging it into outer space. Even from this distance I could hear the shrieks and screams.

A big, hand-scrawled sign fastened to a streetlight pole read: "RVers, Free Parking at Simco Industrial Park" with a big, bent arrow pointing the way.

The lumbering motor home ahead of me turned at the corner, and when I braked at the town's lone traffic light I saw a banner stretched above the street that explained all this unexpected activity. "Welcome to Clancy's Meteor Daze" it proclaimed in jumbled-style print, the words surrounded by a dazzle of silvery shooting stars against a background of midnight blue. Now I also saw posters in windows, with more shooting stars.

Vaguely I remembered reading that August's annual meteor shower would be best visible this weekend. It had never occurred to me that such a celestial event might impact my visit to little Clancy.

Yet impacted it was, and severely so, I found out a few minutes later when I tried to rent a room at one of Clancy's two motels.

"Oh my, no, we don't have a vacancy. We're always booked up weeks ahead for Meteor Daze. Everyone is," the middle-aged woman announced with complacent cheerfulness.

"That's clever, don't you think? The play on words, daze and days. Dooley Bingham thought that one up."

Good for Dooley. "Where would I have to go to find a motel room, then?"

"Dulcyburg is twenty miles, but I know for a fact they're filled up too. Most people come in RVs, you know. Big ol' motor homes and trailers and fifth-wheels. Some people even camp out in tents." Another cheerful smile. "Everyone comes for Meteor Daze."

"Can't people see the meteors from, well, anywhere, without coming to Clancy?"

"Well, I suppose." She straightened her shoulders, a little huffy now. "But we have the very best views. And it's a real *event* here. We have the carnival and Beef Boogie Bingo and a chicken barbecue and a cow-chip throwing contest and a bluegrass festival. Plus a quilt show and flea market, and a rock concert for the kids. A few people even sleep in their cars out there at the industrial park, just so they can be here."

"Doesn't that kind of get in the way of the . . . uh . . . industry?"

"Not so's you'd notice. The industrial park is four hundred acres, and so far Clancy's industry is one chicken-processing plant."

"Oh. The thing is," I said, beginning to feel a little desperate, "I didn't come for the celebration. I didn't even know about it. I'm here on a . . . personal matter. A very important personal matter," I stressed.

"Well, you might as well enjoy the Daze since you're here."

"You wouldn't happen to know the Alexanders, would you?"

"Al and Marcy? Sure."

"This has to do with their daughter, Kendra."

"She and my son worked together at the Dairy Queen,

187

before Kendra went off to college. And then, the leukemia taking her like that, so sudden and terrible . . ." Her look saddened, and she shook her head.

Well, I was here to investigate. The circumstances did not appear to be ideal, but I figured I may as well start investigating. I pulled my photo of the person I knew as Kendra out of my purse. "Do you know this young woman?"

The woman shook her head. "Who is she?"

"Possibly a friend of Kendra's." I brought out the photocopy of the young man's photo. "How about him?"

Another shake of head. "What's this all about?"

I sidestepped the question and asked, "Could you tell me where I might find the Alexanders?"

"They live over on 11th Street, brick house with a red door. But I doubt you'll find them home tonight. Al helps with the RV parking, and Marcy is probably setting up the quilt show."

"I see. Well, thank you. You're sure you don't know of any rooms for rent? Bed and breakfast? Spare closet? Anything?"

I did my best to look little-old-lady helpless and send a guilt-inducing message. *If this was your grandma, wouldn't you want someone to give her a place to stay?*

No sale. But an unexpected bonus as I opened the door.

"That girl in the photo? You might talk to Beth Arlow, well, Bigelow now, she and Kendra were really good friends. She works in Doug Marlow's office. He's the new lawyer."

I drove slowly around the residential area, hoping to see a bed-and-breakfast or room-for-rent sign on a home somewhere. It was a pleasantly old-fashioned small town, wide streets with tree-canopied sidewalks and a mixture of houses from old Victorian to ranch style. There were basketball hoops over garage doors, lawns well-tended but not elaborately manicured. I found 11th Street and a brick house with a red door. Feeling uncomfortably pushy but determined to do what I'd come here for, I rang the doorbell.

Motel lady knew what she was talking about. No answer.

By now dusk had arrived, stains of a flamboyant sunset fading to blue shadows in the west. Decision time. I could drive fifty or one hundred miles to find a motel room. Or I could chalk this up as a harebrained idea and head home.

I put off deciding while I ate barbecued chicken at the Chamber of Commerce stand set up in front of a long-closed hotel. Afterward I found the industrial park, where cars and pickups and motor homes and trailers seemed to be coming and going in all directions. A haze of dust illuminated by blazing headlights hung over everything. Dolly Parton singing from a car radio, motor home generators rumbling, a dog barking, a band practicing somewhere in the distance. Mixed scents of frying hamburger, gasoline and diesel fumes, and dust.

I was just intending to look around, but a busy traffic person was waving vehicles on through to parking places. Al Alexander? But this was hardly the place for investigative dialogue, and, crunched between two big motor homes, I was swept along with the tide. I spotted what looked like a place to turn around and pulled off, only to find that this was a small area set aside for tent campers. Just to get out of the way I pulled into a space between a blue van and a family cluster of tents that looked like gaudy bubbles.

Whew! It was, at least, a relief to be out of the RV traffic. I swiped a tissue across my sweaty throat. Maybe I could manage to find my way out of here when things quieted down.

I spotted some portable restrooms and slid out of the car to pay them a visit. If there were shooting stars, I couldn't see them through the overhanging haze of dust. People came from miles around for *this*, when they could probably have a better view of shooting stars from their own backyards?

Waving dust away from my face, I decided Dix was right. I should keep my nose out of this. My cemetery snooping had gotten my house vandalized. Who knew what I might stir up here?

For once I'd ignore my curiosity and do the smart thing. Go home.

On the way back from the restroom I passed one couple who'd just discovered they'd brought a tent but no tent poles to set it up. They were laughing as they spread sleeping bags on top of the flattened tent. Three little girls, apparently returning from the carnival, carried puffs of cotton candy bigger than their heads. The woman from the blue van was frying hamburger over a folding Coleman stove.

No one threatened to mug me, grab my purse, or sell me anything. No one, in fact, paid any attention to me, and I unexpectedly found myself feeling comfortable, safe, and nicely invisible among the busy campers.

I didn't necessarily have to go home, I reasoned. There were worse places to spend the night. And it seemed a shame to come all this way without finding out *something*.

I crawled into the backseat of the Thunderbird and took off my shoes. I found three packets of Handi Wipe things in my purse and did a mini-cleanup. The night was warm, and I left the windows partway open, but I figured it might get chilly before morning so I was glad to remember the "survival box" Harley had long ago insisted we carry. Among the assorted items I found when I dug the box out of the trunk—first aid kit, flashlight, reflectors to set out in case of accident—were two serviceable blankets. I punched one into pillow shape, curled up on the backseat with the other over my feet, and considered the novelty of the situation.

It wasn't the St. Louis Hilton, where Harley and I had spent one extravagantly expensive night when we went to a pharmaceutical convention. But neither was it as uncomfortable as, say, a cardboard box or a park bench.

Although I had to wonder if Nancy Drew, Miss Marple, or even that tough V. I. Warshawski ever had to sleep scrunched in the backseat of a car, with what sounded like a dog leaving his mark on one of the tires.

But I had much to be thankful for, I reminded myself, and I gathered my thanks to give them to the Lord as I did every night. I had arrived here safely. I was comfortably full of barbecued chicken and three-bean salad. And I had a promising lead on a friend of the real Kendra's.

21

I lay awake for quite a while, but at some point things quieted down—or I was just too tired to let noises or lights bother me any longer—and I slept peacefully.

I woke once in the night and peered out to watch a handful of shooting stars pass over in the now clear sky, followed by a celestial explosion that was almost like fireworks. Maybe shooting stars really were more spectacular in Clancy.

I woke to a pink predawn sky, scent of coffee brewing nearby, and an unexpected surge of anticipation. I was going to learn something important here in Clancy! I could feel it in my bones.

I could also, I realized as I sat up and ran my fingers through my hair, feel a few other things in my bones. Like stiffness, creaky joints, and odd poppings.

I staggered down to the portable restrooms, early enough that no line had formed yet. Back at the car, I washed up again, blessing the time I'd stuffed Handi Wipes in my purse. I combed my hair with the help of the rearview mirror. I felt sticky and grimy, furry-toothed, much in need of a shower, change of clothes, and a brisk session with my electric tooth-brush. I reminded myself that women in covered wagons had managed for months without such niceties.

I also made a pleasant discovery. Polyester may get a bad rap for style, but if you're going to sleep in your clothes it can't be beat. Scarcely a wrinkle in blue pants or lavender blouse.

"Hey, want a cup of coffee?" my next-door neighbor called.

"Why, yes, that would be very nice."

"It's strong," the woman warned. "I need industrial strength to face three days of camping with three kids. But we wouldn't miss the Daze. We come every year."

If she was curious about a lone LOL sleeping in an old Thunderbird, she didn't show it. I sipped my coffee from the Styrofoam cup. Yes, indeed, strong enough to lubricate creaky joints . . . and probably dissolve meteorites as well. I decided I didn't feel any worse than when I'd spent a night at the cemetery.

Although I had to admit I had hopes for better things for the coming night. Maybe I could find out all I needed to know this morning and head home by noon.

I ate breakfast at a Lion's Club stand, then looked up law-yer Marlow's office. Yes, Beth Bigelow worked there. No, she wasn't working today, wouldn't be in until Monday. By that time the parade had started, and everything else came to a halt.

Yet the parade was so much fun I couldn't complain. The Queen of Meteor Daze was a ninety-eight-year-old woman, gilt crown perched on white hair as she rode in a horse-drawn carriage with the mayor, hand waving in regal Princess Diana style. There were fire trucks and horse-mounted square dancers, floats and bands and high-strutting majorettes, antique cars and 4-H groups. A clown flung candy kisses, and I gleefully snatched one up under the very nose of a teenage boy whose hands were already filled with more than his share.

I'd left my car back at the industrial park and ridden into main street on the open wagon pulled by a tractor that the town provided RVers for transportation. But after standing for an hour and a half to watch the parade, my feet felt like a couple of corn dogs right out of the fryer. I threaded my way through the crowd to the carnival grounds, which was also Clancy's city park, bought a sno-cone, and plopped down on a patch of grass.

After a half hour of people watching and sno-cone slurping I decided I was reinvigorated enough to hoof it over to 11th Street and try the Alexanders again. On the way I paused to watch a carnival ride I hadn't seen before, a little train going round and round inside a vertical circle. Except, almost at the top the train would stop, slip backwards a few feet, and then just hang there. I had to crane my neck to look upwards, and I felt as if all the blood were rushing to my own head as I watched all those people dangling upside down and squealing.

A tap on my shoulder. "Want to take a ride?"

I jumped and whirled so fast that the liquid remains of my sno-cone sloshed all over the arm of the stocky man smiling at me. An arm with the tattoo of a blue motorcycle. I peered at him doubtfully. He looked like . . . No, I must be mistaken. Why would he be here?

The little train whooshed downward in the circle. No, no mistake. It really was Mac MacPherson. In blue shorts, knobby knees and all, with a camera dangling from his shoulder.

"I thought I saw you at the parade," he said. He wiped

his splattered arm on his shorts. "Although I wasn't sure. We were on opposite sides of the street, and then you disappeared."

"What are you doing here?"

"Covering the Meteor Daze for a travel magazine article." Of course. That was what Mac did. "You . . . uh . . . have family here?" he added, obviously puzzled by my presence in Clancy.

We moved out of the flow of people milling around the rides.

"No. I'm . . ." I stumbled to a halt, not quite comfortable with an explanation of myself as an elderly Nancy Drew.

He looked around. "You're . . . uh . . . with someone?"

All these peculiar pauses in his conversation. And there was a hint of something significant in the question, though I wasn't sure what.

"No, I'm here alone."

"For the . . . uh . . . Meteor Daze?"

I was tempted to smile brightly and say "Yes, I'm here for Meteor Daze." At the moment, viewing all this as Mac undoubtedly would if he knew the facts, I felt foolish. LOL on a wild-goose-chase murder investigation. But my inevitable squeamishness with untruths got in the way.

So we just stood there looking at each other awkwardly until Mac finally said, "My motor home is over at the industrial park." He jerked a thumb in that direction. "You're . . . ?"

"I'm at the industrial park too." I was suddenly very much aware of my unshowered condition and squelched an unladylike urge to sniff my underarms. Bag lady in an old Thunderbird. "The motels were all filled up."

"So . . . ?"

"So I slept in my car."

"I see," he said. Which he obviously didn't.

Okay, he was a really nice guy, and after the way I'd run

out on him at Magnolia's barbecue, maybe I owed him an explanation now even if I did come off looking nosy and foolish.

"Look, I was just on my way over to see some people. If you want to come along, we can talk."

"Sounds good."

We looped our way through people, clanging rides, squeals, merry-go-round music, scents of greasy hamburgers and hot dogs, and sounds of tin targets falling in a shooting gallery, and came out of the city park near a street sign saying 5th Street.

We walked and I talked, telling him about the Kendra Alexander I knew and her murder and the surprising discovery that she wasn't really Kendra Alexander. And how I was here with the photos hoping to find out more. I waited for a comment like, "Are you out of your mind, Ivy Malone?" which seemed appropriate.

Instead, Mac, apparently accepting my involvement as if it were a perfectly reasonable situation, said, "It would seem as if your Kendra quite likely knew the real Kendra."

"Yes! Exactly."

We'd reached the brick house by then. Again no answer to the doorbell. I stood there undecided as to what to do next.

"Do Magnolia and Geoff know you're here?" Mac asked.

"Yes." Although I hadn't told Dix, which made me feel a bit guilty. I hoped he wouldn't try to call me, and worry. "Geoff didn't say anything . . . he usually doesn't, you know. Magnolia was horrified at first, but after thinking it over she just told me to be careful."

"You came here to investigate a murder on your own. You spent the night sleeping in your car." Mac looked at me and shook his head. "Ivy Malone, you are a mysterious and remarkable woman."

196

Hearing a hint of admiration rather than censure, I decided I'd quit while I was ahead and not mention my midnight stakeouts in the cemetery. They were irrelevant anyway.

"Someone told me Mrs. Alexander might be at the quilt show. Maybe that would be a good place to try next."

"Lead the way."

Which I couldn't, of course, since I had no idea where the quilt show was. So we asked a strolling chicken. Why a chicken costume? No matter. It seemed appropriate, and the chicken was very helpful. She directed us to the crafts building at the fairgrounds, several blocks beyond the city park. The hike proved fruitless, however, because Marcy Alexander had gone somewhere to pick up a quilt.

But while at the fairgrounds we were educated about Beef Boogie Bingo. It consisted of a nervous cow turned into an arena with limestone-lined squares, the bingo winner being the owner of the square in which said cow made her first plop.

A cheer went up when it came. Mac and I looked at each other. American culture? No wonder foreigners thought we were peculiar. Then we laughed and cheered too, and he took my hand as we walked on.

We caught the wagon going back to the industrial park, where traffic was raising dust again. We picked up the Thunderbird, and I drove it on to the motor home section where Mac was parked.

Inside, Mac waved a hand to invite me on a tour of his on-the-road dwelling. The motor home had a compact bedroom in the rear, bathroom split into two sections on either side of the center aisle, tiny kitchen with stove, refrigerator, and microwave, a compact dinette, a sofa and small chair, and two seats for driver and passenger up front. They swiveled to provide additional seating for the little living room.

"Just right for a man alone," Mac said. "Not much house-work."

Mac fixed ham sandwiches, chips, and iced tea for lunch, and we sat at the dinette to eat.

He cleared his throat. "About tonight," he said.

"If you've never tried it, sleeping in a car isn't as bad as you might think. I was actually quite comfy."

"I'd like you to stay here tonight."

"Here?" Okay, I came across as old-fashioned horrified. Let's face it. I am of a generation that is still old-fashioned about an unmarried man and woman sharing close quarters, no matter the ages of the persons involved.

"You can have the bedroom. It's quite private. There's a folding door . . . see?" He jumped up and demonstrated by sliding the divider back and forth. "And the sofa makes into a good bed. I'll be quite comfortable there."

"Thanks, but I don't think—"

"Ivy, I have spent a night sleeping in a car, several nights, in fact, and I don't like the idea of you doing it."

"I was fine last night. I'll be fine tonight. And if anything should come up, I have my whistle. See?" I pulled out the ever-present silver whistle hanging on a cord around my neck.

His brows scrunched in frustration. "You have backbone, Ivy Malone. But—"

"Not much in the brains department?"

"No, I think your brains are fine too. Stubborn is the problem."

Stubborn. Well, better than that other S word, I decided, even though he sounded frustrated.

Then a crafty look settled on his tanned face. "You could use my shower."

Shower. I almost groaned. A truly lovely S word. Mac MacPherson knew the right button to push. The thought of hot water and being clean again gave me a longing shiver of anticipation. But still . . .

"Well, you give it some thought," Mac suggested diplomatically.

We took the wagon back to the fairgrounds, and this time when I asked for Marcy Alexander, a girl pointed me to a slender, fiftyish woman hanging a beautiful quilt of interlocking rings over a wooden rack. Someone came up to talk to her before we reached her, so we strolled around looking at the displays. There was a crazy-quilt design of angular shaped pieces stitched together with what looked like delicate bird tracks, one labeled "Flower Garden" with tiny appliquéd pieces forming colorful flowers, another with signatures embroidered on each square. *Could I do this?* I wondered, thinking of those hours when I felt guilty because my hands weren't busy.

Finally Mrs. Alexander was free, and we headed that way. She smiled pleasantly. "I hope you're enjoying our show. We have a number of prize-winning quilts here."

I assured her we were enjoying both the show and the Daze, then told her my name and where I was from. She was still smiling, but she also looked a little puzzled now. I pulled out my pictures.

"I wonder if you know this young woman." I handed her the photo.

She frowned at it. "This is the same photo the police showed me. I told them, I don't know her. You aren't with the police, are you?"

"No, but this young woman was a friend of mine. She's been murdered, and so far the authorities haven't been able to find out who did it. Or even who she is."

"I'm sorry to hear that." I heard something hard and stubborn creep into her voice, something that said she was just saying words, that she'd calloused herself against caring about tragedies and death. "But why would you think I . . . ?"

"She lived in my friend's rental apartment. She was going by the name Kendra Alexander. And using your daughter's date and place of birth and Social Security number as her own."

The photo dropped to the floor, and Marcy Alexander staggered heavily against the wooden rack. Mac grabbed it to keep it upright. She looked stunned. "The police didn't tell me that. You're saying this girl stole my daughter's identity?"

I retrieved the photo. "So far I haven't been able to figure out what was going on. You're positive you don't know her?" I held out the photo again. "I think she may have been a friend of your daughter's."

She took a long look this time, as if really wanting to find something familiar so she could nail this girl who had brazenly impersonated her daughter. "I'm sorry, no. She could have been someone Kendra knew at college, I suppose, but I'm sure she isn't from here in Clancy." She handed the photo back. "Look, I'd like to help, but I find this rather . . . distressing."

"I'm so sorry. And I wouldn't ask, except that Kendra, the girl I knew as Kendra, was murdered—"

"Yes, you said that." Marcy Alexander's lips compressed as if she was determined not to let that fact affect her.

"Shot in the chest and dumped in the river."

Mrs. Alexander reacted to that raw information with a convulsive swallow, but she shook her head again. I held out the photocopy of the young man's picture.

"How about him?"

She gave the picture a disinterested glance, started to shake her head, and unexpectedly grabbed the photo instead.

"That's Ray!"

"Ray?"

"Ray Etheridge. Kendra's fiancé."

I just looked at her, more bewildered than ever now.

"Where did you get this?" Mrs. Alexander demanded.

"It was in Kendra's . . . the woman I knew as Kendra . . . in her apartment."

"You mean some woman was pretending to be my daughter and . . . and carrying on a relationship with Kendra's fiancé too?" Outrage trembled in her voice.

"I don't know . . ."

I was as shocked and stricken as she obviously was, and neither of us said anything. Mac put in a soft-voiced question directed to her.

"Are you still in touch with him? Or know where we might contact him?"

"They met at college, Arkansas State at Jonesboro. He was from Little Rock. He came home with Kendra on a few weekends and seemed nice, although we didn't really know him well. He was always driving that car." She pointed to the vehicle I now knew from Tiffany was a sixties-something Mustang. She frowned. "We didn't keep in touch, but I heard once that he'd been in an accident."

"Maybe he'd have family in Little Rock?"

"I don't know." She didn't seem interested, as if her mind was still trapped in shock by Ray's relationship to this unknown woman. "He hadn't given Kendra a ring to make it a formal engagement, but they planned to get married after they graduated. But then Kendra was diagnosed with leukemia . . ." Mrs. Alexander's hands plucked in nervous agitation at a seam on a patchwork quilt. "He seemed terribly broken up after Kendra died. I know he dropped out of college. But then to do something like this . . ."

"I don't know that he did anything," I said hastily. "Without knowing why his photo was in her apartment—"

"He went up to Missouri, I'm sure of that," she said suddenly, as if she'd just remembered that fact. "To that city you said you were from." She inspected me sharply, as if there was something suspicious about the connection.

"He did?" I asked in that stupid way that's more conversation filler than an expression of doubt.

"What was he pulling? Setting some girl up with Kendra's identity. What were they up to? Maybe he was even seeing this woman before Kendra died!"

I wanted to say that couldn't be. But I couldn't, because I didn't know, and I just stood there feeling helpless.

"Kendra didn't seem to be doing anything malicious with the identity," I finally offered. But I didn't know that for sure, did I? It now seemed likely that this guy, Ray Etheridge, had provided the girl I knew as Kendra with the birth date and Social Security information to make the fake identity possible.

Mrs. Alexander shoved Ray Etheridge's picture back in my hands. "I—I'm sorry, but I do find this all very upsetting—" She turned and rushed toward a rear door marked Restrooms.

I looked after her, dismayed that I'd upset her. But also regretful that this obviously ended any possibility of further information from this source.

22

We spent the rest of the afternoon wandering the flea market, riding the Ferris wheel, and sitting on grass at the far end of the park listening to the twang of the bluegrass festival. We missed the cow-chip throwing contest, which did not disappoint me greatly.

It was all fun, but my mind kept jumping back to the encounter with Marcy Alexander and puzzling over what I'd learned from her. Had my Kendra had a relationship with the real Kendra's fiancé? Yet the man she'd been seeing, the one who'd almost bowled Thea and me over, was definitely not the guy in the photo. And how did any of this tie in with murder?

We ate fried catfish and French fries at a Moose Lodge stand and, finally, well-fed and tired, caught the wagon back to the industrial park. Most people had gotten their RVs set up by this time, so the industrial park was neither as hectic or dusty as before. A slender crescent moon hung in the western sky, but Mac said it would set by 10:00, so the sky would be dark by the time the meteor shower should be heaviest, between 2:00 a.m. and dawn.

"And you're staying here, right?" Mac said.

"Is that offer of a shower still open?"

"You're telling me my charismatic company isn't sufficient inducement?" he grumbled.

Mac indeed had a bit of charisma, although I didn't tell him so. "The thing is—" I couldn't squelch a yawn. "I don't think I can stay awake until 2:00."

"I figured we'd go to bed, and I'd set an alarm so we could get up at the best viewing time."

That sounded alarmingly cozy for two people who barely knew each other, but the reality turned out to be comfortably less intimate. Mac dug out clean sheets, and I made up the bed for me while he fixed the fold-out sofa for himself. And then . . . a shower! A hot, beautiful, needles-stinging-the-back shower. And sleep, on a mattress that hit just the right balance between soft and firm, with the sliding door closed.

I heard the alarm when it went off in the living room. I jumped up and dressed in two minutes flat, ready for meteor watching.

Although when I went out, I was suddenly self-conscious of my appearance. "Sorry, no makeup at 2:00 a.m.," I muttered. And hair that looked as if I'd slept through a tornado.

"I never noticed," Mac returned gallantly.

He'd already set chairs outside, and we settled into them with eyes turned skyward. Lots of other people were out too, sitting or strolling. A few generators rumbled, but most were silent, lights out, televisions off. The night was warm, no need for jacket or blanket.

The meteors were already shooting, some mere pinpoints of moving light, others streaking fireballs, some coming singly, others in fiery storms.

"It's hard to believe most of them are only about the size of a grain of sand, or at least that's what the scientists say," Mac said.

"They all seem to be coming from one general area of the sky."

"It's called the Perseid meteor shower, and that's why, because they seem to come from the area of the Perseus constellation. Although they're actually debris from a comet called the Swift-Tuttle. Technically, they're meteors when they're streaking across the sky, meteorites when they land on earth."

"You seem scientifically knowledgeable on the subject."

"Pre-research for my article."

Another burst of exploding stars, one streaking almost to the horizon. "Like celestial fireflies," I murmured appreciatively, if not scientifically.

"Hey, I like that. May I use it in my article?"

"Consider it my contribution."

We sat and gazed in comfortable silence. Mac crossed his arms behind his head. I just slumped down in sloppy comfort, my head against the back of the webbed chair.

"Does all this make you wonder about God?" Mac asked, his tone speculative. "How all this got here?"

"I don't wonder about God. And I know how all this got here. He created it. I can never look up at all the stars at night without being reminded of that." Gazing across the universe always did that to me. It made this truth of God's creation so obvious.

Mac shot me a sideways glance. "You really think so?"

"I don't see any way to explain the sky or the stars or the earth or us *without* God."

"Maybe this—" his arm swept the skies, "was always here."

"But the experts who study these things say it came into being X number of years in the past."

"X number of years?"

"Fill in the X with whatever the current theory is on age of the universe."

"But maybe creation didn't start then. Maybe the 'big bang' they talk about happened then, and started this universe. But maybe some other universe was in existence before that and collapsed in on itself. Then the cycle started over again with another bang."

"And this just happens all by itself, like some cosmic Play-Doh exploding and collapsing over and over in an endless cycle?"

"Well . . ."

"There's a biblical quotation—"

Mac laughed. "There's always a biblical quotation. But go ahead," he added quickly. "I'm interested."

"I probably can't quote it exactly, but it's in Isaiah. 'Lift your eyes and look to the heavens: Who created all this? He who brings out the starry host, and calls each one by name.'"

"Specific enough, if you can trust in the Bible."

"I do. For you skeptics, there's also the bumper sticker version. 'God said *bang*, and it was so.'"

He laughed again, and I was surprised that we could so obviously disagree on something so important and yet still feel comfortably companionable sitting here under stars both shooting and stationary.

"You really don't believe in God?" I ventured finally.

"I wouldn't say I absolutely don't believe. But I can't say I absolutely do believe, either. I suppose I've just never felt any great need for God."

"Not even when you were alone after your wife passed away?"

"I didn't figure God was going to give her back to me, no matter what I believed."

"Not in this life," I agreed, "but . . ."

"My wife was a believer," he said, which rather surprised me. "I guess I've always thought . . ." He hesitated for a long moment before adding, with a self-conscious clearing of throat, "I always figured, if there really was anything to life after death, that she'd find a way to contact and convince me."

That concept startled me. A standard of judging the existence of God and eternal life that I'd never encountered before.

"I suppose that puts me in the weirdo category?" Mac inquired.

I didn't comment on that. "Did you ever go to one of those people who claim to contact the dead?"

"Those charlatans? No way!" he said vehemently, and that much, at least, was a relief. "I just figured if there was anything to it, she'd somehow contact me."

"How long ago did your wife pass away?"

"About three and a half years."

"And after her death you decided to go on the road?"

"Not right away, no. Our home was in southern California. We have three children, and there are eight grandchildren now. But they're scattered from Montana to Florida, so I was there alone. I'd retired not long before Margarite died, and I threw myself into keeping busy with a vengeance. Painting the house, inside and out. Building a new fence. Yard work. Raising a huge garden. Taking classes. That's where I learned photography."

"Very commendable."

"I photographed every flower in the yard. Every vegetable I grew. Every project I undertook."

"And?"

"One evening I found myself taking a potato to my photography class. I was all excited because I thought it looked like Lincoln. I was even thinking maybe I should tell someone from TV or the newspaper. And then I suddenly felt as if I'd been whammed in the head with that potato. That was what my life had come to: I was seeing Lincoln in a potato. And I was excited about it."

"I saw Barbra Streisand's profile in one of my tomatoes," I admitted.

He glanced at me, and we grinned at each other under the light of a flaming star. Two people unexpectedly united in a small conspiracy. "Did you ever tell anyone?"

"No."

"Neither did I. But it tells you something about yourself, doesn't it?" he said.

"It embarrassed me. Even scared me a little. The creeping senility thing."

"Exactly. I thought there had to be something more to life than seeing dead presidents in my garden vegetables, even if Margarite was gone. So I bought this motor home, sold my house, and started making the rounds of the kids and grandchildren."

"Maybe, in a way, it's nice that they're scattered out. Gives you lots of traveling to do."

"I love my children and grandchildren. I enjoy visiting them. They're great, each and every one of them. But it didn't take me long to discover that a merry-go-round of visiting them wasn't enough."

"The Lord fills a lot of empty spaces, if you'll let him."

He skipped that comment. "So that was when I discovered the joy, and small cash benefits, of writing travel articles. Now here I am." He smiled. "Watching Beef Boogie Bingo in Clancy, Arkansas. But I meet lots of interesting people, and there are always new places to go and new sights to see."

Two meteors streaked across the sky, almost as if running a race. I considered Mac's on-the-road life. Was he on to something here, just cutting himself loose?

"I ate some of the peach cobbler you brought to Magnolia's barbecue," he said. "It was very good."

The fact that he remembered it was peach told me he wasn't just making polite small talk. "Thank you. I'm sorry I disappeared." Since he already knew I was dabbling in murder investigation, I went ahead and explained to him about rushing over to Thea's to look for Kendra's photo. "I thought I'd get back in plenty of time to talk to you again. But when I finally found the photo I was astonished to see that the guests were gone and the lights out at Magnolia's."

"So you went on home."

"Yes. Of course."

Silence, as if he were waiting for me to add something. When I didn't, he said, "But you didn't stay there. You left again."

"You saw?" I asked, surprised.

"I heard a car in your driveway. I looked out. And a car was leaving. With the lights turned off."

"I didn't want to wake anyone."

"Stealthy as you were being, I figured that."

Stealthy! I didn't know what Mac was thinking, but I reluctantly realized it was time to explain my midnight jaunts. So I told him about overturned tombstones and my decision to stake out the cemetery and try to identify the vandals. "I'd been going there for quite a few nights, but it was on the very night of Magnolia's barbecue that the vandals finally showed up. Though I didn't really accomplish much because I fell in a ditch before I could get the license plate number on their pickup," I had to admit.

He picked up the chair and turned it to face me. "You're telling me you were running out to this cemetery at midnight, hiding there all night, watching for vandals." He shook his head, obviously flabbergasted as he added this to the list of my other peculiarities. Murder investigation. Sleeping in my car. Now midnight stakeouts in a cemetery. "And here I thought . . ."

"Thought what?" I asked when he broke off.

He squirmed in the chair as if he had just developed a bad itch. "It seemed logical. An attractive woman, a midnight rendezvous . . ."

"A midnight rendezvous?" I repeated blankly. "With whom?"

"That's what I wondered. I never did see you come home."

The light came on in my head like a shooting star blazing across my mind. Now it was my turn to be flabbergasted. My mouth actually dropped open. "You mean you thought I . . . and some man . . ."

"I asked Magnolia the next day if you were seeing someone, and she said no. So then I thought, if he was someone you were sneaking around to see . . ." Another squirm. Neither of us were watching the stars now.

"So that's why you asked me if I was here in Clancy with someone. You thought maybe I was sneaking off for an entire weekend rendezvous."

I didn't know whether to be insulted or flattered. Someone thinking Ivy Malone was involved in a secret relationship, carrying on a flaming rendezvous with some unknown man . . .

I couldn't help it. I started laughing.

Mac straightened in the chair, and I could see I'd insulted his dignity. "Apparently I was wrong," he said, his tone lofty.

"Yes. You were wrong."

"I apologize."

210

I couldn't help it. I laughed again at the preposterousness of it all. Finally Mac laughed too.

"But it wasn't a totally preposterous thought," he insisted. "You are an attractive woman. You have sparkle and energy. You're not afraid to try new things. You cook a fantastic cobbler. Why wouldn't you be in a relationship?"

23

Mac was already up when I woke the next morning; he cooked scrambled eggs with diced ham for breakfast. Today I followed him around as he interviewed people for his article. Some were officials overseeing the event, others average people he stopped on the street to get their take on shooting stars, quilts, and Beef Boogie Bingo.

Late afternoon, when he was checking the list of events on a poster to make certain he'd covered everything, I spotted the Community Worship Service scheduled for tomorrow morning in the park. "Oh, that sounds good. I think I'll go." Tentatively I added, "Maybe you'd like to come along?"

"Actually, I'll be moving on first thing tomorrow morning."

"You will?" I'm sure my surprise showed.

"I can get everything I need for the article wrapped up today, and I promised my daughter that I'd be with them for my granddaughter's eighth birthday on Tuesday. It's going to take me at least two days to drive to Montana."

I didn't know why the news gave me such a jolt. No reason for Mac to hang around. Moving on was what he did. And it wasn't as if some big romance had developed between us. Although sitting under the stars together last night had felt a smidgen romantic.

"I'll be staying until Monday so I can see Kendra's friend at the lawyer's office," I said. A little awkwardly I added, "There should be plenty of motel rooms available by tomorrow evening."

"That's what I figured."

My jolt of surprise—and, okay, a sliver of disappointment—was over by the time we ate fried chicken for supper at yet another civic club stand. We wandered the carnival again in the evening, shared a fuzzy bundle of cotton candy, and watched more 3:00 a.m. shooting stars. On Sunday morning, I cooked buttermilk hotcakes while Mac showered.

Immediately afterward, Mac started readying the motor home for travel. He tucked the jacks that leveled and stabilized it into a side cubbyhole, cranked down the TV antenna, rolled up the carpet under the steps, and checked the gauges that showed battery, water, and holding tank levels. By the time I was ready to leave for the 9:00 worship service, he was putting things away inside so they wouldn't fly around during travel.

He followed me out to the car and leaned his elbows against the window as I put the key in the ignition. "You will get a motel room tonight, won't you? I don't want to be worrying that you're camped out in your car. Even if you do have a whistle."

"No need to worry."

"I really did like your cobbler at Magnolia's. And your being here made Meteor Daze a lot more fun."

"I've enjoyed it too."

There was still much I didn't know about Mac MacPherson, and I was mildly regretful. We hadn't gotten around to talking about what occupation he'd been in before he retired. How he happened to have that motorcycle tattoo. What his real name was, behind the Mac. If he intended to stay on the road indefinitely.

"I'll probably be back this way one of these days," he said. "I've been thinking about doing something on Lake of the Ozarks."

"If you get back to Madison Street, I'll bake you another cobbler."

"I'd like that."

For a moment I thought he was going to lean inside the car and kiss me, but instead he squeezed my shoulder and backed away. I wheeled the Thunderbird in an arc, and when I looked back he was checking the oil in the motor home's engine. Moving on. Would I ever see him again? Well, not something I planned on worrying about.

The worship service was nice. Chairs were set up on the grass. Small crosses made of wired flowers stood on either side of a wooden pulpit. One of the groups we'd seen at the bluegrass festival provided the music and did a credible job. The message was brief, on the simple theme of loving your neighbor.

After lunch I felt at loose ends. I'd seen pretty much everything there was to see at the Daze, and now it was just a matter of waiting around until I could talk to Beth Bigelow at the lawyer's office tomorrow. Then the thought occurred to me: Was it necessary to wait? This was a small town . . .

I found a phone booth outside a gas station and looked up the Bigelow name. One Bigelow had an address that sounded distantly rural, but an Andy Bigelow lived on 14th Street. Should I call?

I decided not. I remembered reading in a detective book that the element of surprise is always good. I didn't know why that should matter here, but I was out of my unlikely could-this-be-romance state (a daze of my own?) and back into investigative mode.

The house on 14th was a neat clapboard, with an older blue Honda in the driveway. I rang the bell. A young woman in her midtwenties came to the door. She was wearing a bulging maternity top over red shorts.

"I'm looking for Beth Bigelow?"

"That's me." Friendly smile, not a hostile glare, for a stranger at the door in small-town Clancy.

"I'm a friend of—" I broke off, thinking I should have choreographed this better. I didn't want to upset her the way I had Marcy Alexander. Although maybe that was inevitable, given the circumstances. "You were a friend of Kendra Alexander?"

"Oh yes. We went all through school here together and then roomed at college together too. She was always so energetic and healthy, I couldn't believe it when she . . ." She trailed off with a hard swallow and quick glisten of tears in her blue eyes. "And then to have her go so fast. She was a bridesmaid at my wedding just a few weeks before she died."

"I have a photo here. I think she was a friend of Kendra's, but I need to identify exactly who she is."

Beth took the photo and studied it. "I'm sorry. I don't recognize her. I didn't know everyone Kendra knew at college, of course. But I'm pretty sure I'd recognize anyone who was really a close friend." She handed the photo back.

I held up the other picture. "I think this is Kendra's fiancé, Ray Etheridge."

"Oh yes. Ray." She smiled. "A wonderful guy."

215

"Could you tell me something about him?"

For the first time her open friendliness took a step backward. "Why? What's all this about?"

"It's complicated, but this woman—" I indicated my Kendra's photo, "was murdered up in Missouri not long ago, and I'm looking into—"

"You're a policewoman?"

Obviously, from her incredulous question, I doubted she'd believe in the existence of some Special Geriatrics Force, even if I wanted to lie. "It's just that she was a friend and neighbor, and so far her killer hasn't been caught. But I have reason to believe she had some sort of relationship with Ray Etheridge."

"Relationship? You mean he was dating her or something?"

"I'm not sure."

"Well, you can be sure Ray didn't kill her! And he certainly wasn't cheating on Kendra. He . . . fell apart when she died. He was really crazy about her. He'd never kill anyone."

"The thing that concerns me is that my friend had this photo of Ray in her apartment." I took a deep breath, hating to go on, because what I had to say seemed to reflect so badly on my Kendra. "And she was using the real Kendra's name and identity."

"Pretending to be Kendra? That's awful!" I could see Beth rising toward outrage now, and I hastily said the same thing I'd said to Marcy Alexander.

"I don't think she was using the name maliciously." Which came off as lame as it had with Marcy Alexander.

"How long ago was this woman murdered?" Beth asked.

"Just a few weeks ago."

"I hadn't thought about it for a long time, but I remember hearing sometime last year that Ray was dead too. Though I never heard if it was true or not. Somewhere up in Missouri, I think it was supposed to be."

"Did they say how he died?"

"Accident of some kind, I think. Although I remember thinking at the time, oh my gosh, did he commit suicide because of Kendra? He was so devastated when she died. But you know . . . Let me see that picture again."

I started to hand her Ray's picture, but she grabbed the photo of Kendra instead. She put her thumbs over the dark hair and tilted her head as she studied the oval face partly hidden by a hand.

"Ray had a sister. She was going to college too. Not there at Jonesboro with us, but she came to see him a few times, and we all went out for pizza and beer. Except for the hair, this does look rather like her. But she was very light blond, just like Ray."

I felt a rush of excitement. "This Kendra in the photo dyed her hair dark. Underneath, I'm sure she was quite blond."

"Really?" Beth bent her head to study the photo more closely. "I didn't know Ray's sister well, of course, just met her those few times. But I never saw her in anything even close to this sexy outfit. And I can't imagine why she'd pretend to be Kendra."

I put the two photographs together, and we studied them side by side. Yes, if I mentally blocked out the dark hair, there just might be a family resemblance between the two.

Beth nodded agreement. "It could be her."

"What was the sister's name?"

"Um, I'm not sure . . . Oh, I remember. Debbie."

"I'd really appreciate anything more you could tell me about either Debbie or Ray."

"I remember Debbie was supposed to be a real computer whiz—"

A phone rang somewhere back in the house. Beth looked

that way but didn't move. "Ray was majoring in some kind of engineering. I don't think they had any family. Ray had insurance money from when their folks died to pay his way through college, so I suppose Debbie did too. But Ray was no goof-off, taking it easy. He was a great guy," she added, as if she wanted to be certain I understood that.

My thoughts were more on Debbie. A college-educated computer whiz. With insurance money paying for a college education. But if Debbie Etheridge and my Kendra were one and the same, why would such a person use someone else's identity and work at sleazy Bottom-Buck Barney's? Had Ray perhaps bought a used car at Barney's, and she thought some defect in it had caused his accident?

"Hey, Beth, where'd you go?" a male voice yelled from somewhere back in the house. "Your mom's on the phone."

"Do you have any idea where I might get in touch with Ray or Debbie, in case one or both of them isn't dead?"

"The Alexanders might know."

"I talked with Marcy Alexander, but . . ."

Beth nodded understandingly. "I know. They've stopped going to church, and they won't talk about Kendra at all. I don't remember where Debbie was going to college, but Arkansas State might have an old address for Ray."

"Which they undoubtedly wouldn't give *me*."

"That's probably true."

From somewhere in the house, "Beth! Are you coming?"

Beth rolled her eyes, and I got the gist. Husband and mother-in-law were not friendly chitchatters.

"I won't keep you," I said. I pulled out my notebook and scribbled my name and phone number on a page. "But if you think of anything, give me a call. Collect," I added, since the modest house and car and pregnancy suggested they hadn't funds to spare.

"Aren't the police handling the murder investigation and the identity theft and everything?" she asked, obviously puzzled by my involvement.

"Oh yes. I just . . ." I floundered for a reasonable explanation of my being here. I couldn't think of any, maybe because my involvement wasn't all that reasonable. So all I said was, "The Kendra I knew was my friend, even though there were . . . puzzling circumstances in her life."

"I hope you find out what happened to her."

I hadn't been worrying that my house might be vandalized again, but I was relieved to find everything safe and normal when I got home the following day.

First item on the agenda, I decided, was to figure out what to do with my new information about Kendra. I was certain I might have something important here. So, steeling myself for the reaction, I dialed Dix's number.

24

I tried to ease into the situation diplomatically. I asked how he was feeling and what the doctors had to say. To which I got skimpy answers of "Okay" and "Not much." So then, very casually, I slid into, "Has Kendra's body been identified yet?"

"Not as far as I know."

"The body is still in the morgue?"

"All I know is what's in the newspaper."

"What's in the newspaper?"

"Nothing."

The strong, silent . . . grumpy . . . male.

"Is Haley still helping you out?"

"She cooks. She cleans. She runs errands and chauffeurs. I have to go for physical therapy now. She drives me. I'm supposed to exercise with my walker. She nags me."

"You don't sound particularly grateful for the help."

"She's always sermonizing at me."

"About exercising?"

"About God. Jesus. The whole enchilada."

"Haley preaches at you?"

"Well, not out loud. But she wears those T-shirts with all their God messages."

The man was complaining about T-shirts. "You really ought to work on your attitude, Detective Dixon," I snapped. "If I were Haley, I'd be inclined to wrap one of those T-shirts around your neck—tightly—and shove you off that balcony."

Silence big as some black hole in space.

"Maybe you're right," he muttered finally. My next thought was that if the T-shirt messages were getting to him, maybe they were doing their job.

"Okay, look, I've just acquired some information that may be helpful." I told him that the guy's photo was definitely identified as the real Kendra's fiancé, Ray Etheridge, and that the girl I knew as Kendra was possibly Ray's sister.

"Identified by whom?" Dix growled skeptically.

Now we were down to the nitty-gritty, and to give the information credibility I had to tell him where and how I'd acquired it. So I told him about Clancy and then held the phone away from my ear for the blast I knew was coming.

"Mrs. M., I told you to stay out of this! What have you got anyway, some mutant curiosity gene? Why don't you just sit around and knit or play pinochle or gossip like other little old ladies? This isn't your job, and it could be dangerous. You've already been vandalized once."

A mutant curiosity gene! Well, maybe I did have one. But I wasn't about to admit it. "That was cemetery business, nothing to do with Kendra and murder. But I guess you're not the person I should be giving this information to anyway, are you? You can't do anything with it or find out anything more anyway." A blatant challenge to his blue funk, of course.

"I'm still on the payroll. I still have friends in the department. I'm not completely out of the loop."

"Oh?" I deliberately painted the word with my own skepticism.

"You say someone says this Ray Etheridge may have been killed in an accident, maybe around here?"

"Possibly."

"Car accident?"

"I don't know. It's possible he committed suicide." Then I added a possibility of my own that no one in Clancy had mentioned. "Or maybe he was murdered, just as Kendra was."

Another silence. Detective Matt Dixon, I suspected, might have been reluctant to encourage my thinking along these lines, but he had a curiosity gene of his own. Finally he said, "I might be able to talk to a guy. Or look through some records myself. I may take a desk job before long anyway. *Temporarily*," he added, though I wasn't certain if the emphasis was for my benefit or his own.

"Well, you do whatever you think is right."

"I thought going after that crook at the house was right. And look where that got me. A leg full of more metal than a junkyard, Haley on my case, and Harmon running my murder investigation."

"Feeling sorry for ourself, are we?"

"Ivy Malone, you can be a thoroughly aggravating woman."

"I'll decide later if that's a compliment or an insult." Along with considering whether Mac's temporary suspicion about my having a midnight rendezvous with some man was flattering or insulting, a matter I still hadn't settled.

Dix warned that I should consider the information I'd gathered confidential and not discuss it with anyone.

"But you'll tell me what you find out? We had a deal, you remember," I reminded.

"I'll see." A silent P.S.: *Don't hold your breath.*

222

After hanging up with Dix, I unloaded the car and put a load of wash in the machine. The phone rang just as I was closing the lid. Magnolia, of course. Mindful of Dix's admonition, I skirted around the edges of what I'd learned in Clancy. I had something else with which to divert Magnolia's attention, anyway.

"I ran into Mac MacPherson there."

"Mac!"

"The town was having a meteor celebration. He was covering it for a travel magazine article."

"Well, well, well." I could almost see her squashing the phone closer to her ear in gleeful anticipation of juicy details.

Even if I'd been willing to share juicy details, I hadn't any to offer, so all I said was, "We had a nice time at the flea market and carnival and bluegrass festival. And watching the shooting stars, of course."

I left out my two nights in the motor home bedroom, afraid she might give that some erroneously juicy interpretation. Even holding that back, she pounced on what I'd told her.

"I'm getting vibrations of romance!"

"Just a casual friendship." Quite casual, in fact, considering how fast Mac had zipped out of there.

"Oh." She sounded disappointed, but then she took a philosophical view. "That's how the best romances start."

I'd barely hung up when the phone rang again. This time it was the deacon, Charley Mason, whom I'd talked with at the church.

"I didn't see you at church yesterday, so I thought I'd call and bring you up to date on the cemetery matter."

"I appreciate that. I was out of town for the weekend."

"I talked with the pastor and other deacons and the board

about the possibility of the church taking over restoration at Country Peace. They'd read in the newspaper about the vandalism there, of course, and everyone is interested."

"Great!"

"Several of us drove out to look the situation over, and a couple of our members have been looking into details. Brad Englebretson works for the county, and he's been checking up on ownership, who's buried there, county regulations, et cetera."

"Does it look possible?"

"We think so. It's a murky situation, with all the officers listed on the Country Peace Association papers being deceased. But using information Brad gave me, and the Internet, I've personally located family members of several people buried there, distant relatives in most cases, but they've all been concerned and cooperative. I think we can count on some donations. It's going to take a fair amount of money, of course. Getting those big headstones back in place will require heavy equipment."

"Perhaps that Mr. Braxton would help. Even though his subdivision is some distance away, he was concerned about vandalism spreading to his equipment. Maybe he'd even contribute funds, since he was so generous with his offer of moving the graves and providing land for a new cemetery."

"Actually . . ."

"Actually?" I prompted, sensing a bit of wariness here.

"Jordan Kaine, our other member looking into this, is a retired lawyer who's had some courtroom dealings with Mr. Braxton. Jordan is a bit—" Charley Mason broke off, as if trying to come up with a proper word.

Surprised, I filled in the one that Charley's reluctant tone suggested. "Suspicious?"

"Concerned," Charley corrected carefully. "The reputation of Braxton Building and Development is not altogether savory. There have been lawsuits against them concerning shoddy construction and loan irregularities. Jordan thinks Mr. Braxton's generosity may be motivated by a certain amount of self-interest."

"If what he means by self-interest is that Mr. Braxton would benefit from favorable publicity, that may be true. But I'd think a generous donation would entitle the company to some publicity."

Actually, I felt rather indignant about this attitude toward Mr. Braxton. Anybody could sue anybody over the most trivial of matters, and lawyers were sometimes all too eager to help them. Harley had even been sued once, by some woman who claimed he hadn't put the pill bottle lid on tightly enough, so her expensive pills spilled, causing her both loss of pills and mental anguish. It came to nothing, of course, but the trouble it put us through . . .

"It's just that there are some peculiarities about the cemetery and nearby property that Jordan is looking into," Charley said.

"I see." Although I didn't, of course. "Will Mr. Kaine's doubts about Mr. Braxton affect whether or not the church is willing to take over restoration of the cemetery?"

A moment of silence. "No, I don't think so."

That was all I considered important. Although Charley's next cautious words were less reassuring. "Although it depends, of course, on how many roadblocks we run into."

I didn't hear anything from Dix the next day about Ray Etheridge's accident. Or the following day. I decided maybe he was right. I should take up some age-appropriate hobby instead of muddling around in murder. I wasn't enamored with knitting, pinochle, or gossip, but those quilts at Meteor

Daze had looked interesting. I got a bunch of old scraps of fabric out of a sack in the closet and started cutting and fitting them together in a crazy-quilt design like the one I'd seen at the quilt show.

But by Thursday morning my eyes felt dizzy from all the different shapes and patterns of fabric, I'd stabbed myself with a sewing machine needle, and I started an allergic sneezing. My bird-track stitches looked more like drunken turkey trompings, and I was bored. I could admire the results of dedicated quilting, but doing it personally was about as interesting as counting beans. Another day and it would be me, not the fabric, that was crazy-quilted.

I stuffed everything back in the sack, tossed it in the closet, and drove down to the main branch of the city library. Sensibly, I should have been after quilting instructions. Instead I headed for the shelves where they kept out-of-town telephone books. Marcy Alexander had said Ray Etheridge was from Little Rock, and in the Little Rock book I found listings for half a dozen Etheridges. Back home, I closed my mind to the cost and started dialing. Each time someone answered I explained in my most grandmotherly voice that I was trying to contact Debbie or Ray Etheridge.

No one knew either person. But there was one number, the number I most wanted to reach because it was listed under the name Etheridge, D. R., at which I got no answer. Not during the day, not during the evening, not all next day.

Important? Or irrelevant?

Dix finally called me Friday evening. "I've been doing some checking," he said.

"Good."

"A Raymond Etheridge was killed in an accident here on October twenty-third last year."

"What kind of accident?"

"He was employed by an outfit called Thrif-Tee Wrecking.

226

It's kind of a cross between an auto junkyard and a repair shop. They buy old or wrecked cars and dismantle them for parts, or, if they're repairable, fix them up for resale. Ray was alone there, working on his own vehicle after hours."

"That Mustang in the photo?"

"Yes. He had the car up on ramps, both rear wheels off, and was working under the car. Somehow it slipped off the ramps. His chest was crushed. Another worker found him the next morning."

"How terrible!" My chest felt tight and breathless just thinking about being trapped and crushed like that. Yet at the same time another thought occurred to me. There was still a pair of metal ramps out in the garage that Harley had used when he wanted to work under our car. I'd always assumed they were quite safe. How did a car slip off them? "It was definitely an accident?"

"Given the circumstances, there was an investigation, but the death was determined to be accidental. Etheridge hadn't set the emergency brake, and apparently whatever he was doing jarred the car enough to start it moving and rolling off the ramps."

"Maybe somebody released the emergency brake. Maybe somebody pushed the car off the ramps."

"Mrs. M.—"

"Okay, okay, I know. You said it was investigated."

"And determined to be an accident."

"But aren't murders, especially successful ones, sometimes made to look like accidents?"

Big silence, until he finally muttered, "It's happened."

Working in a junkyard/repair shop seemed an unlikely job for a bright college guy studying engineering. But both Kendra's mother and Beth Bigelow had said Ray was all broken up by his fiancée's death. Maybe he was just marking time until he pulled himself together enough to return to college. "Was a next of kin listed in the records?"

"A sister, Deborah Etheridge. She had the body sent to . . ." Dix trailed off, as if deciding whether I was trying to sneak in one question too many. "A suitable location."

I didn't bother asking him for Debbie Etheridge's address, since he obviously wasn't going to tell me. I had my own theory about that anyway. "Was the sister satisfied with the conclusion that his death was an accident?"

"It was mentioned in a couple of reports that she'd complained, apparently quite vehemently, that the investigation was inadequate. But that's not an uncommon response when someone loses a loved one under unusual circumstances."

"So nothing was done?"

"The case was reviewed. The review affirmed the previous decision of accidental death and determined that the case did not need further investigation."

"Did you talk with anyone at the place where the accident occurred?"

"I'm not on the case. I got this much because a buddy let me dig around in the records."

"Have you given the information I picked up in Clancy to Detective Harmon?"

"Yes, of course." His tone went stiff. Stern law officer doing his duty regardless of personal feelings or conflicts. "He's the officer in charge of the case."

"Is he looking into the possibility of Kendra really being Debbie Etheridge?"

"He's a competent, responsible officer. I'm sure he will."

Something hung unfinished at the end of that statement. I suggested a possibility. "Eventually?"

Noncommittal grunt.

"I'd guess that Detective Harmon doesn't give high priority to BLOL information," I suggested.

228

"BLOL?"

"Busybody Little Old Lady."

Dix ignored that. "According to a guy I talked to, Detective Harmon has a theory that the local Kendra's death is connected with a drug case he's also working on."

That boyfriend of Kendra's who had almost bowled Thea and me over had acted peculiar enough to be into drugs, I had to admit. "I suppose, even if she really was Debbie Etheridge, that her murder could involve drugs. But it doesn't explain her using Kendra Alexander's name."

"I'm sure Detective Harmon will take all that into consideration. Perhaps he'll want to talk with you."

Right. And maybe Sean Connery will call and ask me for a date.

I tried calling the D. R. Etheridge in Little Rock again Saturday morning. Again no answer.

I threw myself into a distracting frenzy of housecleaning. Sunday morning I went to church, of course. I'd called and asked Dix if he wanted to go, but he said a flat no, not bothering with some polite excuse. Tiffany called me Sunday afternoon, just to see how I was doing. And because she was a sweet person.

"Just fine," I said. "Keeping busy."

"You haven't met Ronnie Hilderman yet, have you? He's a police officer friend of Detective Dixon's who I've been seeing."

"Dix—Detective Dixon—mentioned him."

"Ronnie went to church with my folks and me last week and again this morning."

"I'm pleased to hear that." On impulse I asked her an unrelated question. "Tiffany, do you know if Bottom-Buck

Barney's does any business with an outfit called Thrif-Tee Wrecking?"

"Yeah, we get a lot of stuff from them. Their used parts are way cheaper than new ones. Sometimes we send a vehicle over there to get something big, like a second-hand engine, installed."

I remembered Dix saying that Thrif-Tee also restored damaged cars. "Does Barney's sell any vehicles for them?"

"I don't know. That's computer stuff that Jessica handles."

"She's the woman who took Kendra's place?"

"Right."

"Is there any connection between Bottom-Buck Barney's and this Thrif-Tee place, other than buying parts from them or having them do repair work?"

"Not that I know of." She paused. "Although, come to think of it, a relative of Mr. Retzloff's works there. Jessica is another relative. Actually, I heard once that Mr. Retzloff is related to the owner here. Isn't there a word for that, when relatives hire relatives for all the good jobs?"

"Nepotism."

But I wondered if there wasn't a much more ominous connection than nepotism. Ray Etheridge worked for Thrif-Tee. Sister Debbie, under disguise, worked for Barney's. And now both were dead.

25

I ate breakfast and then stopped at a gas station to pick up a city map. It had taken me until late evening yesterday to reach Little Rock. The motels here, blessedly, had plenty of vacancies. Although all the money I'd recently been spending on motels and gas and phone calls was becoming worrisome. I'd told Magnolia I was going down to Arkansas, and she, in a dither about a genealogical connection who flatly refused to answer family questions, hadn't questioned me about the trip. I think she assumed I was visiting DeeAnn again, an error I somewhat guiltily hadn't corrected.

Now I rolled along Little Rock's Boldway Avenue looking for 2478, the address listed in the phone book for D. R. Etheridge. It was an older section of the city, houses big enough for families with ten children, sweeping lawns, graceful old trees. But it was not the elite section of town it probably had once been, and many of the big places had been divided into apartment rentals. As had 2478 Boldway, I realized when I pulled the Thunderbird to the curb in front of it.

Okay, I was here, now what? I could almost hear Dix yelling in my ear, *Stay out of this, Mrs. M!*

But people who listen to voices no one else hears, I reminded myself, get put in the weird, crazy, or S-word category. I briskly ignored the voice and slid out of the car.

I walked up the cracked sidewalk to the old-fashioned front porch. The house was of no particular vintage or architecture. Maybe Victorian to begin with, but chopped and remodeled, with a peculiar stucco addition. Even so, the wooden-railed porch had a homey, old-fashioned charm. There was a separate mailbox for each of four apartments. The name D. R. Etheridge was in the slot above #4, and an arrow on the railing pointed around back.

I found the basement apartment and rang the bell and knocked. Repeatedly. No answer. Which didn't surprise me, of course. I went back to the porch and rang the bell marked Manager.

The woman who answered was my age, small-boned and slightly built, her gray hair almost a match for mine. She was wearing a pretty, pastel blue pantsuit, pearl earrings, and high-heeled white sandals. Which reminded me of Thea. We do hate to give up our high heels, don't we? A little dog with a pug nose and a pink ribbon bounced up yapping and sat down beside her. She glanced at her watch as if hoping this wouldn't take long, but her voice was friendly. "May I help you?"

"Debbie doesn't answer her doorbell. I'm wondering, would you happen to know when she'll be back?"

The woman looked me over and apparently decided I wasn't casing the joint for later burglary. Perhaps one of the advantages of being, if not always invisible, at least a harmless-looking LOL. "Debbie's out of town. I don't expect her back anytime soon."

232

I felt a surge of elation. My guess had paid off. D. R. Ether-idge was Debbie! "She's still on that job up in Missouri?"

"Yes. She's been there for several months now. But the job's supposed to be only temporary, you know, and she left most of her clothes and things here."

"Have you heard from her recently?"

Small, worried crease between her eyebrows. "No, I haven't."

"But her rent is up to date?"

"Actually, this month's rent is somewhat past due. But I'm sure she'll send a money order in a few days, just like she always does," she added hastily, as if she didn't want to suggest Debbie was irresponsible.

"She's such a dependable and trustworthy young woman. Unlike some tenants." I spoke from Thea's experience, not my own, but that throwaway comment hooked me into what was apparently a sore point with this landlady.

"Oh yes! You can't imagine some of the wild excuses they come up with for not paying the rent. 'I don't have the money because I had to get the tattoo on my leg removed,' a young man told me last week."

"Because it said something, um, undesirable, or wasn't the current girlfriend's name?"

The woman rolled her eyes. "I didn't ask for details. But Debbie always pays on time. That's why I've been concerned about not hearing from her. This just isn't like her."

What I wanted was to get inside Debbie's apartment and look around. A sympathetic fib would come in handy here. *I'm Debbie's great-aunt, her grandmother's sister Ivy. I haven't heard from her, and I'm worried about her too. Perhaps I could just step inside the apartment and see if everything looks okay?*

But, however devious my inventive mind, I was, as usual, stuck with my conscience and the truth. "Actually, the reason I'm here is because I'm afraid something *has* happened to Debbie."

She put a hand to her mouth. "Oh no."

I pulled out my pictures, beginning to feel I should put them on flash cards for easy access. "I have this photo."

"That's Debbie?" she asked doubtfully. She pulled the picture closer to bring it into better focus with her trifocals. "Oh, well, yes, of course it's Debbie. But what in the world has she done to her hair? And that dress!"

"This woman was murdered up in Missouri a few weeks ago."

"Debbie was murdered!"

"She was using a different name at the time. But it is Debbie, isn't it?"

"I don't understand. Why would she use a different name?"

"I don't understand either," I admitted honestly. "But her body was found in the river—"

"Oh no!"

"She lived just down the street from me, and I cared about her, and I want whoever killed her brought to justice. So that's why I'm here. I have this other picture of her brother. Did you know him?"

She glanced at her watch again before studying the copy of Ray Etheridge's photo. "I don't recognize him, but I remember Debbie mentioning she'd had a brother. But he'd died, an accident or something, before she came to live here."

"Was Debbie working when she was here? Going to school?"

"Both. She was taking college classes but working part-time for a lawyer. What she really wanted was to get into a job with the police department, but there hadn't been any openings."

"You mean she wanted to become a police officer?"

"Oh no. I guess there's a lot of clerical work with a police department, and she thought it would be interesting. She was very good with computers, you know. But then this other job in Missouri turned up."

So she was working when she had insurance money to pay for her college education. Working for a lawyer. Was that just chance? I doubted it. She could well have thought she might be able to use the lawyer's legal connections to find out more about her brother's death. And had computer-whiz Debbie then decided a job in the police department would give her access to police channels for some deeper investigation into her brother's death?

"She quit both school and job to go up to Missouri?"

"I guess so. I don't remember exactly what she said, something about this being a temporary but high-paying job up there, I think."

High pay, I was quite certain, was not Debbie's motive for going to work at Bottom-Buck Barney's. But why Barney's, if Ray's death had occurred at Thrif-Tee Wrecking?

The woman handed Ray's picture back. She looked at her watch again. "I'm really sorry to rush off, but I have a doctor's appointment in forty-five minutes."

"I was hoping we could look around Debbie's apartment together and figure out what's going on here. Why she was using a different name."

The woman hesitated, but I didn't know if she was concerned about the time or the legalities and ethics of going into the apartment.

"I'd like to find out who her next of kin is," I added. "Would you happen to know?"

"No. I don't usually ask for that information from prospective tenants. Maybe I should."

"So far, her body is still in the morgue because they haven't the name of a next of kin to claim it."

Her knuckles touched her lips. "The morgue!" she repeated, obviously horrified. She looked at her watch again. "Perhaps if you come back later . . ."

Now it was my turn to consult a watch. "I was hoping to get started home as early as possible. I hate to be on the road after dark."

"Oh, I know. I do too. But I can't skip this doctor's appointment." She touched her midsection, hand moving from her stomach area up under the right side of her ribs. "I've been hurting all over in here, sometimes really sharp pains up under my ribs, and they're thinking it may be my gallbladder."

"If it's gallbladder trouble, you don't want to let it go, that's for sure. I kept letting mine go, always telling myself, well, maybe it'll quit hurting by tomorrow. It's so difficult having to go to the hospital when you're alone."

"Oh yes. I don't have anyone to collect rents or take care of Mitzi or anything." The dog wagged a stub of tail, apparently at mention of her name.

"And getting tangled up with Medicare is always such a hassle," I added.

"Tell me about it. I went round and round with them when I had thyroid trouble. And the price of prescriptions these days!"

"Exactly. You feel like you're swallowing gold nuggets. But then I wound up being hauled off to the hospital in an ambulance for gallbladder surgery. So don't let it go," I repeated.

"Where did you hurt?" she asked, and for five minutes we exchanged information about gallbladder pains and Medicare hassles and surgery. She'd known some woman whose gallbladder surgery had left her with an eight-inch scar and all kinds of complications, but I told her about my much simpler laparoscopic surgery, with just tiny incisions.

She looked relieved. Finally, with another glance at her watch, she said, "I do have to go, but it probably wouldn't hurt if I unlock Debbie's door, and you just have a look around . . . ?"

The suggestion ended on an upswing, as if seeking my opinion on the propriety of this. On a strictly legal basis, I doubted this was a proper course of action for a landlady. But I also knew I wasn't here to rip off Debbie's belongings, and maybe I could find out who her next of kin was. Along with some clue that would lead to her killer.

"I'll stay until you get back from the doctor's. And I'll keep the door locked so no one else can get in. By the way, I'm Ivy Malone." I held out my hand.

"Letitia Stone."

We shook hands and smiled at each other. She handed me the keys. "I hate to think of Debbie lying in some awful morgue," she said. "She must have family somewhere."

"I'll see what I can find."

Locating a next of kin to claim Debbie's body from the morgue was important to Letitia, as it was to me. But I knew it was a different connection that was truly at work here.

We were two of a kind, two little old ladies with gallbladder trouble, a bond not to be taken lightly.

When she got back I meant to ask her if she sometimes felt invisible too.

26

A light layer of dust covered every surface, including the TV screen, and the air smelled like something left over from another decade, but otherwise the apartment was scrupulously neat. Pillows plumped on the sofa, beauty and exercise magazines, all several months old, neatly stacked on the coffee table. Kitchen counter and appliances spotless, refrigerator empty.

A framed photo stood on the top shelf of a bookcase. Ray Etheridge and Debbie/Kendra in happier times, blond teenagers smiling with the carefree exuberance of youth and good health. I had to swallow, hard, as I thought about the last time I'd seen her. Bloodless and dead in the morgue.

The bedroom was equally neat. I pulled a dress out of the closet, beige linen, conservative hemline, with a matching jacket. Skirts, some with hemlines short but not minuscule, others calf-length. Pants, mostly dark. Bright T-shirts and blouses. A dressy black dress, low-cut but not immodest. Walking-length shorts, jeans. On the floor below were jogging shoes, black pumps, and scuffed sandals.

Not the kind of clothes Debbie had worn when she was living as Kendra Alexander and working for Bottom-Buck Barney's. Why the change in wardrobe? I saw only one likely answer. Man bait. A man she thought would go for the type of woman who dressed in flashy, revealing clothes, flaunting maximum sex appeal.

But what man? And why? I turned and stared at another item in the bedroom. A computer. Did it hold answers? Possibly. But they were as inaccessible to me as if they were locked in a burglar-proof safe. I didn't know how to turn the computer on, much less extract information from it.

A situation I vowed to remedy. I might not be able to get interested in the intricacies of quilting, but I could get interested in computing. I'd talk to Haley about courses at the community college. I could find out what surfing the Net was all about!

Which was no help at this point, however.

But even with a computer, maybe Debbie had kept something on paper. Where? There wasn't much storage space in the small apartment. I looked under the bed. Dust bunnies and fuzzy slippers.

I went back to the closet. Cardboard boxes on the top shelf! I got a chair from the dinette set, stood on it, got hold of a box . . .

Which was twice as heavy as I expected and immediately crashed to the floor. My aging body followed, along with the clothes I plunged through as I went down. And there I was, a clothes hanger tangled in my hair, a high heel jammed into my armpit, and papers flying everywhere. With Dix's voice in my ear. *See, I told you to stay out of this.*

Shut up, Dix, I retorted grumpily. *It's no big deal.*

I untangled myself, ascertained that nothing was broken, and, sitting on the floor, started going through the scattered contents of the box.

There were Christmas and birthday cards she'd saved. A long-dead corsage. A graduation program showing that Debbie had been salutatorian of her high school graduating class. A program from a play in which she'd had the lead, no doubt good experience for her later role at Bottom-Buck Barney's. Ribbons she'd won in college swimming events. A couple of photo albums, which interested me but which I didn't feel I had time to peruse. A guest book and memorial folder from a funeral. A double funeral for her parents, I saw with a pang. *Oh, Kendra*—a part of me clung to the name by which I'd known her—*how sad*. This was her memory box, I realized with a rough catch in my throat.

Memories that ended with a body in a river. And the man who'd dumped her there still running free.

I kept out one item when I put everything back in the box. It was a birthday card signed "With love from Aunt Chris." So somewhere there was a next of kin. I'd show it to Letitia when she returned.

I was more careful with the next box and managed to get it to the floor outside the closet without catastrophe. The box was actually labeled Important Papers. Bank statements, receipts, warranties for a CD player and television, letters from a lawyer about estate and insurance matters, college records, some from a college here that I'd never heard of, some from the University of Arkansas in Fayetteville. All informational but not helpful for my purposes.

In the third box, however, which was wooden rather than cardboard—pay dirt. This was brother Ray's box. Maybe one he'd left with her for safekeeping? Within minutes, I found the answer to one question, how Debbie had assumed Kendra's identity so accurately. Ray and Kendra had filled out an application to rent an apartment together in Jonesboro. Apparently they'd never submitted it . . . maybe second thoughts on how Kendra's parents would react to

240

their living together? Or perhaps her illness had intervened. The crucial information was all there: Kendra's birth date. Kendra's Social Security number.

By now I was pretty sure why Debbie had borrowed a name. She was looking for the truth about her brother's death, and she didn't want the Etheridge name to expose her relationship to him.

Papers about Ray's college records were also in the box. Payment records on the Mustang. And something else—a packet of a half dozen letters wrapped in a rubber band.

The envelopes, with Ray's name in the corner, were addressed to Debbie in Fayetteville. Apparently, after his death, she'd dropped out of college there and come here to Little Rock. I studied the Missouri postmarks. The last one was dated October 19 of last year, four days before Ray's "accident." I went back to the letter with the earliest postmark and slid the two handwritten pages out of the envelope.

Then I stopped, halted by a squeamish feeling that I was invading Debbie's privacy. Her brother Ray's too. And another feeling that, for all I knew, I was committing some ghastly crime here. Should I be turning the letters, untouched, over to the local police or Detective Harmon in Missouri?

I listened for Dix's voice in my ear. Nothing.

What I could see was Detective Harmon's exasperation if he looked at the letters and found Ray writing mundane missives asking for a loan until payday or griping about the weather.

My legs were beginning to stiffen. I stood up to stretch them and unfolded the letter. It looked well-worn, as if Debbie had read it many times.

And I was reading it before I'd come to a decision about the ethics of the situation. By then, of course, it was too late. I couldn't stop reading any more than I could stop halfway down in a fall from a ten-story building.

The letter appeared to continue a conversation that had started elsewhere, perhaps in a phone call or earlier letters that Debbie hadn't saved. *"Yes,"* it said, apparently in response to nagging by Debbie, *"I'll probably go back to college sooner or later. But not yet. And I'll never be able to go back to State, not without Kendra."*

Then small talk about his paranoid landlord, a temporary job as a telephone solicitor *("My ear has blisters from having the phone slammed down on it so many times"),* and a microwave disaster with an egg. The attempt at upbeat humor sounded forced. Ray's real feelings came out in the next paragraph.

I know no one ever said life is fair. I remember Dad being a stickler for honesty and dependability, all that do-gooder, do-unto-others stuff. But don't you ever get the feeling, what's the point? Mom and Dad live good, upright lives. Pillars of the community. They die in a freak accident that traps them in a burning house. Kendra is the sweetest, most caring and wonderful person in the world. So what happens? Her life ends at twenty with a disease that many people survive. I'm beginning to think you may as well grab whatever you can, because there's sure no payoff for the nose-to-the-grindstone, white-knight kind of life.

The letter ended by saying that he'd run into a guy he knew from back home, someone he thought could help him get a job at the "car outfit" where the friend worked.

I dropped to the edge of the bed with a shiver of dismay. If Magnolia were here, she'd mutter that the letter had bad vibes. Ray was headed for trouble.

I had no idea what Debbie wrote in response to that letter, or

242

if she perhaps talked to him on the phone rather than writing. But in the next letter, after some small talk about a new apartment and some movies he'd seen, Ray sounded defensive.

I know you don't like Danny, you think he's leading me "astray," and I should run back to college and be a happy camper. But I like the job. Who knows? Maybe my life's calling is to be a mechanic, not a college-educated engineer. To tell the truth, without Kendra it just doesn't seem to matter much. But there's something funny going on here. I know Benny in the office figures we grease monkeys are too dumb to figure it out, but when you're changing numbers it doesn't take a rocket scientist to figure out something peculiar is going on. And I'm pretty sure what it is. I suppose at one time it would have bothered me, but now it doesn't seem so bad. So a few people get ripped off. They don't really lose anything. Their insurance covers it. It's a pretty clever scheme, actually.

I was troubled by Ray's air of admiration for something that wasn't on the up-and-up. The letter didn't mention Thrif-Tee Wrecking, but I had no doubt that Thrif-Tee was where the Danny of whom Debbie didn't approve had gotten Ray a job.

The next letter was ordinary stuff. A move to a different apartment. Some car races he and Danny had been to. A reference to a friend's accident that Debbie had apparently written or talked to him about, and congratulations on her good grades. A comment that, *"One of these days I've got to get a computer so we can get on email. This writing letters by hand is killing me. So you better appreciate it!"* But there was a troubling last paragraph:

Okay, I know you think I should run to the cops with what I know. But I'm not going to do it. You know why? Well, for one thing, why should I? The way I look at it, why not just get in on it? There's big money here, but all Danny and I are getting out of it is peon wages. But I think I've figured out the system, and there's no reason we can't do this on our own. Although we'd have to figure out the selling angle, of course. And our oh-so-respectable, big-shot boss would probably go into orbit if he figured out we'd latched on to his scheme. But I can handle it.

There's no point moralizing at me about this, Sis, so don't bother, okay? I love you. If you want to stick to the straight and narrow, fine. Just don't tell me what to do.

It's beginning to tie together, I thought uneasily. Ray's job at Thrif-Tee Wrecking concerned something illegal. The "selling angle" sounded like a possible link to Bottom-Buck Barney's. I couldn't tell if Debbie, at this point, knew the details of what was going on, but she apparently knew enough to upset her.

Did Ray and friend Danny decide to go out on their own? Had their "big shot boss" gotten wind of it, with a reaction far more violent than going "into orbit"?

There was a long interval between that letter and the postmark date on the next one. This one, after some talk about possibly getting together with Debbie over the Labor Day weekend, had a different tone, as if Ray were developing doubts. Or disgust.

Maybe all that old work-hard, honesty-is-the-best-policy stuff that Dad tried to instill in us runs deeper than I figured. Because this is beginning to get to me. Part of it is what goes on here, of course. But there's also knowing what else our oh-so-respectable boss is doing. Pulling phony deals with wrecked cars is bad enough, but it's just "stuff," you know? But knowing how he cheats on his wife with his bimbos really gets to me. (More of Dad's principles rising to the surface here?) I've never seen the guy, did I ever tell you? He keeps his connection with us very much under-the-table, though I think he comes over and checks things out after hours. To make sure no one's cheating him, I suppose. But he isn't as anonymous as he thinks he is. The wife of a guy who works here used to do housecleaning at his fancy house. She works in a motel now, and she says she's seen him in there several times. Not with his wife. But not alone, if you get my meaning.

Well, I suppose it's none of my business. For all I know maybe his wife is playing the same sleazy game. But right now I'm feeling pretty full-up with sleaze.

I opened the last letter with mixed feelings of hope and dread. Ray had recognized that whatever was going on at the shop was wrong, and he was no longer talking about getting into it himself. Yet I knew there was no happy ending.

The letter started out on an upbeat air. Debbie had apparently driven up to see him in Missouri over the Labor Day holiday weekend. It sounded as if they'd had a good time, but there had also been serious talks. Ray got very serious in the last paragraph.

Okay, Sis, you and Dad have finally gotten to me. It's time to get out. The last straw hit a couple days ago. It isn't just cars getting stolen and numbers getting switched and insurance companies getting ripped off. It's people dying. An elderly couple in Alabama were killed in the theft of this Camry we got in last week. I'm sure this isn't the first time something like that has happened, and it's too much for me. So I'm going to the cops. It's going to take some undercover work to get the proof to take to them. I'm sure everything on the office computer is squeaky clean. No help there. Although that's one of the beauties of this operation. Ol' Bo may be crooked as, to use one of Grandpa's old sayings, a dog's hind leg, but he isn't dumb. They do enough legitimate business that it's easy to hide the not-so-legit stuff. But I'm sure there are records somewhere. Probably in the wall safe. Big problem, you say? Oh no. Because I've seen Benny putting the key right there in the file cabinet.

So, wish me luck, Sis. Dad would be pleased, don't you think?

But Ray had never made it to the authorities.

27

I'd just gotten the boxes back on the shelf when Letitia rang the doorbell. I unlocked the door and let her in. Her wispy hair had wilted around her face, and she immediately stepped out of the high heeled sandals. I could almost see the lumpy bunion on her right foot throbbing. I pulled out a chair at the dinette set. She plopped into it with a small groan of relief.

"Did the doctor decide anything?"

"More expensive pills. More tests. Come back next week." She rolled her eyes. "How about you? Have you found anything?"

I showed her the birthday card signed by Aunt Chris.

"Are you going to contact this Aunt Chris and tell her about Debbie?" Letitia asked.

"So far, I don't have her last name or address. Can you use a computer?" I waved toward the blank-eyed machine. "It might be in there."

"Mitzi knows as much about computers as I do." Letitia shook her head. "It's just so hard to believe someone I knew was murdered. The world isn't the same, is it?" She sounded as much wistful as horrified.

"I guess there have always been murders."

"Not to people I know."

We silently contemplated the changed world for a minute.

"Do you ever feel invisible?" I asked.

She looked at me as if I'd asked if she ever flew around the room on a broomstick. "Invisible? No one is invis—" She broke off, her tired eyes widening. "Oh, but that's it exactly, isn't it? It happened today! The doctor's office was crowded, and these three young women wound up squeezing onto the sofa where I was sitting. I felt awkward, because they were talking about some birth control thing, and I couldn't help overhearing. But they didn't even realize I was overhearing, did they? They weren't any more aware of my existence than they were of the jade plant on the end table."

"Not truly *invisible*—"

"But not *visible* either," she said. "I guess it's an age thing."

"Don't let it bother you." I patted her shoulder. "I've discovered it's really quite useful."

"Useful?" She sounded doubtful. Then she tilted her head, eyes narrowing. A nod and unexpectedly foxy smile followed. "Yes. I'll remember that. Quite useful, indeed."

"Well, I'd better get started home. I'll have to stop in a motel somewhere along the way."

"It would probably be okay if you stayed here overnight."

We both looked around. The apartment was clean and unoccupied, and Debbie surely couldn't care. But the idea gave me too much of a walking-across-someone's-grave feeling.

"I think I'll just head on home," I said, and she nodded as if she understood. I realized I was still holding the bundle of letters. "I found these. They're letters Debbie's brother wrote to her. Would it be all right with you if I take them along to give to the authorities investigating the murder?"

She looked undecided for a moment, again considering legalities, I assumed. Then she cast aside whatever her worries were and nodded firmly. "If they can help catch Debbie's killer, by all means, take them. And the birthday card too."

Letitia picked up her sandals, and together, she in her pantyhose feet, we walked around to the front porch.

"I'm going to have to do something about the apartment," she said. She sounded worried. "I need the income from the rental."

"I'll talk to the police about getting Debbie's body identified right away. I'll give you my address."

Once more I scribbled everything on a scrap of notebook paper. Maybe I should have business cards made: "Ivy Malone. Invisible Lady. Specializing in Neighborhood Murder Investigations. Cemetery Stakeouts, and Oddly Shaped Vegetables." I handed her the scrap and hugged her. "I wish we'd met under happier circumstances."

I stayed in a motel just across the Missouri line, but I didn't sleep well and felt frazzled with heat and weariness by the time I got home. Maybe I should trade the Thunderbird in on something compact, with working air conditioning? Although that would mean dipping into a CD, and I need all the interest I can get in these times of miserable interest rates.

I was also rather stiff from that fall I'd taken from the chair, with a blue bruise developing on the inside of my left knee. I tried not to notice that it was shaped like Australia.

I was relieved to see the shades were pulled in Magnolia's house, which meant she and Geoff were away. Dearly as I love Magnolia, I'm not always up for her flamboyant energy.

Even though I was tired, I tried to call Dix right away. I wanted to discuss the letters with him. But there was no answer at Dix's apartment all afternoon and evening, not even when I tried one last time a little before 11:00 p.m., after I'd soaked my sore bones in the tub. Not like him to be out so late these days. I was worried enough that I called the hospital to see if he'd been readmitted. No, no Matt Dixon there. I couldn't call Haley because she had only a cell phone, no home phone, and I didn't know the number.

Next morning I tried Dix's number several times. No answer. I called the community college library and learned that Haley wouldn't be in for several days. Unlikely as it seemed, it almost looked as if they'd gone somewhere together.

Reluctantly, thinking the letters and information about Aunt Chris were too important to delay, I called Detective Harmon. He didn't sound particularly interested but said that when he had time he'd come out to see what I had. When I pinned him down, he reluctantly agreed to maybe later today.

While waiting for him, I called Tiffany. She recognized my voice, of course. Before I could say why I was calling, she said, "Oh, I'll bet you're wondering about Detective Dixon and Haley, aren't you?"

"I did try to call him . . ."

"Ronnie said Detective Dixon's brother called—he's been in the Mideast, you know? And he was going to be passing through Chicago, just a layover there at the airport for a few hours. Detective Dixon hasn't seen his brother for over two years, so Haley is driving him up to Chicago."

Chicago! Well, Dix had better appreciate that. Above and beyond the call of duty, I'd say.

"They left just yesterday, so it'll probably be at least a couple of days before they get back. They were going to stay with some relatives of Haley's along the way."

I appreciated the information, even though this wasn't why I'd called. "Tiffany, I wonder if you could do me a special favor?"

"Sure, Mrs. M.," she said promptly. "What is it?"

"Could you find out if a Benny or a Danny work at that Thrif-Tee Wrecking place where you get used auto parts?"

"Does this have something to do with Kendra's murder?"

"Possibly. Dix—Detective Dixon—keeps telling me to keep my nose out of this, but it seems as if nobody's doing anything, and I think this could be important."

"Remember that old saying, 'Whatever a woman does, she has to do twice as well as a man to be thought half as good'? I figure a woman's nose belongs wherever she wants to put it," Tiffany said.

This was not an old saying I was familiar with, and I wasn't sure I got the connection, but I wasn't going to argue.

"Anyway, I can tell you right now that there's a Benny out at Thrif-Tee," Tiffany said. "He handles the office work, if you can call that greasy hole-in-the-wall an office. I had to run some papers out there one time. Girlie calendars on the wall, old tin cans for ashtrays, dog ugly as a stomped-on Halloween mask, oil stains everywhere. Yuck."

"Maybe you can think of some casual reason to ask him if they have a Danny working there?"

"Sure. I have to call out there every once in a while anyway."

"Do any women work there?"

"I think the guys there are all those macho types who figure no woman can tell a carburetor from a spare tire. I doubt if they'd hire a woman, even if she could tear a car apart and put it back together with her eyes closed."

Which perhaps explained why Debbie investigated her brother's death from a position at Barney's instead of at Thrif-Tee.

251

Tiffany giggled. "But Benny sounds an awful lot like a woman. He got really mad the first time I called out there and mistook him for one. But I recognize his voice now, of course, and try to keep him buttered up."

"One more thing. Do you know who owns Bottom-Buck Barney's?"

"No, but if it's important I can try to find out."

"It might be important." The boss at Thrif-Tee had "bimbos," according to Ray. Debbie had seemed to be trying to pretend she was one. Connection? "The owner never comes around?"

"If he does, he's doing it incognito. Although I think I've talked to him on the phone a few times."

"A nice man?"

"I don't think he calls here unless he's mad about something. Mr. Retzloff always jumps up and closes his door when this guy calls. I got the impression somewhere that he owns some high-class business and would rather people not know he's associated with a grubby used-car lot like Barney's."

Which sounded a lot like Ray's comment about the "oh-so-respectable boss" at Thrif-Tee. "Let me know what you find out, okay?"

I'd been neglecting my garden, so I went out and watered everything. My tomatoes, without attention, appeared to be taking on odder shapes than ever. Remember Jimmy Durante? I could definitely see his nose on one. The cucumbers had taken the opportunity to expand to small dachshund size. One even had beginnings of a tail.

The phone was ringing when I went back inside. I expected it to be Officer Harmon telling me he couldn't come after all. Instead, an unfamiliar voice identified himself as Jordan Kaine.

The name fell into a blank hole before I finally managed to drag it out. "Oh yes, I remember Charley Mason mentioning you. You were looking into some legal aspect of the problems out at Country Peace."

"Yes, that's right." He had a deep voice, youthful sounding for a retired man. A voice that had undoubtedly impressed many a jury with its authoritative depth.

I was not, however, feeling too kindly toward this man who had apparently taken an adversarial stand against the generous Mr. Braxton, who'd offered assistance at Country Peace. In fact, I had to admit to a certain prejudice against lawyers in general ever since the pill-lid incident.

"Charley Mason pointed you out to me at church, but you disappeared before I had a chance to talk to you. I think you may be interested in information I've acquired about Country Peace."

"Concerning Mr. Braxton?"

"Yes, basically."

"Yes, I'm very interested."

I thought he meant to tell me whatever he knew right then, but instead he said, "I was thinking we might have dinner together. Perhaps Friday evening at Victorio's Seafood?"

Thea's and my special place for birthday celebrations. I had to give the man credit for excellent taste, but I still wasn't eager to share dinner with a lawyer. Then I had to chide myself for that discriminatory attitude. In spite of my sour experience with the lawyer handling the loose-pill-lid case, it was a lone experience, and there were no doubt any number of decent, honorable men in the profession. And Jordan Kaine apparently was a respected member of Tri-Corners Community Church.

"Yes, I think I can make Friday evening."

He said he'd make reservations for 8:00 and pick me up about 7:45.

Magnolia and Geoff got home later that day, and she came over to tell me they'd made a rush trip down to Oklahoma and to let me in on her latest genealogical findings. She was wearing moccasins and feather earrings, which I uneasily suspected indicated something meaningful.

"What I found out—"

"From the guy who didn't want to talk about family connections?"

She waved a dismissive hand. "Not him. I located this other fascinating woman. And you know what I found out from her?" Magnolia didn't wait to find out if I wanted to hear. "There's American Indian blood in our background, on our great-great-grandmother's side!"

Magnolia's theory of genealogy, I once decided, was that if one illustrious bloodline is good, ten are even better. And now she had this new one to add to her dazzling array of French, Hawaiian, and Russian royal ancestry. Magnolia looked no more American Indian than I looked Italian Mafia, but I didn't dispute the claim. Who really knows what any of us is, anyway? "That's great. Any particular tribe?"

"Cherokee!" she gushed. "Isn't that marvelous? I'm thinking we'll probably visit the reservation next summer. Maybe take in a powwow or something."

"Where is it?"

"Oklahoma, I think. Oh, but what I really came over for is to tell you we're having some RV friends in for stew and Indian fry bread Friday evening, and I want you to come. I also have some fantastic CDs of American Indian drumming."

"I'd like to come, but I have an appointment."

"On a Friday night?"

"It's about Country Peace. A man from church has been

looking into the problems there. We're going to have dinner together so he can tell me what he's found out."

Magnolia pummeled me with her usual questions, and by the time I'd told her what I knew about Jordan Kaine, she'd jumped to her own conclusions.

"That isn't an 'appointment,' Ivy, it's a date."

"No, it is not a date. I don't even know that he's unmarried."

"Did he make this dinner 'appointment' with you for himself and a wife?"

"He didn't say." Although deep down, I knew. No wife was involved in the dinner, and neither was Jordan Kaine hiding one.

"This is a date," Magnolia stated with assurance. "If he hadn't wanted to see you personally, he'd have told you whatever he knows on the phone instead of asking you to dinner. He got this guy at church to point you out, he liked what he saw, and he's using the Country Peace thing as an excuse to ask you out."

I could think of arguments against that theory, but I didn't have time to present them because the doorbell was ringing. "I've got to go. Someone's at the door."

"Wear something . . ." Magnolia paused, and I expected her to come up with something outrageous. My answer was ready. *No, Magnolia, I am not going to wear anything sexy, seductive, or scintillating.* As if I even owned anything in those categories.

But after a thoughtful pause, the word she chose gave me pause. "Wear something enchanting," she said.

28

Detective Harmon strode in, mirror sunglasses and all. I showed him the letters and birthday card and told him that the Little Rock landlady had definitely identified the earlier photo as her tenant, Debbie Etheridge. "And, as you know, that other photo has already been positively identified as her brother, Ray Etheridge. Who was engaged to the real Kendra." I had the uneasy feeling I sounded as if I were giving a summation of a TV soap opera.

He inspected the birthday card first, without taking off the sunglasses. "This doesn't tell much," he said.

True. "But more information may be on the computer in Debbie's apartment in Little Rock. If you could locate this Aunt Chris, she could surely identify the body."

He didn't respond to that, although he did deign to take the sunglasses off to read the letters. Which he sped through as if he'd stopped in on his way to an emergency call to chase down a bank robber. When he snapped the rubber band around the letters again, I thought he was going to dismiss their importance and hand them back, but he didn't go quite that far. "We're quite close to tying this murder into a drug case, but I'll take these along. They might prove useful."

Right. And I might locate something enchanting in my closet.

"Couldn't you get a search warrant for the office at Thrif-Tee Wrecking, and especially for the wall safe Ray mentioned? And the computer system at Bottom-Buck Barney's also? Something illegal must have been going on at both places. Something that probably resulted in Ray's death, and then in Debbie's also."

I thought I knew now what Kendra/Debbie had meant when she said she was almost through here. She had the goods on both the illegal activities and her brother's killer and was about to go to the authorities.

Detective Harmon looked at me with an air that said I was wearing on his patience.

"Mrs. Malone," he said with strained politeness, "I appreciate your interest and . . . uh . . . theories, but there's no mention of Thrif-Tee Wrecking or Bottom-Buck Barney's anywhere in this material, and we can't get a search warrant based on hasty assumptions. We have to have more to go on than this." He shook the bundle of letters lightly, and I suspected he'd like to shake me as well. Meddlesome little old lady. He wanted his drug deal to work out, wanted to prove he was right.

Detective Harmon left, backing his car out of my driveway with a bit more speed than I thought was called for.

Tiffany phoned later in the afternoon. She'd called Benny at Thrif-Tee with a pretense of checking the name scribbled on an old invoice. Benny had told her a guy named Danny used to work there, but he'd quit last fall and moved away. To Alaska, Benny thought. Or maybe it was Argentina.

Probably not much chance, then, of running Danny down to ask what he knew about activities at Thrif-Tee. Definitely no chance of my doing it, anyway. I hadn't enough information about Danny's leaving to know if it was before or after Ray's death, but I wondered: Had the death scared him, and he'd decided to get out before a fatal "accident" happened to him too?

"What about the company owner's identity?"

"I approached it with Jessica. I told her I thought it would be nice if we had his name and birth date so we could give him a birthday present from the office."

"And?"

"She looked . . . startled, I guess you might say. She said she didn't think that would be appropriate, then she rushed into Mr. Retzloff's office and shut the door." Tiffany hesitated. "I'm not sure why, but it makes me kind of uneasy."

Me too, and I made a quick resolution. No more dragging Tiffany into any of this. I also wasn't feeling good about the fact that my questions were encouraging her to use fabrications to get answers.

Jordan Kaine arrived promptly at 7:45 on Friday evening. I watched him come up the sidewalk from the driveway. Medium height, a little on the stout side, but his walk was light and brisk. Hair gray, but more iron than possum. His suit was a conservative gray, his tie conservative maroon with narrow diagonal stripes of silver. He rang the bell, and I opened the door.

He smiled. "I have the advantage. I know you're Ivy Malone, but you don't know me. Jordan Kaine."

I could easily see him disarming a witness with that affable manner. I felt a bit disarmed myself. If Jordan Kaine were giving out approval ratings, I could see a nice gold star for me as he discreetly looked me over.

258

Was this not strictly an appointment to discuss church business? Was it, at least on some level, a date?

My life a manless moonscape for years. And now two of them?

I quickly discarded the idea of myself as some late-blooming femme fatale. In spite of Magnolia's claim of Mac MacPherson's interest in me, he'd spun out of my life almost as fast as Detective Harmon spinning out of my driveway. And Jordan Kaine just wanted to talk about overturned tombstones.

"I'll get my purse," I said.

We small-talked on the drive to Victorio's. I learned he'd lived and practiced law here for over thirty years. His wife had passed away five years ago, and he had two daughters and four grandchildren. I cautiously supplied corresponding information about myself. By the time we were seated at Victorio's, Country Peace had not yet surfaced in the conversation.

I looked around the candlelit room with pristine white tablecloths and gliding waiters and thought about the times Thea and I had come here. Although Jordan Kaine seemed passably okay, I had to admit I'd have happily traded this "date" for one more birthday celebration with Thea.

He asked if I'd like a glass of wine, and I declined. He ordered halibut, and I chose the shrimp scampi. While we waited for our dinners, he got down to business.

"I've been checking into Drake Braxton's interest in Country Peace."

"I understand you've had some courtroom dealings with him in the past." I kept my tone neutral, but I couldn't help adding, "His offer to provide the land and move the graves to safer ground certainly seems admirable."

"Perhaps. Did you ever notice a tombstone at Country Peace for an Emma Littleton?"

"No, I don't think so."

"It's rose granite, with an oversized chicken on top."

Oh yes, the chicken. Who could miss that chicken? I'd been so astounded by it that I'd never noticed the name. "Yes, I've seen that one."

"Emma was the young daughter of a couple named Earlene and Dolph Littleton. She had a pet rooster she was very fond of, and the parents apparently wanted to memorialize that relationship when she died. They also didn't want her buried in some far-off cemetery—or perhaps they encountered some resistance to the chicken—so they arranged for the opening of Country Peace on a portion of their own land. Their home was back in the hills behind what is now the cemetery."

"I remember seeing an old shack or something way back there. It looked as if the road goes through the cemetery to get there."

"Right. When Earlene was alive, I think it was a reasonably decent place, but Dolph apparently turned eccentric after she died. Chickens became his main companions, and he let the house deteriorate. He died last year, leaving everything to the only relative who, as his probated will pointed out, ever came to visit him. A grand-niece named Alana Littleton."

I didn't see what all this had to do with Mr. Braxton, but I assumed Jordan was headed somewhere with it and didn't comment.

"Alana married years ago. She was probably married even when old Dolph made out his will. But the different name didn't change her inheritance of the property, of course, when Dolph died."

"And her name now is . . . ?"

"Alana Braxton."

"Braxton!"

"As a builder and land developer, Drake Braxton undoubt-edly realized the development possibilities of his wife's inheritance. Someone I'd guess was a representative of Braxton's, although he didn't identify himself as such, approached the county about subdividing the property into two- to five-acre estates, and you perhaps know the kind of money those bring these days. But there was one huge obstacle. The only access to the property is that twelve-foot-wide road easement through the cemetery that Dolph retained to get to his house. A twelve-foot easement does not enable Drake and Alana to divide and develop the property behind the cemetery. A big subdivision requires a road wide enough to meet county standards, on land that can then be given over to the county."

I knew nothing about such regulations, but Jordan obviously did.

"But crafty old Dolph put in a special provision when he provided the land for Country Peace. It says that if, at any time, the land is no longer used as a cemetery, ownership reverts to him or whoever owns the main property at the time."

I felt a dawning dismay. "Which means that if the cemetery no longer existed, Drake Braxton's wife would get that land back. And they could then develop both it and the valuable property behind it."

"Exactly."

Where he was going with this finally hit home. It came out of me in a big gasp. "Are you suggesting Mr. Braxton himself may have had something to do with the vandalism at the cemetery?"

"It strikes me as a distinct possibility. There are big bucks involved here. And big bucks drive Drake Braxton's life. Ethics are so far down on the list it would take a submarine to find them."

Our dinners arrived, and I stared at my shrimp swimming in butter sauce. Was what Jordan Kaine was suggesting possible? I didn't want to believe it. I'd been so impressed with what sounded like genuine concern and generosity on Mr. Braxton's part. Then I remembered something. I dug in my purse, thankful that I seldom cleaned it out. I found what I was looking for.

"Something that I haven't told many people is that I happened to be at the cemetery on one of the nights it was vandalized."

Jordan looked at me in astonishment. "You *happened* to be—"

"The details don't matter," I cut in hurriedly. "The men didn't see me, but I got a good look at one of them. This is a sketch of him." I handed the paper napkin with Dix's drawing on it across the table. The sketch was blurry where the napkin had been folded, but the man's mean little eyes and beefy face and neck still showed.

"Of course, Drake Braxton surely wouldn't involve himself personally in the tombstone vandalism. He'd have some flunky do it, probably one of the many relatives in the clan, so even if you did see—" Then Jordan looked down at the napkin. His jaw dropped. "Well, I'll be. That's him. Drake Braxton himself."

"Are you sure?"

"I faced the man in a courtroom enough times to recognize him. Did you do this sketch?"

"No, I described the man to a police officer friend, and he did it. But neither of us could identify him."

"He's certainly identifiable here." Jordan shook his head, his expression troubled. "But from a legal standpoint, I doubt it's enough to nail him. Could you pin down when you saw him committing the vandalism?"

"Yes, definitely." The night of Magnolia's barbecue, the night Mac originally suspected I was midnight-rendezvousing with some unidentified man. "I could also identify him in person."

262

"But he'll come up with some unbreakable alibi for the night, and he might well be able to convince the authorities that your identification isn't reliable. He'll swear he doesn't know anything about the vandalism, condemns it as much as anyone, et cetera. Was he alone at the cemetery?"

"No, there were two of them. They had a big pickup and a cable. The other man was smaller, kind of wiry, I think, but I didn't get a good look at his face, just heard him speak. He had a high-pitched, almost squeaky voice."

"Well, we can give it a try with the authorities, if you'd like. I'll do whatever I can to help. But if it should actually get into court, they'll attack your nighttime eyesight, your memory, and anything else they can come up with."

Including, no doubt, my age. I was willing to risk personal attack, I decided, if it would bring Braxton to justice, but I had only to look at Jordan's frown to know that justice for Braxton on this skimpy evidence was highly unlikely. Jordan was experienced in these things; he'd know.

I sighed. "I suppose the important thing here is simply getting the cemetery restored, whether or not the culprit is caught. Although there is one other thing."

I told him about the destructive vandalism of my house, including the dragging of Harley's bench that was so much like the toppling and dragging of the tombstones. "I think whoever committed the vandalism at Country Peace also vandalized my house, as a warning to keep my nose out of the cemetery situation." I told him about my letter to the editor and described the lipstick warning on my mirror. "I'm sure, if Mr. Braxton wants the graves moved and cemetery disbanded, he wouldn't have appreciated my interference. And if he'd vandalize the cemetery, he wouldn't have qualms about vandalizing my house too."

"It appears Drake Braxton may be even more slimy than I thought." Jordan frowned again. "Maybe even dangerous."

"But again there's no way to prove anything."

"Right. That's one of the discouraging elements of being involved with the law for so many years. You see a lot of people you know are guilty go free."

"Sometimes lawyers help them go free."

"True." He was still frowning, and I wondered if he was thinking of some culpability of his own in this area.

"But the Lord deals with them eventually."

Jordan nodded. "Yes, he does."

We looked at each other, and I could see he took comfort in that thought, as I did. It was an invisible bond. I leaned forward. "Jordan, have you ever considered selling your home and just roaming the countryside?"

He blinked at the abrupt change of subject. "Roaming? You mean like a hobo?"

"Not quite that primitively. In a motor home, perhaps. Or one of those big travel trailers."

"I wouldn't mind doing some traveling. Georgia and I had talked about seeing Rio de Janeiro and Hong Kong and the Seychelles, but we always put it off, something we'd do 'later.'" He sounded a little wistful, as I sometimes felt when I thought of things I'd never done. "Although I know I'd never want to cut all ties and just become . . . rootless. And the idea of doing it alone certainly doesn't appeal to me."

A world-type traveler. But one who wanted to hold on to his roots. And who looked at me thoughtfully when he said he didn't want to travel alone. *Hey,* I thought, *this really is a date.* And I was unexpectedly glad. Even if he was a lawyer.

My next thought was that he was also a lawyer who was very good at digging into things. "How difficult would it be to find out who owns a company?"

Jordan looked a bit taken aback by this next sudden change of subject. But he was up to it. "It depends, among other

264

things, on whether it's corporate or private ownership. And whether or not someone is trying to conceal ownership."

"Ownership can be concealed?"

"You can usually dig into city business licenses, corporation papers, property tax records, et cetera, and find out something. But a deliberate tangle of interwoven corporate ownerships can get quite complicated." He tilted his head, his expression curious. "Did you have something specific in mind?"

"There are two local companies, Bottom-Buck Barney's and Thrif-Tee Wrecking. I'd like to know who owns them, and especially if it's the same person."

"Does this have to do with the cemetery?"

"No. It's just something I'm curious about." I could see that roused his curiosity, but he was too gentlemanly to be snoopy. "I could pay a minimal fee," I added.

"How about I see what I can find out, and as a 'minimal fee' you have dinner with me again?"

We smiled at each other. Deal. And, right then, for a moment at least, I felt almost enchanting.

29

Jordan and I exchanged waves at church on Sunday, but he was involved in a deacon's meeting right after the service and we didn't talk. Dix called when he and Haley got home Sunday evening. He seemed to have mellowed out somewhat and didn't grumble about Haley or her T-shirts. He also said he was going to trade his stick shift car in on an automatic so he could drive himself and would start part-time work at a desk job in the police department in a few days.

I told him about the letters, wishing I'd made photocopies before giving them to Detective Harmon. Dix's reaction to the other detective's lukewarm interest was noncommittal, though I suspected that was because he felt one officer didn't criticize another to someone outside the department, not because he didn't feel frustration with the other detective.

On Monday, Letitia Stone called from Little Rock. She'd been going through her rental papers and discovered that Debbie's rental application did list a Christine Stanton, with an address in Nashville, as next of kin. I debated calling Aunt

Chris myself but finally decided that since this was a murder and it involved identification of the body, I'd better let Detective Harmon handle it. He wasn't available, but I left the message for him.

Okay, I'd probably involved myself in this too much already, I acknowledged. I was reasonably certain the information I'd obtained could help identify Kendra/Debbie's body, but maybe Ray Etheridge's suspicions had been totally off base. Maybe everything was totally legitimate at Thrif-Tee. Maybe Ray's death was simply a careless accident. Maybe Debbie was mixed up in drugs, as Detective Harmon thought, and both the borrowing of her brother's fiancée's identity and her murder were connected with that criminal activity.

This was Detective Harmon's case, not mine. Time to become uninvolved.

I called Haley, and she said yes, the community college had beginner computer classes, new ones starting in a couple of weeks. She could help me get signed up. I cleaned the kitchen, paid some bills, washed pantyhose, and bundled newspapers for recycling.

Which left me thinking that there was one tiny thing I wanted to do before I backed away from Kendra/Debbie's murder completely. Something kept gnawing at that mutant curiosity gene. I found the address in the phone book, located Ludlow Boulevard on a city map, and drove out there at about 4:00.

Ludlow Boulevard was on the very outskirts of the city, a busy, noisy area of warehouses and industrial plants. Unseen machinery clanged and chugged and whistled and blew off smoke and steam from the sprawling buildings. The metal skeleton of some new construction rose behind a chain-link fence. Sounds of a jackhammer rattled my teeth. A long freight train rumbled over a railroad crossing in front of me. The swinging red light clanged, adding to the noise. Big

267

trucks crowded the street. Huge wheels passed within inches of my face. A piece of yellow machinery with forward forks big enough to impale a dinosaur darted around me. The Thunderbird felt as if it had shrunk to toy size.

I pulled into the parking lot of a tavern to catch a claustrophobic breath. A sign plastered to an electric pole showed a picture of a lost poodle. A lost poodle hadn't much chance of surviving here, I thought with dismay as two passing trucks blasted horns at each other.

After a few minutes I gathered my courage and resumed my search for Thrif-Tee Wrecking. I found it two blocks away, identified by a dirt-spattered sign. Below, the business hours were faded, but, slowing to a crawl, I finally deciphered them: Mon–Sat 8–5:30. Closed Sun. Another sloppy sign said Used Auto Parts, and below that, Barrels for Sale. Any view from the street was blocked by a solid board fence with two gates, one person-sized, one truck-sized. Both gates were also solid boards.

The whole place struck me as suspicious. What were they hiding behind that fence? Anything from drugs to stolen cars to a bomb factory for terrorists could be back there. The thought then occurred to me, however, that concealing junk cars from view was probably some city or county ordinance and didn't necessarily mean anything nefarious was going on.

But I was certain something nefarious had gone on there, and was probably still going on. If I could just get inside, get into that wall safe Ray Etheridge had mentioned, get proof of whatever illegalities that were motive for both his and Debbie/Kendra's deaths . . .

Yeah. Right. And maybe I could sneak into the White House and write an intimate exposé about the First Lady's lingerie drawer.

But if I didn't try to sneak in, if I simply made a straightforward entrance and looked around . . .

Remember what curiosity killed, Dix's annoying voice in my ear warned. "Go away, Dix," I muttered. "Go read T-shirts."

There was no real parking lot, but a narrow area next to the board fence allowed space for a couple of vehicles to pull off. I wheeled the 'bird over there and braked. No one could see me through that solid fence, but, as soon as I stepped through the gate, someone would surely pounce on me and ask what I wanted.

What could I say? "I'd like a transmission for the Thunderbird, please." *Sure, lady, you want that wrapped to go, or you gonna get down and install it here?*

Then I thought of something.

In a fractional lull between trucks, I whipped back into the street and returned to the parking lot at the tavern. I carefully removed the lost dog poster from the electric pole. Which I would bring back later, of course.

I returned to Thrif-Tee, but now the minimal space was taken up by a green van with the name of a car repair shop on the side. I suppose I should have recognized the difficulty in parking as a warning to clamp down on my curiosity and head home, but instead I returned to the tavern and slid the Thunderbird in behind a pickup with a flat tire at the edge of the parking lot.

There were no sidewalks in this area, so I walked along the sloping shoulder, dodging beer and soda cans, electric poles, fast-food cartons, and plastic sacks. Although I did pick up a stray quarter and an interesting looking bolt. I've always been adept at finding little things on the ground. Maybe because I'm built closer to it than most people.

Late afternoon heat blazed down from the sun and rose in waves from the pavement. I hurried to get to the gate before closing time, and rivulets of sweat ran down my sides by the time I reached the high board fence. Each board, I now noted, had been sawed to a sharp point on top to further discourage unauthorized entry. Two guys carrying a rounded chunk of blue metal were coming out the people gate. They headed for the van, their gazes passing through me as unseeing as radio waves as they congratulated themselves on their success. "Where else would we find a fender for an '84 Mazda?" one of them crowed. I pushed the gate open, rattling a chain with a dangling padlock.

A shack bore a tilted sign that said Office. The shack was attached to a sprawling metal building with a large sign that practically shouted No Admittance in bright red. A big sliding door was partly open, emitting noisy clangs and sizzling flashes of light from a welding machine. A tow truck stood by the door.

Had Ray Etheridge's "accident" happened in there?

In back of the buildings and beyond another stern sign saying Keep Out, Employees Only stretched an incredible tangle of whole cars and skeletons of cars and pieces of cars. There was a lineup of engines, a stacked pile of vehicle hoods, others of fenders, wheels, and hubcaps. The mechanical graveyard looked as if it covered at least a couple of acres. Several blue metal barrels, apparently the ones for sale, stood along one edge of the fence. Weeds that looked big and mean enough to be man-eating grew around them.

I stood there warily, but no one appeared to challenge me or offer me assistance. A car and two pickups that looked to be in working condition, probably employee vehicles, were parked to one side of the office. I approached the door cautiously. A big air conditioner in the lone window blocked the view of the interior. No sign suggested this area was off limits, so I pushed the door open. A tinny bell jingled. A short, scrawny man was bending over the drawer of a file cabinet. He turned and looked at me.

I held up the lost-dog sign, my justification for being here. "Have you seen this dog?"

"Lady, if that mutt ever came in here, ol' Duke would eat 'im alive."

Ol' Duke, apparently answering to his name, came out from behind the metal desk he was chained to. Muscular, short-haired, brindle-colored, snub-nosed, his leather collar punctuated with spiky metal studs—obviously the dog Tiffany had described as ugly as a stomped-on Halloween mask. And I couldn't help noticing a distinct resemblance between dog and man. Don't they say people and their pets grow to look alike? Or is that husbands and wives? In any case, jowls of both dog and man drooped, and they both looked as if they might like to gnaw on raw bones. But it wasn't jowls or resemblance that riveted my attention. It was the voice.

The voice.

The squeaky, high-pitched voice from the cemetery. I'd swear it.

And yet . . . how could that be? No, no way was that possible. I didn't have Tiffany's sensitive ear for voices, and this was just some peculiar similarity or coincidence or error on my part.

"You sell used auto parts here?" Dumb question, but I was stalling for time, taking in everything I could. Metal file cabinet, just like Ray's letter had said. Key to the wall safe in one of the drawers? Wall safe . . . where? Behind that calendar? Oh, dear. I squelched an urge to rush over and hang my lost dog poster to cover the calendar picture of an extremely under-clothed young woman.

"Yeah. We sell used parts. You need somethin'?" He made it sound as if I'd be imposing on him if I did. "We're gonna close in about five minutes."

271

I took in as much as I could in the next thirty seconds. Scents of cigarette smoke and some sharp but not quite identifiable blend of grease and oil and other vehicle-type fluids. Big fire extinguisher on the wall. Closed door from office out to shop. Restroom door open, exposing the corner of a dirty sink and cigarette butts on the floor. The air conditioner wasn't working, and a small window in the bathroom was open. Computer on the desk. Mr. Squeaky-Voice didn't look as if he could tell a computer from a hat rack, but apparently he could.

But what I took in mostly was vibes. Unpleasant vibes. Ominous vibes. Also a smell of garlic from Squeaky-Voice himself.

"Well . . . uh . . . I guess I don't need anything today, thank you." I ventured one more question. "Do you sell used vehicles?"

"Nah. If we get something repairable in, we sell it through a car lot over on Sylvester." He picked up an unopened envelope and slashed it with a plastic letter opener.

"Well, uh, thank you, Mr. . . . ?"

"Benny. Have a nice day." He frowned as he yanked something out of the envelope, leaving me to ponder a phrase that had become so overused and meaningless it even came out of the mouth of a grumpy Benny in a junkyard.

I went back outside. Okay, I'd come. I'd seen. Curiosity satisfied, right? Though it was odd about the voice . . .

No, I wouldn't concern myself with that irrelevant detail. Time to get on home and microwave something for supper. Maybe tackle quilting again.

Then, halfway to the gate, I spotted a car. Part of a car, actually, standing some hundred feet back in the metal jungle beyond the shop. The rear half seemed to have vanished, but the remaining front end was small and red. Exactly like Kendra/Debbie's car.

Forget it. You've already been wrong about one red car. A red car is a red car is a red car. But the front end appeared intact, and if it held the key Kendra said she'd hidden . . .

I looked around. The industrial noises of the area roared on, but clangs and welding flashes in the shop had ceased. The only sign of life I saw was a big bird perched on the board fence. No one was paying any attention to me.

I bent low and zigzagged around vehicles in various stages of dismemberment. I'd gotten only halfway when voices made me duck behind the remnants of a station wagon so old it still had wood panels on the sides. I turned and watched three men come out of the shop. They were in workmen's clothing, all carrying lunchboxes. Two walked to parked vehicles. The third opened the big truck gate. One pickup and the car drove through the opening. The gate swung shut, the gate operator apparently a passenger in one of the vehicles.

No one had noticed me. Invisibility in full operation.

That was when the new idea surfaced. I didn't leap on it like Wonder Woman swooping down on a bad guy. I mean, this struck even me as questionable. Dix would not approve. Detective Harmon would not approve. I didn't know him well, but I was reasonably certain Jordan Kaine would not approve. Even Mac, who'd shown tolerance for both my cemetery sitting and my foray into murder investigation in Clancy, probably wouldn't approve.

How about you, Lord?

I listened, but sometimes the Lord is silent. Or maybe he just gives us a chance to use our own good sense.

Benny came out of the office and tossed something in the bed of the pickup still parked by the office. I scrunched lower into my hiding place. Benny returned to the office. The next time he came out he'd probably get in his pickup and leave, locking the gates behind him.

273

Decision time.

Make a run for the gate before Benny locked it or hunker down in this scrapyard for the night? Once he left, I'd be in here alone. With all night to locate the key to that wall safe and get inside.

Was that doable?

It wouldn't be a comfortable night. I still felt those bad vibes. It would also be a hungry night, because I'd eaten only a carton of yogurt at lunch, and I couldn't exactly call out for pizza from here. This cemetery of vehicle skeletons and dismantled parts also struck me as considerably more scary than the cemetery of tombstones had ever been. And that motionless bird on the fence was beginning to look a lot like a hungry vulture.

But wasn't the chance to get something on Thrif-Tee, which would provide a motive for Kendra/Debbie's murder, worth a night's discomfort?

Yes.

I'd lost track of the red car, but I crept farther back into the metal cemetery of old vehicles until I found a gray sedan with an intact backseat. The car, without wheels, sat low to the ground. It had long ago lost the glass in its windows, but that wouldn't matter on this warm night. The door worked. I crawled inside.

The scent immediately hit me. My first thought, given a general jitteriness, was, *Is this how dead bodies smell?* But after a moment's consideration I decided it was merely the smell of musty mice nests. Not an appealing situation, but I'd never been one to squeal at the sight of a mouse. There was even some reading material spread on the rotting floorboards. A magazine cover showed a bodybuilder with enough muscles to hoist this old car with his little finger. Maybe I could learn how to improve my pecs.

I worried about the Thunderbird for a few minutes. It

274

had looked a bit noticeable when I left it in the parking lot of the tavern, but I hadn't seen any of those ominous signs about towing noncustomer cars, so hopefully it would be safe until morning.

I checked my purse and was pleased to find some mints dispensed by the drive-through window at the bank and four packets of crackers left over from chili I'd had somewhere. Again I blessed my habit of stuffing everything in my purse and seldom taking anything out. I was also relieved to see my keychain flashlight was still in there. I'd need that once I got into the office. But how was I going to get in the office? Maybe through that bathroom window, if I could find something to climb up on to reach it. Or maybe I'd have to break the front window.

Okay, I was in good shape for a night of investigation. All I had to do now was wait. Thunderclouds that looked heavy with rain were gathering off to the southwest, and I doubted my shelter would keep out much rain, but maybe I wouldn't have to stay all night. Once I had incriminating information to give to Dix or Detective Harmon so they could come back with a search warrant, maybe I could climb on those blue barrels, crawl over the fence, and drop safely to the other side.

I scrunched low in the mouse-scented seat and started reading about a man who'd added fourteen inches to his chest.

Industrial activity boomed on, and the area was only fractionally quieter than it had been during the day. I ate a packet of crackers and a mint and wished I had some water.

By 7:45, the fact that Benny was still in the office was beginning to make me edgy. A distant rumble of thunder joined the noise of a passing freight. Was it possible Benny lived here, that he stayed on the premises all night? Or could this be one of the nights Ray had mentioned, when the "boss" came to do an after-hours checkup on receipts or records?

Even with the clouds moving in, it didn't get really dark until quite late on these long summer evenings, but by the time big overhead yard lights came on Benny still hadn't left. I'd almost resigned myself to the fact that he wasn't leaving and this was one dumb idea. Then two sharp blasts sounded over the general rumble of traffic and industrial noise. A horn outside the gate.

With surprising alacrity, Benny ran out and opened the gate. A pickup towing an enclosed, windowless trailer pulled in. Benny closed the gate, then opened the big sliding door to the shop. The pickup driver backed the trailer inside. Then I couldn't see what was happening, but a few minutes later pickup and trailer came out. Benny again opened the gate in the board fence, and the pickup and trailer disappeared into the night.

If I'd blinked twice I'd have missed the whole thing, leaving me wondering what had just happened here. Had the quick, and what certainly seemed to me to be clandestine, night visit been to bring something in or haul something away? A legitimate bit of after-hours business or something on the nefarious side?

Was this what Benny had been waiting for? Would he leave now? Only my eyes rose above the level of the sedan's window frame to watch as he got in his pickup and drove out through the gate. He closed the gate from the outside, his arm reaching through to fasten the chain and padlock. Yes! He was gone!

No. Not yet. He came back in through the people gate and went to the office again. The lights went off, and this time he came out with a handhold on Duke's collar, the metal studs gleaming under the yard lights. The dog lunged against the restraint, big body twisting with eagerness.

I felt a jolt of nerves. Eagerness to do what?

Two seconds and I found out. Benny turned the dog loose, and ol' Duke immediately dashed back and forth along the board fence, nose to the ground. Now the stomach-knotting fact got through to me: Duke wasn't just an ugly pet keeping Benny company. He was the junkyard's night guard.

Cancel one expedition into Thrif-Tee's wall safe. With the Hound of the Baskervilles out there, I wouldn't dare stick so much as a finger out of my hiding place. I scrunched lower on the seat.

The dog started barking. Deep, I'm-gonna-eat-you-alive barks. The barks got closer and louder. I didn't have to peek out the window to know Duke's nose to the ground was now following my zigzag trail. A minute later he was at the car door, heavy claws scratching, snarls mixing with the ground-shaking barks.

The Hound of the Baskervilles had found his prey.

Me.

30

Now I wished this old wreck had glass in the windows. Slobber flew over the frame. One paw caught on the edge, and the head, like a canine gargoyle out of a nightmare, loomed in the glassless window.

"Go away! I'm not hurting your precious wreck." I whacked at the dog with the magazine. He caught it in his overtoothed jaws and yanked it away.

How to distract him? Food? I hadn't any raw hamburger on me. I dug frantically in my purse. I tried to tear the cellophane wrapper off the crackers, but with Duke's big jaws lunging at me I just tossed whole packets at him. He downed it cellophane and all, one gulp for each packet.

What else? Mints. I tossed them too.

Then I realized something as I pawed through the purse. The tough private eyes and sleuths I read about, even the female ones, always came prepared for perilous situations such as this. They packed pepper spray or a hidden derringer. Or even more formidable weaponry. A Glock. Or a Sig, maybe. What was I packing? A purse full of checkbook and keys, paper clips and coupons.

I tossed out a lipstick and a bottle of Tums. Then the bolt I'd picked up along the road. Maybe Duke would find them edible. Or break a tooth.

Oh, Lord, did you tell me not to do this . . . and I closed my ears? Help me, please . . . what do I do now?

The dog's head came through the window again. My offerings of food had not warmed his attitude. I wasn't sure if the rumble I heard came from him or the thunderclouds overhead. I whacked him with the purse. It felt like hitting a wall with teeth. The purse went the same route as the magazine. But just when I thought Duke was coming through the window and I was going to be dog chow, a hand grabbed his collar and yanked him back. Now something else appeared in the window, something darkly metallic gleaming under the yard lights.

The double barrels of a shotgun. Was this an improvement over Duke's teeth? Not necessarily.

"Okay, c'mon outta there," Benny growled.

"I'm coming," I said, and I was the one whose voice was high-pitched and squeaky now.

"What?" he said, and I realized then that he couldn't see me in the shadowy interior of the car and hadn't known that I wasn't some six-foot male packing a baseball bat.

"Is the dog still loose?" I asked.

"You just come out. I'll worry about the dog."

I thought I had a lot more worries about the dog than he did, but I opened the door and eased my feet onto the glass-strewn ground. The dog snarled, and Benny said, "Git back." I hoped the dog knew what the words meant.

"What're you doin' here?" Benny demanded. "I thought you left." He sounded indignant, which I found somewhat encouraging. At least he was asking questions before letting go with both barrels of the shotgun.

"I . . . uh . . . haven't found the poodle yet." True. I smiled and tried my best to look grandmotherly. I was willing to go for eccentric if need be. Even senile.

"Look, we don't allow no bag ladies campin' out in here for the night. You're gonna have to move on."

Bag lady? Fine by me. I was also more than willing to move on. I bent over to retrieve my now tooth-pocked purse, but both Duke and Benny had other ideas. Benny, with another threatening "Git back," won.

I headed toward the front gate. A bolt of lightning lit up the sky. A junkyard full of metal did not strike me as a desirable place to be in a lightning storm. I walked faster. I wasn't going to worry about the purse. Let Benny and Duke fight over it. *Lord, were you waiting for me to exhibit some good sense here tonight . . . and I blew it?*

We passed the sliding door to the shop. Another sharp bolt of lightning cracked, close enough to make my scalp prickle, like the time Thea left a home perm solution on my head too long. I tried to act as if I were casually exiting a mall. *Thanks, Benny, I appreciate this. Have a nice day.*

"Hey, not so fast," Benny said. He jerked the shotgun barrels toward the office. "We're going in there first."

I thought about making a run for the gate, but I knew what my chances were at outrunning Duke. I suspected he was looking for any excuse to chomp down on any available portion of my anatomy. I turned in at the office. The lights were already on. Benny must have turned them on when he ran back in to get the shotgun. One of the overhead fluorescent bulbs sizzled. Benny snapped the chain onto Duke's collar. He set the shotgun on the desk, then dumped the contents of my purse beside it.

He went straight for my wallet, flipped it open, and studied the windowed contents. Driver's license. Two credit cards. AARP membership card. Medicare card. Library card. Dirk's Subs & Salads punch card, buy ten, get one free. Old photo of Thea and me, another of Colin. I couldn't say why, but I was glad I'd removed that incriminating sketch of Drake Braxton that Dix had made.

Benny looked a long time at the driver's license, his gaze flicking from photo to me and back again. He studied each of the other cards with equal care, then went back to the driver's license. It gave the most information, of course, including birth date and address. The intensity of his interest was making my palms slippery with perspiration. I wiped them on my pants leg.

"Please keep whatever cash is in the wallet," I said brightly. I knew there were two twenties, a ten, and four ones in there. I usually know exactly how much I have, especially toward the end of the month. I was willing to eat grits until the next Social Security and interest checks came, if I could just get out of here. "For all the trouble I've caused you."

He didn't respond. He picked up the purse again and checked the other compartments. That netted him a couple of old packets of taco sauce, my little red New Testament, a "Cathy" comic strip clipping, and miscellaneous scraps of paper. Plus the photo of Kendra in her exotic dress and the photocopy of Ray with his Mustang. The temperature in the cluttered office seemed to plunge about twenty degrees when Benny spotted those items. I shivered, not blessing my tendency to leave everything in my purse now.

Benny grabbed the phone on the desk and punched in numbers. He turned his back to me, revealing a pink bald spot in his mousy colored hair, but I could hear him plainly enough. "I think you better get over here. We got a visitor. I stayed late because that '01 Malibu was coming in, and I caught her hidin' out back. Driver's license says she's Ivy

Malone." Brief silence while the person on the other end of the line said something back to him. Then, "Yeah. That one. From the house on Madison Street."

That one. From the house on Madison Street. I didn't like the sound of that. It singled me out as someone not unfamiliar to both Benny and the person on the other end of the line.

We waited. I asked if I could sit down. Benny kicked a chair in my direction. Duke retired into a dog bed barely big enough for his heavy body. He'd lost interest in me, the chain apparently signaling to him that he was off duty. I clasped my hands together and pushed back the cuticle on my right thumbnail with my left thumbnail. All trace of the blood blister was gone now. The storm seemed to have moved on, rumbles receding into the distance, but the air still felt humid and heavy. Benny didn't stare at me, but he kept sending me speculative glances.

I felt that if I were really clever I could coax all sorts of incriminating information about Thrif-Tee out of Benny. But I wasn't that clever. And I was afraid I knew too much for my good health already.

"May I have a drink of water?" I finally croaked. My throat was so dry that swallowing my fear had ceased to be an option.

He jerked a thumb toward the restroom. My legs felt both stiff and wobbly as I walked over to the tiny room. I found a lone plastic glass there. Neither it nor the sink looked as if they'd been cleaned in this decade. I decided I wasn't thirsty after all, but I ran the water anyway and came out trying to look refreshed. Insulting Benny about the state of his restroom did not at the moment seem a prudent thing to do.

Twenty minutes later headlights flared outside the office. Benny hadn't gone out to open the gate, so the person apparently had a key to open the padlock. There was enough delay after the car lights showed that I realized he was taking time to close the gate again. For some reason, that felt distinctly ominous.

The office door opened. By then I was fully expecting Drake Braxton. I'd been doing some heavy-duty thinking, and I thought I had it figured out. The reason my name and address were familiar to Benny was because he and Braxton had been there when they trashed my house over the cemetery deal. Now I was about to learn that Drake Braxton not only owned a building and land development company, he also owned Thrif-Tee Wrecking and Bottom-Buck Barney's.

Wrong.

Not that I didn't recognize the tall, lanky, black-haired man who swaggered inside. I did. The man who had almost bowled Thea and me over one night. Kendra's maybe-married boyfriend.

Harley used to love to play pool, and my brain now felt like a pool table with the colored balls chunking into the pockets as things fell into place. Clunk, clunk, clunk. Debbie had come here to start up a relationship with an oh-so-respectable boss who liked bimbos. To find out who killed her brother. She'd done it, and paid for the knowledge with her life. And the killer she'd uncovered was right now staring down at me.

My life felt precarious too. A spinning eight ball poised on the end of a cue stick.

But one colored ball didn't click neatly into any pocket. Benny. If he worked for this guy, what was he doing at the cemetery with Drake Braxton?

The first thing Benny did was shove my driver's license and the photos over to the angular-faced man. The guy studied them carefully, without comment, then used one bony forefinger to poke carefully through the contents of my purse as if he felt something might contaminate him. He latched on to an item Benny had ignored. A matchbook from the motel in Little Rock. I always pick up free matchbooks. Not because I collect them. You just never knew when you might want to start a fire.

"What're you doing here?" he asked.

A truthful answer wasn't going to help my case. I detoured with, "I wasn't hurting anything. I was just sitting in the back-seat of one of the cars, until your watchdog . . . objected."

"That's his job."

"He does it well." I stood up. "Now, if you'll excuse me, it is rather past my bedtime, so I should be getting home—"

"You're not going anywhere." He appraised me as if I were a used car. Maybe one he was considering chopping up for parts. He flipped the matchbook open. He struck a match, and all three of us watched it burn down to a stub. I wasn't sure what the symbolism was, or why the tiny flame was so mesmerizing, but it scared me right down to my guzzles, as Colin used to call them. My throat twitched in a non-swallow, and I sat down again.

"What were you doing in Little Rock?" the guy asked.

Did he know that Debbie Etheridge, masquerading under the name Kendra Alexander, had come from Little Rock? Probably. I gave him another string of non sequiturs. "I'm very fond of my niece, who lives in Arkansas. By a lovely lake just outside Woodston. Their twins are starting college this fall."

He frowned at my snow job of irrelevant information. "You live on Madison Street. Not far from where a . . ." He paused and then spun the photo toward me. "A young woman named Kendra used to live."

"Yes. She's dead, did you know?" I said, hoping to suggest that no suspicions of him lurked in my mind. "It's been most upsetting. Especially since I also just lost my very best friend, Thea, and now we'll never be able to celebrate our birthdays

284

together again. We always went to Victorio's Seafood. Have you ever been there? Their lobster is awesome."

He frowned again. Or maybe that was his permanent expression. "What do you know about Ray Etheridge?"

"I've never met anyone named Ray Etheridge." True.

"You're carrying a picture of him."

"Oh. Him."

"Why were you flashing this picture of him around Bottom-Buck Barney's?"

Oh dear. So that's what had gotten me sucked into all this. "I didn't know who the young man in the picture was. I found it in Kendra's apartment and thought he might be the person who'd killed her."

"She knows a whole lot more than that or she wouldn't be here or carrying those pictures," Benny cut in, squeaky voice rising almost to dog-whistle range. "Even if we didn't find anything in her house—"

"Shut up, Benny."

I looked at Benny with shocked realization. Drake Braxton hadn't trashed my house. The destruction had nothing to do with the cemetery. Benny and this guy had done it. Someone at Bottom-Buck Barney's had told them I'd come in with that picture of Ray. Then they'd used the phone number on the back of the picture to track me down so they could search the house for any other connection to Ray Etheridge.

The thought struck me that when you're being a busybody in more than one area, it's harder to know who's out to get you.

I also wondered which one of them had been the artist on my bedroom mirror. Benny, I decided. Not that it mattered at the moment.

"You know Kendra wasn't her real name, don't you? That she was really Debbie Etheridge. Ray's sister." The lanky guy's tone was soft, speculative, even mild. Which somehow made it all the more ominous. Like a rattlesnake quietly coiling for a strike. I doubted he'd be discussing this with me if he intended to let me stroll out the front gate.

I wasn't about to admit to anything, however. "My neighbor Thea and I thought she was a very sweet young woman."

"Sweet?" He laughed cynically. "Conniving little schemer, that's what she was. Leading me on, making me think—" He broke off abruptly. "What did she tell you?"

"About you?"

"About anything."

"Nothing! Kendra was a very . . . private person. She kept things to herself."

"How'd she get here?" He spoke to Benny now, but his head jerked toward me and his eyes never left my face. "I didn't see a car."

"I dunno. I never saw a car either. I thought she was just some bag lady looking for a place to spend the night until I found the name on the driver's license. And those pictures. Then I figured she must be on to something and snoopin'."

"How'd you get here?" the guy demanded of me.

I didn't think his knowing my Thunderbird was parked two blocks away would help my situation. He could dispose of a vehicle easily enough. He'd apparently done it with Kendra/Debbie's red Corolla. "If you're asking how I'm going to get home, you needn't concern yourself about my transportation." I made my tone lofty, as if I could quirk a finger and summon a limousine on a moment's notice.

He was not impressed. "Kendra leave anything with you? Papers or anything?"

So that was why they'd gone through my place! A search disguised as vandalism. He thought Kendra may have made a written record of everything she'd uncovered, and left a copy with me for safekeeping. Oh, if only she had!

I tried a bluff. "What would it be worth to you if she had?"

That brought a laugh from him. "You trying to blackmail me?"

For the first time I noticed a heavy sag in the pocket of his light jacket. He was packing something more lethal than a purse, I was sure of that. Could I make him think I had incriminating evidence against him stashed somewhere? And would it be helpful, or a death sentence, if he did think that?

I didn't know, so I opted for lofty again. "I have no idea what you're talking about."

A sharp blast of thunder made us all jump. Even Duke looked up. The storm had circled around and returned. The thunder sounded as if all those junked cars out there had come to life and were advancing on the office.

"What're we gonna do, Bo?" Benny asked, his voice hitting plaintive now. He repeated what he'd said before. "She knows somethin' or she wouldn't be here. This ain't good."

The guy named Bo repeated himself too. "Shut up, Benny." He touched the sag of the gun in his pocket, his angular head tilted thoughtfully. "Go bring your pickup over to the door. I don't want to use my car this time."

This time. Not like last time, when he'd used his car to dump Kendra's body?

"Maybe we oughta—"

"Just get the pickup," Bo growled.

I swallowed hard. Did he mean to shoot me here and carry my body out to the pickup? Or were we going for an end-of-the-line ride in the pickup?

Benny disappeared out the door.

"Get a rope too," Bo called after him, and for a split second his eyes weren't on me. I dashed for the door to the shop.

Locked. An explosion of noise, and something crashed

into the door just below my hand on the knob. I stood frozen for a split second as I realized what had happened. This guy named Bo had shot at me!

I couldn't get around him to the front door. I ran for the other door, the one to the bathroom. Another shot. Something crashed to the floor as I slammed the door behind me. I threw the bolt that fastened the door. Which would crumble under one good kick. And even if it didn't, what had I accomplished? I was trapped in here.

Trapped like a duck on a rail in a shooting gallery, I realized as another gunshot ripped through the door and thudded into the wall behind me. I pressed my back up hard against the wall by the toilet stool, trying to make myself as skinny as a grease smear.

Didn't he care that he was shooting up his own property? Apparently not. Wasn't he afraid someone would hear gunshots? No problem there. In the general deluge of industrial noise and traffic on the boulevard, plus the thunder, not even a machine gun would have been heard.

So he could just keep shooting until he nailed me. And he couldn't miss many more times.

Another bullet. This one hit the sink, and a shard of porcelain flew across the room. It wouldn't even matter if I managed to dodge every bullet until he ran out of shells, I realized. All he had to do then was crash through the gunsplintered door and grab me. Or let Duke do it.

I closed my eyes for a bare second. *I trust you Lord. Yesterday, today, and tomorrow. If this is my time . . .*

Maybe not!

Frantically I climbed up on the stool and then on the tank at the back of it. Another bullet. This one grazed the mirror over the sink and sprayed splinters of glass around the tiny room. Carefully, or as careful as I could be when I was shivering and shaking, I stepped from the porcelain tank over to the sill below the small window, balancing myself with a clutch on the flimsy paper towel holder beside the window. I kicked out the screen and, blessing my scrawny frame, slithered through the narrow opening. I didn't give any thought to what was below, just dropped as a bullet sang out the open window.

I hit something that boomed hollowly—another of those blue barrels, like the ones beside the other fence? Had Bo heard that? How could he not hear it? I rolled into a ball beside the barrel, listening as if my whole body were an ear. Two more shots whanged into the wall above me.

I unrolled and blindly crawled away from the office shack, my eyes not yet adjusted enough to see anything. The shop and office blocked the area back here from the yard lights, but a yellowish beam shafted from the bathroom window behind me. Then a flare of lightning lit up a metal jungle of barrels between me and the fence, some lying sideways on the ground, some stacked two high by the wooden boards. *If I can just reach those, climb up and over the fence before Bo and Benny realize I've escaped from the bathroom . . .*

Another crash, this one different from the gunshots. Bo breaking into the bathroom. An outraged yelp. "Hey, she's not in here! Where'd she go?"

Benny squeak-yelling something indecipherable. A flare and crack of lightning. Ping of raindrops on the barrels. Heart churning in my chest like some out-of-control cement mixer, heartbeat clogging my throat and ears.

A shape blocked light from the window as Bo peered through it. A sudden burst of rain blurred the figure. I huddled against a barrel, hoping he'd think I'd disappeared into thin air. But even if Bo thought it, Duke would know differently. A Bible verse plopped into my head: *A prudent man sees danger and takes refuge, but the simple keep going and suffer for it.* Was that me, simple and now about to suffer for it? Like Mac said, a Bible verse for every occasion. But no time to contemplate my errors now. If I was going to get out of here alive, I had to get over the fence before they turned the dog loose.

I scrambled toward the barrels as Bo let go with three shots through the window. I bumped into a barrel lying on its side, and pain hammered through my knee. Now, in the deluge of rain, I couldn't see anything but shapeless blurs of barrels.

Rain was good. If I couldn't see them, maybe they couldn't see me. *Thank you, Lord.*

My reaching hand found an upright barrel. Above it another one, with the fence right behind them. But no way could I get on top of the barrels stacked two high. Okay, then I'd have to knock a top barrel off. With all the junk around here, there had to be something I could pry with.

"She's around back here, Bo!" Benny screeched. "I seen somethin' moving."

I peered in the direction of the voice. Even in the veil of falling rain I could make out a blurry figure standing at the corner of the office, on the line between light and shadow. Then another bigger shape joined the first one. Bo was outside now.

Random shots bonged hollowly into the barrels. Whatever happened to the good old six-shooter with a limited number of shots? Bo's gun seemed to have an unlimited supply of ammunition.

I slithered farther into the haphazard stand of barrels, trying to put one between me and the gun. A barrel should at least slow down a bullet.

"Get in there, Benny! Run her out so I can get a clear shot at her!"

"I'll go get Duke."

"She's going to try to go over the fence. We've got to get her before—"

"She's an old lady! She can't go over the fence!"

She's going to give it a good try, I thought determinedly. But all the barrels by the fence seemed to be stacked two high, unclimbable as the sheer face of a mountain cliff. Could I roll one of the other barrels up to the fence and stand it upright so I could climb on it? No, no time.

I tried to shove one of the top barrels off, but it wouldn't budge. A bullet hit the barrel right next to me, close enough to vibrate the metal against my shoulder. Was Bo shooting randomly or was he zeroing in on me?

I got partway around two stacked barrels, right up next to the fence. Bracing my back against the fence I put my shoulder to a top barrel and pushed, straining like ol' Atlas trying to lift the world. And over it went!

"She's right over there!" Bo yelled as the barrel crashed to the ground.

"I'll get 'er!" Benny yelled back.

I heard a crash that sounded as if Benny had run headlong into the rolling barrel. I scrambled on top of the barrel below the one I'd just shoved. If I could just get over the pointed ridge of boards . . .

"I can't see nothin', Bo!" Benny yelled. "Don't shoot until—"

I grabbed the peaked top of a board and tried to swing my leg up, but it had been a long time since I was a tomboy playing backyard pirate and climbing fences. My foot hit another barrel, and this one toppled as if balanced on a needle point.

And then the whole junkyard world came unglued. The falling barrel hit another one, and that crashed into two more. Moving barrels everywhere, crashing and colliding and booming and bonging. A new game: bowling with barrels. Screams. Shouts. Shots. I lost my footing, tumbled to the ground, and saw stars and lightning when my head hit something.

Did I lose consciousness for a few seconds, maybe more, in the sea of moving barrels? I wasn't certain. But it felt oddly peaceful just lying there with rain pattering my face as the storm deluge softened to a gentle drizzle. Sounds of the industrial plants and traffic had receded, and the junkyard was almost silent as the barrels stopped rolling. Or maybe the silence was only in my head. My mind felt as if it were looping gently overhead, too disconnected and distant to make my muscles move.

This would be a good time to be all-the-way invisible, I thought dreamily. I had a nice vision of Bo and Benny and even Duke dashing around, asking themselves in bewilderment, "Where is she? Where'd she go?"

But I knew I wasn't that invisible. In another minute Benny or Bo or Duke would find me. And then I'd be looking into the barrel of a gun.

31

I waited. The wooziness in my head slowly cleared, and still no one had shoved a gun in my face. How come? Did Bo and Benny think I was dead, killed in the avalanche of barrels? Were they even now inside conferring about where to dump or bury my body?

Then I realized how imprudent I was being, lying there wondering anything. *Don't ask questions, lady. Just run, run while you have the chance!*

I headed for the fence, crawling through the maze of fallen barrels with all possible speed, ignoring bits of glass and metal biting into my hands and knees. I grasped the rim of a barrel to pull myself to my feet. I was trying to climb on top of it when a second thought struck me. Did I have to take this difficult over-the-fence route? I didn't understand why no one appeared to be gunning for me now, but maybe I could just sneak out the front gate.

I stood poised by the barrel, trying to make sense out of the odd situation. Yellowish light still streamed from the bathroom window, but all it illuminated was the jumble of fallen barrels. I could read the printing on one now. Hydraulic fluid. On another, motor oil. No sounds came from inside the office. The area by the wall of the shack below the window was all in dense shadow.

Were they toying with me? Planning to shoot me in some way that they could claim they'd mistaken me for a burglar? If that was so, making a silhouette of myself on top of the fence might only be playing into their scheme.

Standing bent-bodied in hopes of making myself a smaller target, I felt my way around the fallen barrels and slid toward the darkest shadow under the open window. From there I planned to slip over to the corner of the office and reconnoiter. Then, if the way looked clear—and Duke didn't sink his teeth into my leg—I'd head for the gate. *Thank you, Lord! Thank you for giving me this chance.*

I was almost to the office wall when I stumbled over something on the ground. Something not metallic. Something different, softer . . .

I shrieked when I groped with one hand and found what it was. A body.

I found an arm, followed it up to neck and face. Encountered wetness warmer than rainwater. I stood up and thrust my hand into the shaft of light from the restroom. Blood.

I knelt down and felt around again. A big body. With a lot of hair on the head. Wearing a lightweight jacket that was now soaking wet. Bo.

My first instinct was to jump and run for the gate. My chance to get out of here! But something—Christian conscience?—made me reluctantly put my fingers to Bo's throat and feel for a pulse.

Yes. He was alive. I tried not to feel disappointed. Apparently the avalanche of barrels had knocked him down, and he'd hit his head on something harder than I had, and he was out cold. But for how long? And where was Benny? Had he heard my shriek?

I wanted to just cut and run and put Ludlow Boulevard in my rearview mirror, but instead I started around the office to get to the door and phone. A second thought made me turn back. Where was the gun?

No clever searching on my part found it. I stumbled over it where it had fallen, a few feet from Bo's hand. I cautiously picked it up and took it with me. It occurred to me that I was mixing my fingerprints with Bo's, probably not a good idea. But at this point I was less worried about fingerprints than about Bo regaining consciousness and finishing me off.

I passed his car as I circled the office. The vehicle was big and long and foreign, expensive enough to finance a portion of the national debt.

Inside, I dialed 911. For the first time I realized I was soaking wet too, hair plastered to my head, clothes stuck to my body, shoes squishy. Duke, still chained to the desk, appeared unconcerned about me or my wet state. I gave the 911 people what was undoubtedly a garbled account of events here, given that both my brain and muscles were beginning to dissolve into wet mush. A businesslike woman interpreted it well enough to say they'd send police and an ambulance immediately.

"Are you in danger now?" she asked.

I eyed my available artillery, a double-barreled shotgun and a heavy handgun. I wasn't too sure how to use either, but I figured I'd give it a good try if Bo or Benny showed at the door.

"I'll be okay."

I went in the bathroom and, ignoring the washbasin filth, washed the blood off my hand. A hint of wooziness returned as I watched all that red swirling down the drain, even if it

wasn't my own. I returned to the desk and scooped everything back into my purse.

Then I realized something. This was my chance to accomplish what I was here for. I tiptoed over, keeping an eye on
Duke, and slid the girlie calendar aside. Bingo. Wall safe. Now
all I had to do was find the key in the filing cabinet. Which I
did, right up front in the second drawer. Ray knew what he
was talking about. All I had to do now . . .

Then conscience got to me again. A man was lying out
there injured and unconscious. Shouldn't I be doing something? A couple of jackets, dusty enough to have been hanging there since last winter, were draped over hooks by the
door to the shop. I grabbed them, put one around my own
wet shoulders, and headed for the door with the other. On
second thought, I went back for the handgun.

The good Samaritan with a gun. I didn't stop to ponder
the inconsistencies inherent in that.

Behind the shack, I was relieved to find Bo still alive. Even
more relieved, I had to admit, to find that he was still out cold.
I covered him with the jacket so he wouldn't get chilled. Since
the thunderstorm and rain, the air had cooled considerably.

I still didn't know what had become of Benny. It didn't
seem likely he'd also been conveniently knocked unconscious.
I tentatively called his name a few times. No answer.

The answer came a few minutes later, after two police cars
and an ambulance arrived in a screaming parade of sirens
and flashing lights. The medics loaded Bo, still unconscious,
into the ambulance and sped off with him, sirens wailing. The
police had a spotlight on their vehicle, and its roving beam
picked out another body among the fallen barrels.

Benny didn't need an ambulance. He was quite dead from
the gunshot wound in his back. One of Bo's shots meant for
me had accidentally nailed Benny instead.

There was a bit of confusion about what had gone on here,

since one man was dead, another was unconscious with a head injury, and I, a soaking wet LOL, was in control of the guns when the officers arrived. I supposed they didn't encounter this particular scenario on too many occasions.

"Do any of you know Detective Dixon?" I asked the two police officers eyeing me with a combination of consternation and suspicion. We were in the office now, clustered around the desk. "I think he can vouch for me."

Under the circumstances, I wasn't certain just what Dix might vouch, but his name seemed to have a favorable effect on the officers at the moment.

"I also think, if you check the gun I gave you and the bullet in Benny against the bullet taken from a young woman currently in the morgue, the one whose body was found in the river a while back, that you may find they match."

"And why would that be?" an officer asked skeptically.

"Because Bo killed her when she found out that he'd also killed her brother, or had someone kill him, right here at Thrif-Tee Wrecking and I'm pretty sure if you check that wall safe—" I nodded toward the metal corner exposed by the tilted calendar picture, "with that key—" I motioned toward the key I'd set by the computer, "that you'll find interesting details about some very illegal activities in stolen vehicles and altered VINs here."

I'd like to be able to say I concluded these dazzling revelations with a graceful, enigmatic smile, but what happened was that Duke suddenly decided maybe he should pay attention to all this activity, even if he was chained up. He came around the desk with a snarl, I jumped backward and skidded and tumbled to the floor with a noticeable lack of grace.

Which is how, having survived the Hound of the Baskerville's attack in the car, a killer gunning for me, a jump out a window, and an avalanche of blue barrels, I wound up in the hospital with a broken arm.

32

Medicare patients are not encouraged to linger in hospital beds, but the hospital kept me for almost forty-eight hours while they checked out my working parts, X-rayed everything, and kept me under observation for a possible concussion. I was amazed at the parade of people who rushed in to see me. I wasn't certain how all of them found out about my situation, but Magnolia and Geoff showed up. Tiffany and her Ronnie. Jordan Kaine. Charley Mason and the pastor from Tri-Corners Church. Dix and Haley. Even Cecile called from the nursing home, saying she'd read something in the newspaper.

Everyone was helpful. Magnolia and Geoff zipped off to pick up my car from the tavern parking lot. Tiffany had quit her job at Bottom-Buck Barney's and didn't know what, if anything, might be going on there, but she and Ronnie offered to drive me home from the hospital. Jordan Kaine overrode that offer and insisted he'd do it. The pastor prayed. I had to fight off Cecile's determination to give me her treasured blue starfish necklace.

Everyone also had questions, most of which I answered with an I'll-have-to-talk-to-the-authorities-first primness. Two officers showed up to question me. So did Detective Harmon. To my surprise, Detective Harmon said he'd already contacted Aunt Chris and that she was supposed to arrive the following day to identify the body.

Dix, however, was the only one who came with information to answer my questions, information he'd acquired through his new desk job at police headquarters. He sat beside my hospital bed with his plaster-encased leg stretched out in front of him.

Bo's full name, Dix said, was Beaumont Zollinger. He'd suffered a serious concussion, but he'd regained consciousness and was expected to recover completely. He did indeed, through a series of interlinked corporations, own both Bottom-Buck Barney's and Thrif-Tee Wrecking. He was also the more open owner of a prestigious foreign car dealership, and was married with three children. He had no criminal record. Which to my mind, of course, didn't necessarily mean he wasn't a criminal.

Benny was Benny Littleton, age forty-seven, currently unmarried, with a record of small-time crimes some years ago, nothing recent.

Duke had been taken to an animal shelter and, since he had committed no crime beyond being an excellent watchdog, would probably be released to Benny's married daughter.

I was still mulling over the name Littleton. It sounded familiar. Then it came to me. Emma Littleton, the little chicken girl! And Alana Braxton, nee Littleton, the woman who had inherited the land behind Country Peace: I summarized the connection for Dix.

"So that explains why Benny was helping Drake Braxton vandalize the cemetery. He was a relative of Braxton's wife. And he was so fond of his and Drake's loop-and-drag system of vandalism from the cemetery that he and Bo used it on Harley's bench at my house."

Dix didn't congratulate me on the brilliance of my logic. He was still a bit grumpy about my having further involved myself in all this. But he nodded grudging agreement. "You could be right."

"So, what about this Beaumont 'Bo' Zollinger? Has he been charged with murder yet? And what did they find in the safe?"

"We're still awaiting results of the comparisons of the bullets from Bo's gun, Benny's body, and the body of the girl in the morgue. The papers in the safe are under investigation."

I sighed. The feet of justice tramp slowly.

Jordan took me home the following morning. He was extremely kind and solicitous of my welfare and comfort. He returned that evening with a takeout Thai dinner. Tiffany and Ronnie showed up with pizza, and Magnolia brought over fry bread made into what she called Indian tacos, so we had a fine multicultural meal.

The broken arm was inconvenient and the cast awkward, but it was no big deal. Except it meant I couldn't enroll in a computer class because I couldn't use that hand.

A few days later Dix reported that the comparison tests on the bullets had come in. Until then, Bo had been held in jail on the basis of attempted murder for trying to gun me down in the junkyard. After the tests showed a bullet from Bo's gun had killed Kendra, who by now had been officially identified as Debbie Etheridge, murder charges were also filed against him. Aunt Chris had Debbie's body shipped back to Arkansas for burial.

300

The papers in the safe were minimal but enough to show what was going on at Thrif-Tee. The fact that there was a stolen '01 Malibu in the shop pretty much confirmed everything. Thrif-Tee Wrecking legally bought wrecked or disabled cars, often from out of state. They then, through what appeared to be an ever-widening network, matched them up with appropriate stolen cars. The VINs on the stolen cars were altered to show the numbers from a legal vehicle, and the cars were then sold through Bottom-Buck Barney's, also using the titles from the legal vehicles. If no suitable wrecked or disabled car from which to take numbers was available, the stolen car was chopped up and sold for parts in what Dix called "chop shop" activity. Some of the wrecked cars were also dismantled for parts, just to make things look on the up-and-up.

It was my personal opinion that that was how Kendra/Debbie's Corolla had been disposed of, because the red car at Thrif-Tee did not turn out to be hers. The system had worked so well because both Thrif-Tee and Barney's did sufficient legitimate business, which included selling trade-ins from Bo's foreign-car dealership, to conceal the illegal activities.

I testified at the grand jury hearing, which indicted Beaumont Zollinger on murder and a bevy of other charges to do with the activities at Thrif-Tee. I'd have to testify again at the trial, scheduled to begin in about three months, but, other than that, my involvement in all this was over.

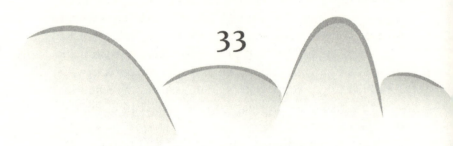

33

The call came about a week later. I was studying a postcard I'd just received from Mac. The postmark was from Idaho, and he wrote that he was doing an article about a week on a dude ranch. No mention of any upcoming trip to Missouri, no address where to reach him. Although he did say he'd been out looking at the stars the night before and thought of me.

When the phone rang I answered it rather absentmindedly, still thinking about the postcard and trying to decide if I was pleased, relieved, or disappointed. "Hello?"

"Ivy Malone?" A deep, growly voice, with none of the energetic enthusiasm of the voice from an hour earlier that had tried to sell me super-potent vitamins.

I jerked to attention. I was holding the phone to my right ear, which still felt awkward, as if I were listening in on someone else's conversation. But I couldn't use my left hand for the phone as I did pre-junkyard brawl.

My first instinct at the sound of the growl was to say, "No,

Ivy moved to the south of France." But I *was* Ivy Malone, so I said, "Yes."

"If you know what's good for you, lady, you won't testify at the trial."

I swallowed. "What trial?"

"Don't play cute. You know what trial. This would be a good time for a nice vacation, a nice long vacation, somewhere far, far away, until the trial is long over. Or you'll find yourself taking a permanent vacation from life, with a view from about six feet under."

He hung up, and I stood there clutching the phone. Momentarily, I was too stunned to panic. Was this for real? Who was it? My first thought was Bo. Beaumont Zollinger. But Bo, though he was scheduled to be released on bail shortly, was at the moment still in jail. Surely he wouldn't be making a threatening phone call from there. Couldn't be Benny, of course. Who else?

I had no idea. But whoever he was, he hadn't sounded like he was playing games. Then panic kicked in, and I called Dix at his desk at the police department. He asked questions that I couldn't answer. No, I didn't recognize the voice. No, I'd heard no accent or identifying peculiarity. No, I had no idea where the call was coming from.

My question was, "Don't the police offer some kind of protection? Guards or something? Or maybe they'd like to send me on a long vacation—yes, the south of France would be nice—and then bring me back to testify at the trial?"

"I might be able to get you a police guard for a few days, but three months . . ." I could almost see Dix shaking his head.

"And there's no money in the police department budget for sending little old lady witnesses on extended vacations?"

"I'm afraid not."

"I should just ignore the call, then? Chalk it up as a crank call and forget it?"

"No. You absolutely cannot do that."

"So I'm just a sitting duck until the trial, waiting for some-one to take a potshot and get rid of me?" I'd been a sitting duck once already, in that cramped bathroom at Thrif-Tee Wrecking, and it was not an experience I wanted to repeat.

"Look, for right now, just lock all your doors and win-dows. Don't go outside and don't open the door to anyone who isn't a best friend. Nobody looking like or claiming to be a delivery person, utility person, long-lost acquaintance, nobody. Haley and I will be over this evening."

"I can't spend the next three months just sitting here with my doors locked!"

A brief silence from Dix, as if he were thinking, *I don't see why not. Take up pinochle. TV soap operas. Quilting.* But what he said was, "Just hold on until Haley and I get there, okay?"

They showed up about 7:00. After a repeat of the ques-tions, which I still couldn't answer, Dix finally said, "Okay, we've worked out a plan."

"Does it involve going to the south of France?"

"Not that far," Haley said. "It involves coming to live with me until the trial."

I looked at her in astonishment. "I can't do that."

Haley put a hand on my arm and squeezed. "Yes, you can. I'd love to have you. My grandma was my roommate for a couple of years when I was a kid, and it was great. She used to tell me wonderful bedtime stories."

"But giving up my home, going into hiding . . . Doesn't that seem a bit extreme?"

"I consider a death threat extreme," Dix said. "Unless you'd prefer that six-feet-under, permanent vacation?"

Well, no.

"There is another alternative," Dix suggested. "You could *not* testify at the trial. And announce that decision to the media."

I shook my head. No way. I would testify at that trial if I had to spend the next three months hiding in a closet eating grits.

Dix discussed the threat with Detective Harmon, and the detective thought moving in with Haley was an excellent idea.

I did it the following day. Dix was adamant that I tell no one where I was going, so all I told Magnolia and Geoff was that I was going "into seclusion." They would pick up my mail and keep an eye on the house and contact Dix if they saw anything suspicious. Dix would collect my mail from them once a week. I had the newspaper discontinued, and I called Cecile at the nursing home to tell her I wouldn't be in to see her for a while. It was a bit disconcerting to realize my life could be wrapped up so easily.

Haley lived in a one-bedroom apartment near the community college. She had a second twin bed moved up from the apartment complex's storage area. I left the Thunderbird locked in my garage so my caller couldn't use it to trace me, and took only a minimal amount of personal belongings. Plus a fair supply of jittery nerves.

The nerves calmed in a few days, and Haley and I settled into a surprisingly comfortable routine. I didn't tell her bed-time stories, but we started studying Romans together before bed. Haley gave me lessons on her home computer, including how to connect with the Internet, where I spent much of each day. It was a bit difficult, given my one-handed limita-tions, but I was soon familiar with Windows and modems and was using spell-checker and thesaurus, entering chat rooms, using the delete key to correct my errors, and back-ing out of websites that looked too much like the calendar at Thrif-Tee Wrecking.

I didn't go to church on Sundays. That was disappointing, but we all agreed it was prudent not to show my face anywhere. Dix's adamance about keeping undercover extended to Jordan Kaine, which brought that budding relationship to at least a temporary halt. Haley went to her church, of course, and I was astonished when, on the third Sunday after I moved in, Dix started going with her.

Haley didn't take a newspaper, another one of her not-until-I-get-my-student-loans-paid-off economies, but from radio and TV news I learned that Bruce Retzloff, manager at Bottom-Buck Barney's, had been charged in connection with the stolen vehicles scheme. Several of the cars in his personal collection were under investigation, including a '64 Mustang. There were also a couple of news items about restoration work begun at Country Peace. No mention of Drake Braxton.

I had several conferences with the prosecuting attorney about my testimony for the upcoming trial. Haley whisked me off to these in a taxi. I was surprised she didn't insist on a paper bag over my head.

From Dix I learned that Tiffany had taken a job with a wholesale plumbing supply company. She and Ronnie were a steady couple, going to church regularly, even joining a Wednesday evening Bible study group. Dix also said there was a For Sale sign on Thea's house now, which brought back again how much I missed her.

But everything else was going along so smoothly that by the time six weeks had elapsed I was thinking maybe I could just quietly move back home. An idea I quickly discarded when Magnolia reported to Dix that someone had come around claiming to be from an out-of-state firm seeking to find me in connection with a considerable inheritance.

Phony as a three-dollar bill, of course, which meant my caller had not forgotten me. I resigned myself to waiting out the trial date.

Which arrived only to be postponed until after the first of the year. Then postponed for another fifteen days.

During that time two pleasing events took place. Dix went forward to acknowledge his decision for the Lord and to request baptism. And he and Haley announced they'd be getting married in mid-February.

At that point, considering how things were turning out for Dix and Haley, and Tiffany and Ronnie, I had to admit that the Lord hadn't needed my matchmaking help. He'd had his own plans all along. He was also a much better matchmaker than I could ever be.

One other nice little event. Mac sent a copy of a travel magazine with his byline on an article about Clancy's Meteor Daze. It was titled "Celestial Fireflies."

Then the long-awaited day was here. The day Beaumont "Bo" Zollinger's trial began. And on the third day it was my turn to testify.

34

I was not allowed in the courtroom before testifying. I was stuck off in a room by myself where I couldn't hear the other testimony, under the logical theory that one person's testimony might be swayed or contaminated by testimony given by another witness. Although I did understand that much of the earlier testimony would be from expert witnesses concerning the bullets and other technical and police evidence.

At this point I already knew the prosecuting attorney had decided there was insufficient evidence to charge Bo with killing Ray Etheridge. I regretted that, but I knew the prosecutors must work with what they had.

The courtroom was crowded when I took the witness stand. I knew Dix and Haley were there, but the faces blended into one big blur. I was uncertain whether this came from nerves or a need to have an eye exam and new glasses. Probably both. Although one face stood out clearly—Bo's glowering at me from between his lawyers at the defendant's table. I kept wondering who he'd put up to making that call to me.

Not that it matters now, I thought with a defiant stare back at him. *Because here I am.*

And testify I did. For almost an hour and a half. Then cross-examination by the defense attorneys.

I could have attended the remainder of the trial, which lasted more than a week after my testimony, but I didn't do it. Testifying had taken more out of me than I realized it would. I'd have had to stiffen up to be limp as a dishrag.

But there was one event for which I was determined to be present, and the assistant prosecuting attorney promised to call me when that time came.

The call came at 10:25 on a Wednesday morning. The assistant said the jury had just been issued their instructions by the judge.

"There's no telling how long the jury will be out, of course," he said. "Could be a few hours or a few days. But if you want to be sure of being here when they bring in their verdict—"

"I'm on my way."

Which wasn't totally accurate. I was in the middle of— what else?—washing my hair. I didn't bother to try to give it any style. I just did a fast towel dry, ignoring the clump that stood up like a toadstool on the back of my head, and called a taxi. I knew Dix and Haley would be disappointed to miss this, but both were working today.

So there I sat in the back of the courtroom, waiting with a whole crowd of people for the jury to return. I didn't want to discuss the case or my part in it with anyone, so I kept my eyes on the magazine I'd brought, Haley's current issue of *Today's Librarian.* A little short on fascination, even if I wasn't nervous enough to shred the pages rather than read them. What if they let Bo go?

Finally, just before 4:00, a kind of wave rippled through the courtroom. The jury was returning. There were the formalities before the verdict was announced, and then it came.

Guilty!

Sentencing wouldn't be until the following week, but this was what mattered. Guilty!

Bo stood there looking as if he'd like to avalanche blue barrels down on the whole world, but I didn't care. Now I knew this truly was over for me. I could go home and return to normal life. Collect my own mail. Resubscribe to the newspaper. Go to Magnolia's barbecues. She'd hinted through Dix that she had a new man for me to meet. Maybe I'd buy my own computer.

So I walked down the hallway with an upbeat swing in my walk—only to get a prickle across my scalp and an uneasy feeling between my shoulder blades. Not anything as specific as a tap on the back or a nudge from behind. Just a feeling as if the spot had been targeted with an icy laser beam. I cautiously turned and looked behind me.

Drake Braxton.

Okay, so what, I said to myself as I took an awkward step backward. He hadn't seen me watching him at the cemetery. He couldn't blame me that his scheme to grab Country Peace hadn't worked. I already knew he hadn't even trashed my house. He probably didn't even know who I was.

His first words disproved that hopeful thought.

"Mrs. Malone," he said, with a smile like an eager guillotine operator sharpening his equipment.

And just why, I wondered uneasily, *is he here at this trial?*

He didn't wait for me to acknowledge or deny the identification. He got right down to business. "We're going to get you. No one does to one of the Braxton brothers what you did and gets away with it. We will get you."

I was scared enough to go lightheaded. For all I knew he

310

planned to carry out the threat right there in the hallway. But I was confused too. "Braxton brothers?" I squeaked.

"The fact that Bo is my half brother doesn't make him any less a Braxton. And the Braxtons stick together. You didn't do me any favors either."

So he had connected me with that letter to the editor urging restoration of the cemetery. "How . . . how many brothers are there?"

"Enough to do you in. So these are your last days, Mrs. Malone. Better enjoy them. Because as of right now, lady, you're roadkill."

I looked around wildly. There were several other people standing close by. "These people heard you threaten me." I motioned to them. "If anything happens to me—"

"Allow me to introduce one of my sons," Drake said. He didn't offer a name, but he gestured toward a young man beside him—big, burly, and as mean-looking as Drake himself.

Another gesture. "That's Bo's son. And their lovely wives, of course."

Four—count 'em, four—feral smiles. Plus Drake's.

I reeled over and slumped against the wall as the family trooped by. I wanted to protest. *Hey, I'm not the only one who testified and convicted Bo!*

But I knew it didn't matter. It was me, muddling around in all this and bowling with barrels out at Thrif-Tee Wrecking, who had been instrumental in bringing Bo down. Was Drake Braxton also the one who had made the pre-trial threatening phone call? I didn't have Tiffany's talent for recognizing voices, and I had no idea. Or maybe it was one of the sons.

Okay, I could go to the authorities with this.

And get where? Drake would simply deny my accusation, shake his beefy head, and act baffled that I'd made up such an incredible accusation. Maybe he'd even imply that my mental state was so unstable that my testimony was worthless and that his brother Bo deserved a new trial.

I could tell Dix and Haley, who would undoubtedly insist on hiding me away even longer. No, I couldn't do that. I was not their continuing responsibility. They had lives to live, a marriage to get on with.

I took another taxi home and drove the Thunderbird over to Haley's that evening to collect my things and thank them both. I kept up a breezy, cheerful front. Trial is over, guilty man convicted, and everything's fine now.

Then I went home to talk to the Lord and see what his solution to this new problem was.

By morning it was there, but I hesitated. *Are you sure, Lord? Wouldn't that be running away?*

But then I reminded myself that I'd trusted the Lord so far in this life, and I wasn't going to stop now. The Lord would most certainly be with me *there* just as he'd always been *here*.

So I decided I'd do it. We'd make it just a temporary arrangement, of course, just until Drake Braxton's hostility simmered down. *Thank you, Lord.*

One invisible lady should surely be able to live a safe and uneventful life hidden in the bosom of a loving family in small-town Arkansas.

Right?

Contact the author:

    Lorena McCourtney
    P.O. Box 773
    Merlin, OR 97532

Visit the website at:
    www.lorenamccourtney.com

Don't miss the next book in
the Ivy Malone Mysteries
by Lorena McCourtney:

In Plain Sight
available April 2005
from Fleming H. Revell

Turn the page for a preview of

In Plain Sight

1

In spite of the threats, I'd held on to a small hope that the danger would, given a little time, fade away. The phone call I've just received has squashed that hopeful fantasy.

The Braxtons are not fading away.

Because of my role in convicting his brother of murder, one mean, beefy Drake Braxton vowed at the end of the trial to make roadkill out of me. There are apparently more Braxtons eager to help in this endeavor. Their homicidal intentions were made all too clear when my house caught fire, with me in it, a couple of weeks ago. Intentions thwarted in the small-blaze stage only because of the observant eyes of my good . . . and nosy . . . neighbor, Magnolia Margollin.

Although I recently discovered that I have aged into a semi-invisible state, I'm afraid I may not be invisible enough to evade the Braxtons' murderous intentions toward me. This phone call threatening dire damage to various portions of my anatomy is further proof of those intentions. The prudent action at this point appears to be to remove myself from the danger zone for a time.

Ever since the death of my best friend Thea, my niece DeeAnn Harrington has been urging me to come stay with her and her family in their big house near the small town of Woodston, Arkansas. She's also suggested I should consider living with, or close to, them permanently.

I'm reasonably certain I don't want to make a permanent move. Harley and I bought this house here on Madison Street in Missouri many years ago, and, though Harley is gone and the area has deteriorated in the past few years, it's still home to me. But I've been talking it over with the Lord, and a temporary visit down there in the lovely Ozarks appears to be a fine solution to my problem.

I picked up the phone and dialed DeeAnn's number. My fourteen-year-old grand-niece Sandy answered.

"Oh, Aunt Ivy, you should see what I just crocheted! It's a candy-pink top that's just awesome. I can't wait for some nice spring weather to wear it."

I'd helped Sandy learn to crochet the last time I was down for a visit. Now, with a certain apprehension about teenage apparel, I asked, "Does it show your belly button?"

"Of course!"

"Does your mother know?"

"I'm going to show it to her." Considered pause. "Soon."

I didn't intend to jump into the middle of that, so I just said, "Could I speak to DeeAnn, please?"

"Are you going to come visit us again? Oh, I hope so! But you need to come right away, before—"

"Maybe," I cut in.

"Okay, I'll get Mom. She's upstairs sorting through some towels and stuff to pick out things that match."

That seemed odd. DeeAnn is a good enough housekeeper,

but she doesn't usually fuss about such things as whether her towels coordinate. She came on the line a minute later.

"Aunt Ivy, how good to hear from you! I heard on the news that they sentenced that awful man who murdered your neighbor, but I couldn't get you when I tried to call. And everything has been in such an uproar here that I didn't get around to trying again."

Uproar was the usual state of existence in the Harrington household. The twins, Rick and Rory, were off at college in California now, but DeeAnn was financial secretary at their church, created puppet shows featuring Korman the Klutzy Kangaroo for the kids, and kept books for several small businesses in Woodston. Sandy practiced gymnastics in an upstairs hallway, zoomed around on her skateboard, kept in touch with people from Arkansas to Zanzibar on the Internet, and sometimes had the guys in a local Christian rock band over to practice. Husband Mike did executive things with an expanding roofing manufacturer and was up to his elbows in activities aimed at keeping the teens in a church youth group busy.

"Maybe I can help," I said to DeeAnn. "There have been some, uh, unforeseen developments here, and I'm thinking I might take you up on your invitation to come visit for a while."

"Oh, Aunt Ivy . . ."

It didn't take extrasensory powers to hear the dismay in her voice. "If it isn't convenient now, maybe some other time," I amended hastily.

"Oh, Aunt Ivy, I feel so bad about this. It isn't that it isn't convenient, and we'd love to have you. But we're moving. Mike has just gotten a promotion, but it's also a transfer. To Hawaii!"

"Hawaii," I echoed. I had a dim vision of palm trees and grass skirts. I finally gathered my wits together enough to add, "Well, this is so exciting! And wonderful news for all of you. Congratulations!"

"It is wonderful news, and we are excited. But it's all happening so fast. We're leaving in less than a week, and there's all this sorting and packing and everything that has to be done. I didn't realize we had so much *stuff*."

I was glad I hadn't mentioned my Braxton problem. Dee-Ann would feel worse than ever if she knew about that. "Throw things out," I advised. "That's what God designed moves for. To make us get rid of our excess baggage."

"Hey, I know what let's do. As soon as we get settled over there, you come stay with us! Sandy has been digging up all kinds of facts about Hawaii on the Internet. We'll eat fresh pineapple and go body surfing and roast a whole pig in a luau!"

A whole pig sounded a bit intimidating, but, in general, a trip to Hawaii might be a fine idea. If the Braxtons didn't roast *me* first. "Maybe I can do that," I said.

"Aunt Ivy, is something wrong?" my ever-perceptive niece asked. "You aren't thinking we don't want you to visit, are you?"

"Well, of course I think that," I said with pretended huffiness. "I'm sure you've invented this wild story about Hawaii just to keep me from coming. I venture to say you may even go so far as to move to Hawaii to make the story convincing."

DeeAnn laughed. "There's one woman I've done some bookkeeping for whom I'd consider moving to Mars to escape from, but not you, Aunt Ivy. Never you."

"I know. And I appreciate that."

"But there is something wrong, isn't there?"

I considered how to phrase my situation to be truthful but not cause DeeAnn concern. "Since the trial, things have felt a bit . . . edgy here. I was just thinking it would be nice to get away for a while. But don't you worry about it. I'll be fine. I'll just go spade up my garden and plant some spring peas. Now tell me all about Hawaii."

DeeAnn bubbled on about how the company had leased a house for them in Honolulu, and they'd already had welcoming emails from relatives of friends in their Woodston church. "Sandy has mixed feelings about the move. She's excited about Hawaii, but she hates to change schools in the middle of the year. And leave her friends, of course. I've found homes for all my house plants. We're down to only one cat at the moment. Celery. And Mrs. Grandy from church is taking her, so no problem there."

Celery, their stub-tailed calico cat, so named for one of her odd food preferences, was a stray that had wandered in a couple years ago. I'd always suspected there must be some sign in generic animal language announcing "Free Food! Nice Folks! Come On In!" posted on the back steps of the Harrington house.

"But we haven't decided what to do about the house, whether to put it up for sale or rent it out. I do love this old place . . ."

"I'm sure everything will work out fine. Well, I'll just let you get back to your sorting and packing. We'll talk again before you leave, okay?"

I didn't mean to cut her off, but I had some thinking to do here. With plan A shot down and the murderous Braxtons gunning for me, it was time to move on to plan B.

Unfortunately, I have no plan B.